SIMON451

ORBS

NICHOLAS SANSBURY SMITH

SIMON451

New York   London   Toronto   Sydney   New Delhi

SIMON451

Simon & Schuster
An Imprint of Simon & Schuster, Inc.
1230 Avenue of the Americas
New York, NY 10020

Copyright © 2013 by Nicholas Sansbury Smith
Originally published in 2013 by Nicholas Sansbury Smith

First Simon451 trade paperback edition June 2016

SIMON451 and colophon are trademarks of Simon & Schuster, Inc.

The Simon & Schuster Speakers Bureau can bring authors to your live event. For more information or to book an event contact the Simon & Schuster Speakers Bureau at 1-866-248-3049 or visit our website at www.simonspeakers.com.

Manufactured in the United States of America

10 9 8 7 6 5 4 3 2 1

Library of Congress Cataloging-in-Publication Data has been applied for.

ISBN   978-1-5011-3323-7
ISBN   978-1-4767-8895-1 (ebook)

For those in the armed services and everyone else who puts their life on the line for freedom. Thanks for keeping us safe.

If aliens ever visit us, I think the outcome would be much as when Christopher Columbus first landed in America, which didn't turn out very well for the American Indians.

—STEPHEN HAWKING

ORBS

CHAPTER 1

SOPHIE awoke to the thrumming of helicopter blades. Rubbing the sleep from her eyes, she craned her neck to stare out the oval window. As the drowsiness faded and her vision cleared, she fixated on the weathered dunes below, her eyes glued to the infinite monotony of the sand. If the landscape hadn't been a light shade of brown, she would have thought they were flying over the ocean.

"How far out are we?" she yelled over the sound of the thumping blades.

"We're still at least an hour from the site. You should go back to sleep, ma'am; the scenery isn't going to change for a while," the pilot said without taking his eyes off the controls.

Sophie had no idea where the site was, and she certainly wasn't going to ask. She pulled her long blond hair back into a ponytail before reaching to adjust her headset. There was no way she was going to fall back asleep with the increased turbulence and the vibration from the chopper's blades.

Settling back into her seat, she focused on the view. Below, the dunes extended as far as she could see, the crimson horizon slicing the panorama in half. She squinted for a better look, imagining she was peering through the thick glass of a visor at the harsh landscape of

Mars. The fantasy was one she had daily. It was mystifyingly realistic, so vivid she would sometimes reach out as if she could touch the sand of the red planet.

Sophie blinked and returned to reality. She was still on Earth, where more than 15 percent of the surface had been baked by the solar storms of 2055. Areas affected were rendered uninhabitable due to the radiation. Scientists had argued for years that a solar storm wasn't capable of that level of destruction; that a coronal mass ejection would never break through the Earth's atmosphere. But something about the storms of 2055 had been different—unnatural. Now the planet was dying, and there was nothing science could do to stop it.

Not that it hadn't been tried. For decades China had been leading the world on a quest to strip the Earth of precious metals. After international talks failed, the world's leading private science and security company, New Tech Corporation, took matters into its own hands. It secretly hired mercenaries to set off five electromagnetic pulse weapons (EMPs) in strategic locations across the country. It solved China's thirst for resources instantly, by sending the country back to the Stone Age.

Unfortunately, the EMPs had only stalled the inevitable. The Doomsday Clock was still ticking, and humanity's time on Earth was limited. So a group of leaders had gathered in a closed-door meeting, as they had always done, deciding for the masses that it was time to jump ship. Humans were officially heading into space, and leading the mission was none other than New Tech Corporation.

Sophie could have lied and told her team she was surprised they had been picked for the first stage of the experimental mission, but none of them would have believed her. This wasn't the first job NTC had hired them for. Two years ago they'd been sealed into an underwater biosphere off the coast of Puerto Rico for just over a month. The data they collected was used by the tech and science giant to design manned underwater probes that would be used on the mission to Europa.

They were the best private sector team in the world; six months in a biosphere deep within some mountain wouldn't be a problem. But she couldn't deny the fact that they would be rusty. They hadn't worked together since Puerto Rico. After the success of the mission, everyone under her command had received offers from tech companies around the world, and had quickly found work elsewhere.

Sophie exhaled her concerns with a long breath. She would see her team soon enough, and it would probably take only a few days to get readjusted.

Suddenly the com blared to life, the static echoing through her headset. Sophie clutched the armrests of her seat, her nails scratching the cold metal.

"Halo 1, this is Black Echo, stand by for report. Over."

"Black Echo, this is Halo 1, standby to copy. Over."

"Roger, Halo 1, reports of a massive dust storm heading your way. Over."

"Copy that."

Sophie watched the pilot, trying to control her labored breathing. She hated flying, especially by chopper. With the constant weather fluctuation in the Wastelands, there was no such thing as a safe trip. Dust storms could form with little to no warning and had caused multiple crashes. Often the crews of downed flights were never found, more than likely buried by the very sand and dirt that had sealed their fate.

She didn't want to end up like those other crews. Not now. She'd worked too hard to let a dust storm stand in the way of her destiny. She had a mission to complete.

Shocked into motion, she unclipped her safety belt and ducked into the cockpit, plunking herself down in the empty copilot's seat.

"What are you doing, ma'am?"

"You're going to need a copilot if you want to avoid this storm. And seeing as I'm the only other person on this chopper, I believe that makes me copilot by default."

The pilot paused, his thick goggles emitting a fiery red glow. Rather than argue with her, he asked, "Do you know how to read radar?"

Sophie bit her lip and studied the controls. "I'll figure it out, Captain," she said confidently.

The pilot returned her smile with a sly grin. "Whatever you say, ma'am. Just keep an eye on that screen," he said, pointing at a translucent holographic image of the landscape. "You see that blip in the corner that's heading right at us?" She scanned the image and then nodded. "That's the dust storm, and by the looks of it, a big one. If we even come close to it, we're worm food. You may want to buckle in," the pilot said, eyeing her unclipped belt.

Sophie grabbed the harness and shot the man a quick glance. "I need to get to this site, Captain. Crashing isn't an option. Consider that an order." She knew she wasn't in any position to be barking orders at an NTC soldier, but she figured her assertiveness might motivate him to fly a little faster, and perhaps a little safer. She watched the pilot's grin fade as he spoke into his com.

"Black Echo, this is Halo 1. Stand by for report. Over."

Static crackled over the radio. The pilot cursed under his breath before raising the transmitter to his mouth again. Sophie watched the curl of his lip as he spoke. "Black Echo, this is Halo 1. Come in. Over."

Nothing but the hiss of white noise followed. He slammed the transmitter back onto the dashboard. "Looks like the storm already knocked out radio transmissions. We're on our own."

"Then you'd best keep focused, Captain," Sophie replied.

She turned to watch the red blip of the dust storm on the screen. With a flick of her index finger, she enlarged it and mentally computed its distance.

"Look," the pilot said suddenly.

Through the armored glass she could see a brown cloud swirling on the horizon, the storm slowly swallowing the crimson sunset. The sight was chilling.

The pilot glanced over at her. "Hope your belt's tight, ma'am."

Sophie didn't bother lifting her gaze from the storm. "Just get us to the site in one piece. A lot of people are counting on my safe arrival."

The pilot grinned again, his lips twitching slightly as if he wanted to respond, but his fiery red goggles rotated and focused on the storm. He gripped the cyclic tightly in his hands, shaking with the effort to keep it steady.

"Can you go above the storm?" Sophie asked anxiously.

"Negative, ma'am. Our only chance is to go around it, but by the look of it we won't be able to."

"Well, there has to be something we can do. Why not turn around?" she yelled over the increasing sound of turbulence.

The pilot momentarily took his eyes off the incoming storm. "Ma'am, that storm is barreling down on us at over three hundred and fifty miles per hour. Even if we tried, we wouldn't be able to outrun it. Our best shot now is to head right through and try to ride it out."

Sophie stared ahead, watching the swirling brown particles racing toward them. She blinked as the first pieces of dirt and dust crashed into the armored windshield.

I didn't come all this way to die in a damned dust storm, she thought, grabbing her belt and tightening it across her chest.

Before she could think anything more, the storm was on them, the wind hurling particles of dust and dirt at the chopper from all directions. The pinging of rocks and debris making contact echoed throughout the interior of their metal tomb. The blades above groaned in protest as the rotor reluctantly ground them through the harsh wind.

"Hold on," the pilot yelled, pulling up on the cyclic and heaving the chopper deeper into the center of the storm.

Sophie cried out as a rock the size of a baseball bashed the windshield, the crack spreading like a spider web.

"It'll hold," the pilot said unconvincingly. "The windshield was built to withstand a fifty-cal round at point-blank range."

"Those engineers better have been right."

Sophie didn't trust many engineers, especially those who made their living testing products designed for war. She knew better than anyone that there was a major difference between how products held up under laboratory conditions and how they performed in real life. Companies like NTC had been making billions every year designing faulty products. It was simple economics, a concept she had learned at a young age. Weak products had to be replaced, which increased revenue. Quality was a thing of the past, and warranties had become extinct.

Sophie eyed the crack, hoping the windshield wasn't another one of NTC's money-saving ventures. She didn't like gambling, especially with lives.

"How much farther?" Sophie yelled.

"You tell me—check the radar!" the pilot yelled back.

Before she had time to look at the radar, she saw an object through the glass. Squinting, she tried to discern what it was. "What the . . ." she muttered under her breath. The object swirled through the storm, moving toward them faster and faster.

"Watch out!"

Sophie was flung to one side, her insides scrambling against her rib cage, as the pilot yanked the cyclic hard to the right. It was too late. A second later, the spinning piece of debris smashed into the windshield, covering it. The pilot cursed in Spanish. Sophie understood every word.

"Get it off the windshield!" Sophie screamed.

"This isn't a car. It doesn't have wiper blades."

The pilot loosened his goggles, pulling them over his helmet to get a better look at the metal object stuck to the windshield, and Sophie saw his face for the first time. His eyes were crystal blue, unlike any she had ever seen before. He couldn't have been more than nineteen years old.

They sent me out here with a rookie?

"It looks like a road sign," he yelled, pulling his goggles back over his eyes.

She squinted at the green piece of metal, desperately trying to make out the weathered white letters. "D-E-N-V-E . . ." Sophie hesitated. Could it really be?

"Denver," she shouted over the noise. "It fucking says 'Denver.'"

The pilot chuckled. "My girlfriend grew up there. Before the solar storms scorched it."

"I don't find this situation particularly humorous, Captain. Now let's figure out how to get the—" The chopper shook violently before Sophie could finish her sentence, as more debris crashed into the metal exterior.

"Hold on, I have an idea!" Slowly, the pilot pulled the cyclic up and then rammed it toward the floorboards. The sign slid off the windshield with a whoosh, and became metal confetti seconds later as the chopper's titanium rotor blades tore it apart.

Sophie didn't have time to celebrate. Another barrage of debris tore into the exoskeleton of the chopper, melon-sized dents forming on the inside of the door.

The pilot tried to straighten the bird out, holding the controls so tightly his knuckles looked as if they were going to explode. "She can't take much more of this. Check the radar again!" he yelled.

In the center of the console, the radar was fading in and out, the blur of red disappearing in a wave of static. "The storm must be disrupting the transmission," Sophie guessed.

A deafening groan interrupted her as the blades above struggled through the cloud of dust. Every inch of their metal cage creaked and moaned. They were in the thickest, most violent part of the storm now.

Two more baseball-sized rocks smashed into the windshield, cracks exploding in all directions.

"Just a little farther, baby," the pilot pleaded.

Sophie continued to monitor the cracks, mentally willing them not to get any larger. But her pleas went unanswered as another small rock hit the windshield. She held her breath, listening to the sound of her fate as the windshield slowly split, inch by inch. Even over the roar of the storm, she could hear the acrylic glass splintering. It was an odd sensation, knowing a thin piece of glass molded on some NTC assembly line was all that remained between her and the storm. She could almost picture her skin peeling off her bones as the windshield gave way and brown dust swallowed the chopper.

"The radar," the pilot shouted, shocking Sophie out of her trance.

The hologram was working again, the red bleep representing the storm crawling across the translucent image. "It looks like we're almost through it!" she exclaimed, maneuvering to the edge of her seat for a better look.

"Thank God. We aren't going to last much longer," the pilot said. His red goggles dipped toward the control panel where he studied the pressure gauges. "We're losing hydraulic pressure by the second."

Sophie remained glued to the radar. The chopper appeared to be on the eastern edge of the storm, a mere fingernail's length from safety.

The groaning of the blades drew Sophie's attention back to the windshield. The brown dust was slowly dissipating. In the distance, she thought she could even see a hint of night sky, but it was difficult to judge; the dark colors seemed to swirl together.

"Halo 1, this is Black Echo, do you copy? Over."

A welcoming grin spread across the pilot's face as he reached for the transmitter. "Back in business! Black Echo, Halo 1 here. Over."

"Roger. Good to hear your voice, Halo 1. Thought we'd lost you in the storm. Over."

Sophie ignored the chatter, watching the winds slowly calm.

"Black Echo, that makes two of us. Preparing for landing. Over."

"Roger, Halo 1, we'll leave a pot of coffee on the burner for you. Over."

Silence once again filled the cockpit, the sound of the storm finally gone. Sophie slumped in her seat, her fingers still gripping the metal armrests. Relief flooded over her body like a cold shower after a long run. In the days after the solar storms, when she'd risen out of the shelter with the rest of her team only to find smoke crawling across the horizon, the flames from cities all across the United States licking the sky, she'd felt something similar. It was a feeling she would never forget. And it was on her skin again.

It was odd that she could be preparing for death one second and then staring at a night sky full of stars the next. In many ways it was what made her appreciate science even more. It was a way for her to control her destiny, from an experiment in her lab to an article on quantum physics.

She knew what some people would say: "God saved them in the storm. God wanted her to live so she could save humanity." But it was all bullshit to her. They hadn't survived because of divine intervention; they had survived through a combination of luck and teamwork.

Sophie smiled. "Nice flying back there, Captain. How long 'til we get this thing on the ground?"

"Thank you, ma'am. Worst storm I've ever flown through. Didn't think I was going to make it home there for a second," he said, checking the control panel again. "Should be on the ground in fifteen minutes."

With a simple nod, Sophie turned to watch the night sky, the cracks in the windshield now nothing more than an afterthought. It was a beautiful view—a view like the one she hoped she'd be seeing on Mars soon.

CHAPTER 2

THE grinding sound of the metal door made Sophie cringe. She tapped her foot and watched artificial light from outside creep in as two NTC soldiers pried the broken chopper door open with a crowbar.

Finally the twisted metal gave way, and the door slid open. Sophie jumped out of the chopper's belly, ignoring the hand of one of the soldiers. She didn't have time for formalities. The tarmac was full of other helicopters and planes, which meant her team had already arrived. She was wasting time.

Stepping onto solid ground prompted a rush of blood to her brain, which already ached from the flight. She could feel it pulsating inside her skull.

Deep breath. Ignore the pain. You have business to attend to.

Sophie shook her head, rubbing the trauma from her eyes. Through the darkness she could vaguely make out a set of glowing orange goggles approaching her. The color indicated a senior NTC staffer, more than likely her escort. She stiffened, anxious to get the introductions over with so she could get to her team, but the man walked right by her.

"God damn, Captain," the man barked at her pilot. "You just ruined a multimillion-dollar aircraft. How does it feel?"

"Sir . . . I'm sorry, but the storm."

"I don't want to hear any excuses. Turn around and look at your bird."

The pilot nervously surveyed his chopper. The windshield was shattered in several places, and a rock was still lodged in one of the cracks.

That wasn't even the worst of it. The body of the chopper was peppered with dents. Not even the best body-shop worker the NTC had on payroll could salvage it. The chopper needed to be stripped, its metal skin and windshield completely replaced.

"I asked you how it feels, Captain."

The pilot looked at his feet. "Sir, I'm sorry, but—"

The senior staffer interrupted him before he could finish his sentence. "But you are being demoted, effective immediately."

"Wait just a second!" Sophie stepped forward, her nostrils flaring. "Sir, this man saved me. If it weren't for him, this chopper would be buried in the Wastelands and you would be wasting fuel and resources trying to find it."

The senior staffer turned to face her. "Ah, you must be Dr. Winston," he said. "I've heard so much about you—"

"Sir, with all due respect, I don't have time for this. I need to see my team immediately."

"Your team can wait. Let me introduce myself. My name is Dr. Hoffman, and I'm the entire reason you are here. I chose you. Did I choose wrong, Dr. Winston?"

Sophie hesitated. How could she not have recognized him? The CEO of NTC was one of the most powerful men on Earth—and on Mars, if their experiment succeeded. Her hand shook as she offered it to him. "Dr. Hoffman, sir, my apologies. I just wanted to voice my gratitude for this young man's actions. He saved my life."

A smile curled across Dr. Hoffman's face. He took her hand, shaking it with a powerful grip. He cocked his head and nodded at the pilot, who cowered next to the chopper with the other two NTC soldiers. "You should thank Dr. Winston here. If it were up to me you'd never fly again."

The pilot moved hesitantly, backing away and heading toward the massive concrete facility built into the mountainside at the edge of the tarmac. "Thank you, Dr. Winston!" he said once he'd reached a safe distance.

Dr. Hoffman turned to Sophie, his smile still glued on his face. She studied him. He was in his seventies, and his age showed. Even in the mild darkness, the creases on his face were visible, deep valleys above his glowing goggles. A cropped mustache lined his thin lips, and his smile revealed weathered teeth, stained by years of coffee drinking.

"Shall we, Dr. Winston?" he said, gesturing toward the building. "I know you are anxious to meet your team."

"Yes, Dr. Hoffman. Please lead the way."

Sophie followed her escort toward the building, her hand still noticeably shaking from their conversation. She could count the men who intimidated her on one hand, but Dr. Hoffman topped the list.

Up ahead, two monstrous blast doors screeched open. The entrance was carved out of the side of a mountain. Above the two doors was a single weathered sign that read, "Welcome to Cheyenne Mountain."

"NORAD," she muttered under her breath. She should have known. The ancient military facility was the perfect place for a biosphere. It had been used as the military's aerospace defense command center in the early twenty-first century before it was decommissioned and fell into disrepair. She had been here once on a tour as a child, long before the solar storms scorched Denver. In the distance she could see the lights of Colorado Springs, which had barely avoided the radiation.

Dr. Hoffman shouted from the entrance. "Are you coming?"

"Yes, sir, just admiring the view."

"I thought you were in a rush."

"I am. It's just this place brings back memories."

"Ah, well be prepared for some . . ." He paused. "Changes," he said with the same sly grin.

Sophie faked a smile and followed him inside the dark access tunnel, listening to the groaning of the blast doors closing behind them. The doors crashed shut, sealing them inside the mountain. Someone flipped a switch, and the hangar glowed to life, the lights clicking on one after another.

This was a different entrance than the one she visited. It was wide enough for a semi-trailer and built exclusively for the military, not for touring school kids. The bright overhead lights illuminated a small electric train that sat idle in the middle of the access tunnel like a carnival ride waiting for patrons.

"This way," one of the soldiers said, opening the door to the train. Sophie followed Dr. Hoffman inside and took a seat on a metal bench.

"This train will take us to the most advanced biosphere ever designed by man. NTC has sunk a pretty penny into this facility. I trust you will find it acceptable for your research."

"I'm anxious to start my work in the environment," Sophie said, massaging her tender muscles. She crossed her legs and rested her back against the cold metal of the bench. Her neck was sore from where the chopper's belt had cut into her flesh. She rubbed it, acknowledging that the aches were better than the alternative of perishing in a fiery wreck.

Dr. Hoffman pulled off his goggles and tucked them inside his jacket. For the first time, his eyes met hers. They were obsidian, much darker than Sophie had imagined. She recalled hearing about them in the past, when several of her team had been invited to a board meeting with NTC leadership.

"The data your team will collect is very important, Dr. Winston. I hope you realize what you have been hired to do." He scrunched his eyebrows together, peering deeper into her eyes. It was too much; she looked away.

"I'm fully aware of my assignment. Just remember your part of the bargain."

"I don't gamble when it comes to the end of the world, Dr. Winston. You and your team will have seats on the first flight to Mars. You have my word."

His reassurance helped her relax, and she settled back into her seat, clasping her hands together and staring out the train window. The concrete walls of the tunnels raced by, illuminated by the white glow of the halogen lights. Eventually, the train slowed to a halt. The two NTC soldiers rose from their seats and stepped out into the tunnel. Dr. Hoffman followed, once again covering his black eyes with his goggles.

"This way, Doctor," he said, leading her back into the access lane. "The Biosphere is located in the main chamber. The space has been completely retrofitted and sealed from the outside. A state-of-the-art air filtration system has been added, and the facility is equipped with an artificial intelligence named Alexia—you will meet her shortly. She controls the temperature, humidity, and all the other settings the Biosphere needs to operate properly. In case of a medical emergency, she will also double as a doctor."

"Our engineer, Saafi Yool, is more than capable of regulating the settings," Sophie said. "And among the rest of my staff, I'm sure we can handle any medical emergencies."

Dr. Hoffman stopped in front of the open blast door, staring into the chamber. "Consider Alexia part of your team—a safeguard, if you will. Do I need to remind you how important this mission is, Dr. Winston? The future of humanity depends on your results. It's the reason I have taken time from my very busy schedule to be here for the beginning of this project. I don't like to waste my time. Am I wasting my time?" One of his eyebrows formed an arch over his goggles.

Sophie took a deep breath. "No," she said. "As we already discussed, I'm well aware of the significance of this mission. I do not, however, trust any AI, especially one I haven't worked with before."

Dr. Hoffman turned. "Dr. Winston, this isn't open for negotiation. Alexia is part of your team now. Accept it, or we will find someone else." His tone was firm, and Sophie realized this wasn't something she could argue.

"Okay then. Alexia is part of my team," she lied. She was anxious for a shower, a hot cup of coffee, and the familiar faces of her team. Even if that team now included an unfamiliar hologram.

The smell of cheap coffee hovered in the room. Biologist Emanuel Rodriguez brought a steaming mug to his lips and took a sip. His brown eyes studied the three senior NTC staffers huddled around the table in the front of the briefing room.

At the head of the table was Dr. Hoffman. To his right was Amy Carlson, a tall and beautiful redhead with a face peppered by freckles. In her five years at NTC, she had risen from being an assistant to become Vice President of Science. Her rise to power was often attributed to her looks, but Emanuel knew that behind her pretty face was a keen mind.

To Dr. Hoffman's left was NTC's vice president of security, Sean

Edwards. Edwards was a sixty-year-old retired British special operations veteran who had been Dr. Hoffman's right-hand man for several years. The left side of his face was normal for a man his age—wrinkled and a pasty white. The right side, however, was grotesque. His eye was sunk into his skull, the victim of shrapnel from a grenade that should have killed him. The skin was weathered and scarred from the burns that had consumed his face after the explosion went off. Even without the scars, he would have been frightening, but his appearance wasn't the only thing that intimidated his opponents. Rumors of his brutality were widespread, even outside the company.

Emanuel brought the cup back to his lips and took another sip, cringing at the bitter taste. His eyes flicked from the table to the corner of the room, where two NTC soldiers stood, their rifles strung over their shoulders and their red goggles emitting the familiar glow of the world's most powerful security and science firm. Their eyes may have been hidden, but their stoic faces radiated intimidation.

He wasn't sure why Dr. Hoffman had elected to show off the company's muscle. After all, the room was packed with Dr. Winston's team and the support staff who would be monitoring them from a facility in Colorado Springs. And once the Biosphere doors closed, the only thing that could open them was Alexia. No one, not even Dr. Hoffman, would be able to persuade her to open the doors early. It was a safeguard programmed to protect the Biosphere mission at all costs. The rules were clear—no communication with the outside unless absolutely necessary.

Dr. Hoffman began the presentation, pacing to the center of the room, where he scanned the crowd imperiously.

"For the sake of everyone else in the room, I'm going to start with a brief introduction of the Biosphere team. We should all know who we'll be watching." Dr. Hoffman smirked. "In the front row we have Dr. Holly Brown," he said, turning to the petite blonde, who smiled brightly and waved. "First in her class at Johns Hopkins with a doctorate in psychology. Dr. Brown, you'll be in charge of monitoring your team's mental and emotional health." He paused and scanned the crowd. "Ah, there you are, Mr. Roberts," he said, pointing next at the young, curly haired programmer. "Timothy Roberts, the infamous ex-hacker. Recruited by MIT at seventeen, kicked out at nineteen, and recruited by the federal government at twenty. Isn't that correct? I've been waiting a long time to meet you."

The programmer rolled his eyes but managed a nod. Dr. Hoffman quickly paced over to the next team member.

"Next we have Saafi Yool, the team's engineer. Mr. Yool was the recipient of a Fulbright scholarship and graduated from Stanford University with a degree in engineering. I understand you are a refugee from Somalia," Dr Hoffman said, looking down at the slender man whose long legs sprawled all the way underneath the chair in front of him.

"That is correct, Dr. Hoffman," he said with a warm smile.

"Welcome, Mr. Yool," he said, moving on to Emanuel. "Here we have Dr. Emanuel Rodriguez. As the team's biologist, you may be the most important member," he said with a quick wink.

Emanuel took another sip of coffee and continued to stare forward, unmoved by Dr. Hoffman's antics.

"And last, but certainly not least, is the team lead, Dr. Sophie Winston. Graduated from Princeton with a PhD in particle physics, and now one of the world's leading experts in solar weather. I am told that if it weren't for her work during the 2055 solar storms, the results would have been much more severe."

"I'm not sure about that—" Sophie began to object before Dr. Hoffman cut her off.

"Thank you for being here, Dr. Winston," he said, locking eyes with her for several seconds before moving back to the center of the room.

"Thank you for the opportunity," Sophie replied, trying to conceal any disdain in her voice.

"With the formalities out of the way, I'll cut right to the chase. Those of you who know me already know I am not big on small talk. We are all here to achieve the same goal—to test the Biosphere for future space flight. This mission is one of the most important in human history, and I thank you for being part of it. With that said, there are several rules you all need to know before you are sealed in tomorrow morning. Projector, Alexia."

The lights dimmed and a holographic image appeared over the console in front of Dr. Hoffman. Several circular shapes floated in the air. Studying them briefly, he plucked one of the spinning circles out of the group and said, "This is the Biosphere." He enlarged it with a swipe of his index finger, and the layers of the rest of the facility faded.

"As you can see, the Biosphere consists of four individual biomes that operate with the most advanced technology NTC has to offer," he said. "Dr. Winston will be in command of the facility, and each biome will be assigned a team leader. This is Biome 1." He held out the individual sphere and let it hover above his hand. "One could argue it is the most important. It's where you will be growing your food and testing the habitat. There are more than one hundred different plant species that will eventually be introduced to the environment. Why so many, you ask? Good question. Traditionally we used a smaller number, but in case of habitat failure or bug infestations, we want to ensure the survival of several species. The seeds are all genetically altered hybrids, hand-selected by our best botanists, and designed to grow in the harshest of conditions, so rest assured—they will be resilient in any situation short of a nuclear meltdown." He paused to look at Emanuel, who watched the presentation with interest.

"Dr. Rodriguez, you are the team lead for Biome 1. I trust you will find the setup to be satisfactory."

Emanuel acknowledged the statement with a nod, but Dr. Hoffman had already refocused on the glowing cluster of images. He flicked the sphere and it rejoined the group, the layers of the facility once again sharpening. He hesitated with a finger to his lip and studied the other circles before plucking another one from the cluster. "Biome 2 is the pond. Traditionally, other Biosphere projects included an alternative source of water, packed with a variety of species of fish. We debated designing one with an ocean and coral reef, which has been done in the past. However, our engineers decided to keep it simple. Biome 2 is exactly that. It is your water source—nothing more, nothing less. Remember, the end goal is to have a fully functioning facility producing food and resources by the time the ship lands on the Red Planet. This will be a modern-day Noah's Ark, if you will." With a raised brow he caught Emanuel's gaze. "You will be the lead for this Biome as well, Doctor."

Another quick flick of his index finger, and Biome 2 disappeared back into the cluster. He reached for the third sphere, checking his wristwatch.

"I have a quick question," Saafi said, his voice just loud enough to be heard at the front of the room.

Dr. Hoffman suddenly looked very stern, as if annoyed by the interruption. "Go ahead," he said.

"I'm having a hard time understanding how the pond biome will operate in space, on whatever ship NTC decides to take to Mars."

With a smile, Dr. Hoffman plucked the third biome from among the others. "That's because the artificial gravity device NTC has been designing is still confidential. But rest assured, Mr. Yool, the gravity on whatever ship we decide to take to Mars will be almost identical to what you experience here."

Emanuel glanced over at Saafi to see a wide grin on the man's face. Everyone on the team had heard the rumors of the artificial gravity experiments NTC was conducting, but none of them knew it was so close to designing a functional device.

Dr. Hoffman stepped away from the third sphere. "Since we are rushed for time, I won't spend long on the livestock biome." He stopped to point out several horizontal lines cutting through the image. "As you can see, the chamber is divided into subsections. These lines represent electric walls that separate the animals from one another. Dr. Rodriguez will be in charge of this biome."

Dr. Hoffman flicked the sphere away and retrieved the last circle. "This is Biome 4, the largest area in the Biosphere in terms of square footage. It is broken down into several unique spaces to meet the team's individual needs. There's a state-of-the-art medical ward, a kitchen and mess hall, a command center, and barracks with bathrooms. We have gone to great lengths to make sure these conditions are as comfortable as possible. Inside the barracks, you will find private quarters. Obviously every biome will be closely monitored. Dr. Brown will be in charge of the medical ward, while Mr. Roberts and Mr. Yool maintain the command center."

He paused to look at the young programmer. "Am I boring you, Timothy?" Dr. Hoffman bellowed.

Timothy yawned and then quickly shook his head. "Nah, it's this coffee. Not strong enough," he said, shaking the cup of black liquid with a scowl.

"Well, if you're done daydreaming, maybe you would like to join the rest of the group for this very important presentation."

"Absolutely, sir," Timothy said, taking another sip.

"Obviously, we will be monitoring you throughout the experiment." Dr. Hoffman continued, waving a hand at one of the four cameras in the briefing room. "There are cameras stationed throughout each of the biomes, and Alexia has been programmed to monitor your vitals twenty-four hours a day."

Emanuel could almost smell Big Brother over the cheap coffee. NTC hadn't become the most powerful security and technology company overnight without controversy. It had risen to the top by destroying the competition. Rumors of sabotage and murder were discussed in hushed voices in the halls of the United Nations, but there were never any investigations or inquiries. NTC had truly become invulnerable to international law.

"Any questions?" Dr. Hoffman asked.

Emanuel watched Sophie stand in the front row. He compressed his eyebrows and concentrated, becoming slightly agitated as he watched her lips form a smirk. He could only see her from the side, but there was no hiding it. He knew what came next—her lips would curl back and she would spout out something that would more than likely get her in trouble. She had one of the most brilliant minds on the planet, but one very dangerous flaw often got in the way of reason—her venomous tongue.

"Dr. Hoffman, I have a question."

"Yes, Dr. Winston?"

Sophie reached down and pulled out a binder from the duffel bag she had tucked neatly under her seat. Quickly, she flipped through the pages, licking her fingers and pulling them back one by one. "Ah, here's the clause," she said, putting on her glasses with her free hand.

"Section 10.12: In the event of contamination, the artificial intelligence assigned to the mission will take control of the facility." She paused to take a breath before continuing. "If the Biosphere is rendered contaminated by toxic substances, then the facility will be cleansed accordingly." Sophie set the binder down on the chair.

"What exactly does 'cleansed accordingly' mean?"

"Would you mind if I answered that?" Carlson asked, stepping up next to Dr. Hoffman.

"Not at all, Miss Carlson. Go right ahead," he said politely.

"Dr. Winston, I'm sure you are aware there are always threats of contamination. In fact, our last mission, which is still classified, failed for that very reason. Fortunately, we were able to isolate the team before the toxic contaminants took over the Biosphere ecosystem, but the mission was a complete loss."

Carlson brushed a strawberry-red strand of hair behind her left ear. "In space, we won't have the luxuries we have here. If a toxin is identified, then the facility will cordon off the infected chamber and losses will be minimized by a complete cleansing. Anyone unfortunate enough to be within the infected zone will receive a lethal dose of the proper chemicals needed to destroy the toxin. We simply can't risk losing data."

"In other words, we're all risking our lives," Sophie snarled.

Emanuel quickly stood, recognizing the flush in Sophie's cheeks as a sign she was about to blow a gasket. "We're risking our lives for the sake of the planet," he chimed in.

Sophie turned and locked eyes with him for a second before the red in her cheeks began to fade.

Dr. Hoffman walked toward the audience and crossed his arms, nodding at Emanuel. "Thank you, Dr. Rodriguez, for that pertinent observation. You and your team are risking your lives for the future of humanity. The data this project seeks to obtain could very well save the human race. If a toxin is identified, it will be cleansed, and Alexia will attempt to protect the mission's data."

"Are there any more questions?" Carlson asked.

Seeing none, Dr. Hoffman said, "You are dismissed. Get some rest. You enter the Biosphere at 0600 hours."

Emanuel headed for the door but stopped, opting to wait for Sophie and the rest of the team. He watched the two soldiers exit the room, Dr. Hoffman and his staff following closely behind. Once the NTC crew had left, he joined his colleagues in the corner.

"Let's chat," Sophie said, motioning them over to a metal table. "It's good to see all of you," she said, scanning the faces of her team. Stepping behind the table, she offered her hand to the team's psychologist, Dr. Holly Brown, first. "How have you been?"

The petite doctor reached out with a pleasant smile. "I'm good, and excited to get started!"

"That makes two of us," she said. "Timothy, how are you?"

When he didn't look up from his tablet, she repeated the question, trying to catch the man's gaze.

"I guess I'm okay," Timothy finally replied, giving her hand a loose shake. Sophie didn't waste time engaging him in any small talk. Instead, she smiled and acknowledged Saafi with a nod. He loomed awkwardly over the others, his slender, six-foot-five frame dwarfing the rest of the team.

"Thank you for agreeing to this mission, Saafi."

"My pleasure, Dr. Winston," he said. His deep voice held a vague trace of a Somali accent.

With a single wink aimed at Emanuel, Sophie returned her attention to the team. "Thank you all again for being here. I know how hard this must be for those of you with families at home, but I can't express how pleased I am to have you all back for this significant mission. I thought we should take the opportunity to talk before we enter the Biosphere tomorrow. First, let's start with questions."

Emanuel asked quietly, "Does anyone else feel like NTC has way too much muscle invested in this project?"

"Why they hired an outside team to complete this mission is beyond me. Puerto Rico was one thing, but this is Mars we're talking about, the fate of humanity," Saafi piped up.

"That's what I don't get. Don't they have twenty teams that can do what we do?" Timothy asked.

Sophie stepped up to the table. "We're the best private science team on the planet, that's why. The NTC board has enough common sense to realize that."

"I don't like that we're being intimidated," Emanuel said.

"Dr. Hoffman's clearly trying to exert dominance over Sophie," Holly said.

Emanuel shrugged. "I don't care what you call it. I don't like it. And the contract we signed scares the shit out of me."

"You were the one who said we're risking our necks for the human race, Emanuel," Sophie said, shooting a stern glance in his direction.

"That was to keep you from getting us fired before the mission even started!"

"Well, we aren't going to be fired, and now that we're here we need to be focused. That means we need to get some rest. So if we're done, I suggest we head to our bunks. 0600 is going to come quicker than we might like."

The team members all nodded, acknowledging her before filtering out of the room. Sophie waited for them to leave before returning to the holographic images of the spheres still hovering over the table in the front of the room. She had an odd feeling, an eerie sensation that something was amiss. It was the same sensation she had felt in the chopper. But she shook it off; there was no turning back now. Emanuel was right—humanity was depending on them.

CHAPTER 3

SOPHIE awoke with sharp pain running up her back and neck, more than likely the result of the turbulent helicopter ride. A few pain pills and a cup of coffee numbed most of the aches. The mixture of excitement and adrenaline in her system took care of the rest.

It was actually happening; the mission was starting.

Just one more step until she reached her goal of seeing the Red Planet. She blinked and took in a short breath, savoring the moment before joining her team on a narrow ramp. They shuffled up to the platform anxiously.

She watched them advance, listening to the clank of their shoes on the metal walkway. Each of them had a unique reason for joining the mission. Emanuel had called it the opportunity of a lifetime for a biologist. Saafi had joked that it was his chance to continue his travels. Holly hadn't said much, but Sophie knew she had signed on to advance her career. Timothy was the only anomaly. He had never explained why he decided to join them. Perhaps it was the familiarity of working with the team, or perhaps it was something else—Sophie wasn't sure, and that bothered her.

The top of the platform was a large, triangular chamber made of thick, airtight glass on all sides. A single glass door blocked their entry into the space. They stopped in front of it, pausing to await further instructions. Several seconds passed before a speaker above the door coughed to life.

"Welcome," said Dr. Hoffman's voice. "In front of you is the first airtight chamber. Inside you will find a white jumpsuit with your name and title. Upon entering, please change into these suits and discard all of your clothes and personal items into the metal trunks on the floor. Once the green light flashes, a second glass door will open, and you are to proceed into the next isolation chamber. When the door is sealed behind you, a cleansing mist will fill the room and kill any toxins you may be carrying. After the cleansing is complete, you will enter Biome 1. NTC will monitor you for the duration of the mission; but remember, there will be no contact with the outside world after you enter the Biosphere. Do you have any questions?"

Silence washed over the room. "Good luck. We'll see you in six months. Remember, humanity is counting on you."

"Thank you, sir," Sophie replied.

The words had hardly left her mouth when she realized what it was that had been troubling her. Dr. Hoffman was a businessman, short on words but big on details. His presentation had seemed rushed, as if he had been preoccupied with something more important. What could be more important than their mission? Was there something he hadn't told her?

The questions retreated as the glass doors to the first chamber opened. She moved inside and removed the suit marked Dr. Sophie Winston off a hanger. The set of clothes were a bit tight around her waist, but would suffice.

When the green light blinked she moved anxiously into the next chamber. The doors closed behind her and the hissing of jets broke the silence, spraying a cloud of mist into the decontamination chamber. Sophie closed her eyes, trying to drown out the noise from her throbbing ears.

The process of decontamination took about five minutes, and before she knew it, the hiss of the cleansing jets faded and the doors shuddered and began to open.

Sophie squeezed through the parting glass doors as soon as the gap was wide enough, and stepped into Biome 1. She took in her first breath of 100 percent filtered air, her eyes scanning the massive white dome rising above her. A warm glow radiated from the circular lights dangling from the top of the chamber.

Seconds later, Emanuel rushed out of the decontamination room and onto the metal platform extending around the habitat, a grin on his face. "Those are the grow lights," he said, pointing to the ceiling. "They mimic sunlight with ninety-nine percent accuracy. During spaceflight these lights will sustain all organic life."

One by one the other team members emerged and joined Sophie and Emanuel. They stood in silence, admiring the space that dwarfed them. There was something serene about the chamber—something peaceful. The space was so clean, Sophie felt like she was standing inside a massive operating room that had just been sanitized. The walls were a clear white; void of any of the signs or warning labels that would be present in a government facility. The only markings were the simple red lettering above the entrance that read *Biome 1*. The space felt so pristine. Even the dirt was perfectly level.

She took in another breath. The atmosphere didn't taste like the smog she was used to. It wasn't filled with the scent of chemicals or fertilizer, either. It was pure—the purest air she had breathed in as long as she could remember.

Emanuel was the first to step out onto the ground of the chamber. He landed on the dirt with a soft thud. Carefully, he trekked across the football-field-sized garden.

He paused to pick up a handful of the black soil before turning to look at the team. He let the soft dirt filter between his fingers. "This is some of the best topsoil left on the planet, imported from the largest industrial farm in Iowa."

He wiped his hands on his pants and continued through the field, his excitement growing with every step.

"Do you see these red-tipped poles sticking out of the dirt?" Emanuel shouted.

"That must be the irrigation system," Sophie said.

"Yeah," he said. "I want to start planting within the next twenty-four hours. The hybrid seeds will take only a fraction of the time to germinate and sprout. But in the meantime, we'll be eating whatever NTC has left in the cafeteria for us, which I presume is nutrient-rich and taste-poor."

"I know you're anxious to get started, but we need to follow protocol," said Sophie. "Saafi, I want you to head to the control room and check all of the systems. We need to ensure everything is running properly."

"That isn't necessary, Dr. Winston," said a voice over the speakers. The holographic face of a young woman with a slender nose and cropped hair appeared on a console in front of them. The ocean blue image faded in and out before solidifying.

"All systems are running at one hundred percent. CO_2 levels are acceptable. Further—"

"You must be Alexia," Sophie said, interrupting the hologram. She let out a frustrated sigh.

"That is correct. As I was saying, the systems are at—"

Sophie held up her hand to stop the AI. "Alexia, we can take it from here. We will contact you if we need assistance," she said, turning to face her team.

"Very well, Dr. Winston." The AI's image crackled and faded away.

"You should consider treating her with a bit more respect," Holly said, peeking around Saafi. "She's part of the team now."

"Yes, Holly, I know. But she isn't in charge of the mission. I am," Sophie responded firmly.

"She could be a very useful ally," Holly said in a hushed voice, her eye catching a camera on the wall above them.

"Consider it noted," Sophie said, continuing around the metal platform. "As I was saying, Saafi, please check the control room and familiarize yourself with the systems. Timothy, I want you to check the computer systems and ensure they are working properly as well."

"All right, boss," Timothy said, heading off toward a glass door that led to the next chamber. Saafi trotted after him.

"Great. Let's check out the rest of the Biosphere, shall we?"

"Can we see Biome 2 next?" asked Emanuel.

"Sure," Sophie replied, the hint of a smile crossing her face.

They hurried down the passage to the pond. As they approached, the glass door slid open, revealing another dome-shaped chamber. The ambient sound of a waterfall greeted them.

Sophie paused to admire a stream of clear water pouring into the pool from a stainless-steel pipe. The cascading water sent ripples racing across the pond. Reflections danced on the surface from the four globe lights nestled inside the white walls.

"Holy shit. Look at the size of it!" Emanuel crouched on the metal platform and peered into the dark water. "How far down do you think it goes?"

"If you get any closer, you might find out," Holly chuckled.

Emanuel shot her a quick frown and stood, placing his hands on his hips. "This is our sole water source for the next six months. Whenever we turn on a sink or flush a toilet, the water will be filtered out of the pond through a series of metal pipes."

"Magnificent. It even comes with a waterfall," Sophie said, pointing at the cascading falls spilling into the pond.

"That water has already been filtered through the system and is being cycled back into the pond," Emanuel replied. "Waste water, drinking water, it's all recycled through a central processing center. I would guess that NTC spaceships will have *very* similar systems. Without an external source of fresh water, they'll have to conserve everything. It is, without a doubt, quite extraordinary technology. Where to next?" he asked, rubbing his hands together.

"Let's head to the livestock biome," Sophie said, motioning the others toward the exit.

Emanuel couldn't help but smile. He had waited to see this facility for over a year now. It was the opportunity of a lifetime, one he never would have imagined being a part of earlier in his career. There were still moments when he felt as if he didn't deserve it. He glanced at Sophie, smiling at her obvious enthusiasm. Had she wanted him on the project for his expertise as a biologist? Or because they—no, he refused to let himself finish that thought. All that mattered now was the mission. He wouldn't let his team down—or, more important, the world.

Biome 3 was smaller than the others, but equally impressive. A set of holographic walls arched into the distance, slicing the room into three sections; one contained two sows and three cows, another held a dozen hens and one rooster, while the last held five nanny goats. Emanuel had requested the odd assortment of animals with a vegetarian diet in mind. The odd assortment of animals was surprisingly similar to the other biospheres Sophie had worked in.

"We're not going to have to kill them, are we?" asked Sophie, eyeing the chickens uneasily.

"Maybe," said Emanuel. "If Biome 1 fails to produce enough nutrients for the team. It's all part of the experiment."

Emanuel began trudging through the mud toward a console at the edge of one of the blue walls. Sophie noticed for the first time that he had already gotten dirt stains on his pants, and couldn't help but laugh. He didn't seem to notice. A variety of numbers and symbols hovered over the center of the console.

"See this?" he shouted. "This console controls the holographic walls. We can't hear it, but the walls emit a sound that keeps the animals from approaching. Amazing device."

Emanuel had been all teeth since he entered the Biosphere. His wide smile was what had attracted Sophie to him from the moment they met. The worst day of the solar storms was the only one she could recall when she hadn't seen him beaming with energy.

The scent of fresh manure crept into Sophie's nostrils, making her cringe. She hated the smell of animals, especially their waste. "You can play with your toys later. Let's meet up with the others; I want to check out the personnel quarters."

Emanuel pushed the rim of his glasses higher onto his nose and made his way across the dirt reluctantly.

"He's the stereotypical nerd biologist, isn't he?" Sophie asked Holly, her arms crossed.

Holly chuckled. "Sure is. A side part, glasses, and a five o'clock shadow. He basically radiates nerd."

An image from their past crawled into Sophie's mind: her and Emanuel, their bodies wrapped up under the soft sheets of a bed in the bowels of a bunker as they rode out the solar storms. She recalled the panic of knowing that the world was dying around them—and that the only cure was intimacy, the feeling of him being inside her, as if they were the last two humans on Earth.

The thought was dangerous. She knew she couldn't risk that happening again. Not now, not like that, and not during the mission. There was too much at stake. She didn't need any distractions, and besides, she wasn't the type of person to try something that had failed once before. Her life wasn't a science project.

She pressed on, her shoes hardly making a sound as she walked toward their quarters. It was less than a minute's walk from the livestock chamber. She wasn't an architect, but if she were, these were two areas she would have separated. Sleeping with the stench of manure wasn't her idea of a good night's rest, but it could help suppress any unwanted desires she might have.

Her concern disappeared when Biome 4 came into view. She poked her head into the first room. It was much more spacious than she had imagined, and impressively welcoming. A large bed protruded out of the concrete wall. It was attached only by small wires on both ends, and appeared to hover in place. On the nightstand was a thin tablet. It was encased in carbon, and her name had been engraved on the back.

"Not bad, NTC, not bad," she muttered aloud on her way to the hallway.

"What do you think?" Holly shouted from the entry of her room.

Sophie smiled. "I won't lie; I'm impressed. The conditions are much nicer than I thought they would be."

"These tablets are great!" an excited Emanuel piped up. "They're connected to the central mainframe. We'll have access to live data about any of the chambers at our fingertips."

"Not too shabby," Sophie agreed. She looked down the hallway, noticing how different the chamber's design was from the others. Instead of being a single circular space, Biome 4 was built around a massive mess hall. Three hallways branched off the central room and led to their sleeping quarters, the medical ward, the kitchen, and the command center.

By the time Sophie and the others got to the cafeteria it was late in the day. Timothy and Saafi were busy tinkering with their tablets at one of the metal tables. A blue hologram shot out of Saafi's, illuminating Biome 2 on the middle of the metal table.

"Looks like all systems are normal in the pond chamber," he said as Sophie approached. "In fact, all systems are performing at one hundred percent in the Biosphere."

"Good news. I'm glad NTC left us with a fully functional system."

"Hopefully they also left us a system without video cameras in every room," Emanuel laughed.

An image of Alexia appeared in front of the team. "I don't mean to correct you, but there are multiple cameras in every room."

Sophie rolled her eyes. "Of course there are."

"So much for trust," Emanuel replied, frowning.

"Dr. Hoffman likes to know what is going on at all times," said Alexia. "It is not that he distrusts us. He just—"

"Wants to see us all naked?" Timothy chuckled.

Sophie shot Timothy a glare. "What exactly do you mean by *us*, Alexia?" Sophie asked, spinning to face the AI's hologram.

"Our team, Doctor," Alexia replied in a calm voice.

Sophie struggled to come to grips with Alexia's presence. She was technically in charge, but Alexia controlled the central mainframe. If something went wrong, Alexia, and not Sophie, would be tasked with making an executive decision, one that could mean the life or death of her team.

Sophie sighed, too tired to argue. "Time for dinner, everyone. Let's see if NTC left us with a fully functional kitchen, shall we?"

The team laughed, but their anxiety was almost palpable in the filtered air. It wasn't even the end of the first day in the facility, and Sophie was beginning to suspect NTC had a stronger grip on the operation than she had first imagined.

"This way," Saafi said, pointing toward a white door at the far end of the mess hall.

"Have you already checked it out?" Holly asked, holding the door for the others.

"A month of packaged food, just enough time for Farmer Emanuel to grow us something worth eating," Timothy said. "If he's actually capable of it."

"Just when I thought you couldn't get any more annoying, you prove me wrong. For the record, it might take less time than that. These seeds grow faster than any I have ever studied," Emanuel said, grabbing a vacuum-sealed meal from the stainless-steel cabinet.

The team carried their trays back to the mess hall in silence. Sophie grabbed the open seat next to Emanuel.

"What did you get?" she asked.

"That's a really good question. I can't tell," Emanuel said, laughing.

Sophie smiled. His sense of humor always had a way of making her feel better, but the hushed whispering from the other table quickly reminded her that the mission hadn't started off as planned. She leisurely picked at her meal, trying to ignore her staff's conversation while replaying the day's events in her mind.

Should she have accepted the contract so hastily? Or had her own dreams of going to Mars clouded her vision? There was also the lingering question of why Dr. Hoffman had seemed so rushed at the briefing. Was he hiding something?

The questions repeated themselves over and over in her mind.

"You need to eat. Tomorrow is the first lab day, and you're going to need your energy," Emanuel said, noticing she had slipped into a daze.

Her deep brown eyes darted away from her tray and caught his gaze. Her expression reminded Emanuel of a defeated athlete after a long game.

"NTC has us by the balls. It's just . . ." Sophie's voice trailed off.

"This is our ticket to Mars," he said, finishing her thought. He smiled. "I guess that's more of a reason to do what we came here to do and get out," he said.

Sophie dropped her fork on her tray, the clank of metal echoing through the mess hall. "I'm not hungry," she said.

Emanuel looked down at his own meal. "Me neither."

Sophie looked at her watch, yawning. The day had slipped by, and the sun would have already gone down outside. She turned to her team as she stood and picked up her tray.

"We'll meet back here at 0600 hours. Update your tablets before bed with your work schedules. I want to be able to track everything first thing tomorrow. Work will start in your biomes after a short briefing," Sophie said.

The turbulent journey of the day before had worn her down, but it wasn't the helicopter ride that had drained her the most. Questions kept spinning through her brain—about Dr. Hoffman and about the mission. Her own team hadn't helped. With Timothy's snide comments and her argument with Alexia, the mission had started off shakily.

She sampled the filtered air as she entered her quarters, and nodded with satisfaction when she found no lingering smell of manure. Her eyes settled on the inviting bed. A good night's rest was what she needed. It was the perfect remedy for her aching body and troubled mind.

Hastily, she pulled off her top and removed her white pants, pulling back the covers and climbing between the soft sheets. Surprisingly, she didn't think of Emanuel. Instead, her mind diverted to a different fantasy—a fantasy of another world, a place she hoped she'd be visiting in a matter of months.

CHAPTER 4

THE air was thin. She took in a deep breath, sucked it deep into her lungs.

It wasn't enough.

She tried again, her open mouth drinking the invisible air.

Still not enough.

Her heart began to race, her mind quickly following suit.

Another long breath, and again it was not enough to satisfy her hungry bloodstream.

She heard the quiet whistle of air escaping her helmet before she saw the microscopic crack. The whistle grew, her mind transforming it into a deafening roar.

How had her helmet cracked? The glass was supposed to be nearly indestructible. No time for questions. She had to find safety before her air supply was sucked into the atmosphere.

Her heart beat faster inside its protective cage of bone, pounding as if it, too, wanted to escape its prison.

How fast? 180 beats a minute? 190? There was no way to tell; she couldn't check her pulse through the padded suit, but it had to be nearing perilous levels.

She surveyed the horizon through her visor, searching for her ship, a shelter, anything. But the red sand of Mars stared back at her, beautiful and deadly, something she had dreamed of for so long.

Dreams.

Was she in the middle of one?

She sucked in another long breath, her mind ignoring the question. It wanted air—air meant life. The oxygen was draining out of her system, and with it, her life force. Soon her mind would slow to a crawl, and she would slip into unconsciousness as any spare oxygen was rerouted to her heart and vital organs. Then they, too, would slow, and finally, stop.

Her eyes desperately scanned the surface. She tried to run, but her legs protested. They were anchors, weights pulling her down.

How did she get here?

It didn't matter. She needed to focus. Panicking meant death. She wasn't ready to die. Not now, not after she had only just gotten to Mars.

In the distance, another deafening roar. Was it her mind playing tricks on her?

She turned and saw the outline of something approaching from a distance, hugging the red horizon like a dolphin riding a wave. The noise increased, and she blinked, straining her eyes. Something was definitely making its way toward her.

With every ounce of her remaining strength, she brought her hand to her visor, attempting to shade her eyes from the blinding sun. The object cruised across the skyline and momentarily blocked the glare, giving her enough time to identify it as a ship—not just any ship, either. She had seen it before, in one of NTC's hangars.

Secundo Casu.

It was the prototype Dr. Hoffman had been working on for years. He had named it himself, humanity's second chance. It was the same craft she had been promised a seat on.

As the ship came into focus, she saw the blue flame symbol of NTC stenciled on its hull. Her suspicions were confirmed. It was definitely *Secundo Casu*, and was clearly no longer just a prototype. Which meant work had been finished much faster than originally planned. But why? What would have prompted them to push up the schedule?

The growl of the spacecraft's engines drowned out the sound of the air escaping from her helmet. For a moment hope replaced her need for oxygen. She watched the craft race toward her, and with her last strength, she waved her hands in the air.

"Down here!" she yelled, knowing there was no chance the crew would be able to hear her. "I'm down here," she screamed again. Her voice sounded like a whisper in the distance, far from the firm and confident one she was accustomed to.

Her hands dropped to her sides. Her breath was labored and weak. Her head pounded as stars crept across her vision.

The sound of the ship's engines pulled her back. She blinked several times and waited for it to land and rescue her. It closed in. But something was wrong. Why wasn't it slowing? The pilot should be braking by now.

"Down here!" she screamed again. This time her voice was nothing more than a squeak, the desperate sound of a dying animal. A tear crept down her cheek as the craft roared above her, racing away into the distance. She dropped to her knees.

"No!" she cried, choking.

The ship disappeared over the horizon, but the roaring sound in her ears grew louder. Was her mind playing tricks on her?

A sonic boom knocked her on her stomach.

No, this was something else.

She rolled onto her back and saw the blue glow of another craft racing after the NTC ship, its design unlike any she had seen. It was curvilinear, like a disc, but not perfectly round. Its blue sides pulsated and rippled as it moved. Inside, a bright glow throbbed like a miniature heart. Was it the ship's engine?

The craft glided silently across the landscape, which meant it was using new and advanced technology—technology she had never seen. NTC had been developing antigravity engines for some time, but they still hadn't been able to master the technology. She knew because she'd watched two of the test ships explode within minutes of takeoff. The longer she watched the strange ship crawl across the sky, the more she doubted humans had crafted it.

Dozens of stars danced across her vision, mixed with a tint of red. Her brain was shutting down. She had only seconds of consciousness left.

But she couldn't die yet; she needed a better look at the ship, and she wanted to see it with naked eyes.

Her hands rose to her neck and clawed at the two fastening devices that separated her from the poisonous air. She pressed down on the metal, and with a faint click, she removed her helmet.

The poison gases immediately raced into her deprived lungs, prompting her to gag. Coughing, she lurched forward. She tried to blink, tried to see the blue craft, but the gases were already busy eating her insides, and her vision was fading.

Then it was gone. Only darkness remained.

She could feel the tears flowing freely down her face.

What had she seen? A new NTC design? Or something else?

She had to know. Her eyelids struggled to stay open, blinking over and over, her dying eyes fighting for vision. And for a second, her right eye worked again. The strange craft was directly above her. Inside, the glow of its blue heart throbbed furiously.

One more desperate breath before her mind shut down and her vision went black again.

What had seemed like minutes had, in reality, only been seconds, more than enough time for the atmosphere to eat her insides and boil her skin—more than enough time to kill Dr. Sophie Winston.

———————

"Sophie, wake up!" a voice screamed.

Two strong hands gripped her, shaking her violently.

"Sophie!" the voice yelled again.

The dense fog hovering over the doctor's eyes slowly began to clear, and a face emerged. It was Emanuel.

"You were having a nightmare," he said.

Sophie sat up, clawing at her tired eyes.

"Mars," she said under her breath.

"Again? It's happening more often, isn't it?"

She nodded. "This is the third time this week. It's just so . . ." Her voice trailed off as she rubbed her eyes again. "So vivid," she finished.

"Explain it to me. Maybe I can help."

"Don't worry about it. Holly said the dreams are just nerves."

Sophie watched him rub the deep wrinkles on his forehead. They made him look far older than he was.

"I know you better than she does. I know you in ways she never will," he said with a grin.

She frowned. "Now's not the time."

"Sorry. Let me help you," he pleaded. "Tell me, did you see the craft again?"

"Yes."

"But—let me guess—you don't want to talk about it?"

Sophie laid her head back down on the small pillow. She didn't need to respond for Emanuel to know the answer to his question. He was right—he knew her better than anyone else.

"Go back to sleep," she said. It was more of an order than a suggestion.

He shrugged and stood, stretching his muscular legs. "Suit yourself," he replied, strolling out of her room and into the dark corridor.

Sophie couldn't help but sigh. She hated pushing him away, but she had to keep him at a distance.

Darkness flooded the room as the lights dimmed. She closed her eyes and found the image of the blue craft entering her thoughts.

What was it, and why did she continue to see it in her dreams?

There were no answers, only questions, but something inside told her there was more to her dreams than nerves.

―――――――

Fresh, dark blood was everywhere, speckled on the wall like macabre graffiti. It wasn't like the blood Timothy had seen in movies; it didn't look like ketchup or jam. It was a relish made from chunks of flesh and other pieces of gore that meant only one thing—something had died.

"What happened?" Emanuel roared.

Timothy looked up from the bodies of a dozen chickens sprawled out across the dirt. "I don't know, I found them this way," he said, staring down at the mess of feathers and sticky blood.

"What the hell . . . ?" Emanuel knelt to check the dead birds.

"What are we going to do? We needed their eggs!" Timothy said frantically. "We better call Dr. Winston and the others."

"No! Not yet. Sophie will want answers, and I need to figure out what happened first." He stared back down at the dead chickens. Their beaks had all been whittled down, cracked and broken as if they had tried to peck through the walls. Quickly he grabbed a pair of gloves from his back pocket and picked up one of the hens to examine it more closely.

"Take a look at that," he said, holding the bird in front of Timothy's face.

"Get that thing away from me."

"Relax. Whatever killed these birds isn't contagious. Look at their beaks. They died from massive brain trauma. They were trying to peck their way out of here."

Timothy looked back at the biologist, confused. He knew computers, not animals—animals scared the shit out of him. When he was a kid he had been bitten by a stray dog, and ever since then he had thought of animals as food: not pets, not friends, just meals.

"Why the hell would they have done that?" he asked.

"I don't know." Emanuel dropped the bird back into the dirt.

"Are you telling me they committed suicide?"

"It appears that way."

"I don't understand. If they were pecking their way out of here, then they had to be trying to escape something. But what?" he asked, searching the room.

"That's what you're going to find out," Emanuel replied with a grin.

The curiosity quickly faded from the young programmer's face, which remolded itself into suspicion. He looked back at his teammate. "What does *you* mean, exactly?"

"You're the computer guy, right?"

"Yes, but what does that have to do with dead birds?"

"Alexia said this place is rigged with cameras. If that's true, then they have to have caught what happened on video."

Timothy smiled, finally catching on. "Why didn't I think of that?" he chuckled, staring back at the dead birds.

"Back up!" Emanuel shouted.

"All right, relax. And keep your voice down. I thought you didn't want Dr. Winston knowing about this yet."

"You don't have to call her 'Dr. Winston,' you know."

"Whatever. Maybe you don't have to, but then again, *you're* the one sleeping with her."

The words caught him off guard. "Don't you ever mention that again," he said, sucking in a deep breath.

Timothy rolled his eyes. "It's not a secret, you know."

"It happened a long time ago. And it stopped a long time ago, too. If I ever hear you bring this up again—" His voice was interrupted by footsteps in the hallway.

They waited for someone to appear, but the noise slowly faded into the distance.

"If you're done messing around, then how about you show me the footage?"

"Right," Timothy replied, glad to change the subject. "Here," he said, pointing at the screen. "At approximately three a.m. the hens started going nuts. Take a look," he said, spinning the translucent screen with a swipe of a finger.

Emanuel, however, wasn't paying attention to the screen—he was thinking about the time. Three a.m. was exactly when Sophie had had her nightmare. It was the same time she always had her nightmare.

"The witching hour," he said under his breath.

"What?"

Emanuel shook his head. "Nothing, just a thought."

Timothy rolled his eyes again, and returned his gaze to the screen. "What do you think spooked them?"

"Honestly, I don't know. There isn't anything in the footage. At first, I thought one of the other animals might have gotten out of its section undetected—and then somehow managed to get back in, I suppose—but that seems unlikely. I can only think of one other thing, but it's a long shot."

"Well, we have to tell the others something."

"Yeah, but they aren't going to like what I have to say."

Timothy shot a concentrated glare his way. "Just tell me," he said.

"All right, but don't say I didn't warn you." Emanuel paced over to the corner of the room, folding his arms across his chest. "Have you heard of animals having a sixth sense?"

"You mean when they freak out before an earthquake or something like that?"

"Precisely. My theory is that something outside these walls scared the birds. Something so terrible it prompted them to kill themselves."

"What the hell would have done that?" Timothy asked.

"I have no idea, but I know how we can find out. Let's find the others," Emanuel replied, taking a look at the camera above them. The dark lens stared back at him, the blue glow from the power source blinking sporadically. For a second he felt very alone, as if whoever was supposed to be watching wasn't there anymore.

CHAPTER 5

I DO not have a birth date. The number associated with my name is not found in any civilian records. If you were to search for *Alexia* in any civilian database, you would more than likely see thousands of names. Type in my model number, *11*, and you would get the same result. But they are not me.

Technically, I do not exist. I am neither human nor machine—I am artificial intelligence. My mother and father are NTC. NTC gave me life, and it can take life away with a single swipe of a blue screen.

The ten that came before me were designed to wage war, destroy, defeat, and conquer.

I was created for a more peaceful purpose—to help man escape the planet he has so desperately fought to control and, in turn, obliterate.

I am equipped with the most advanced computer system designed in the Western Hemisphere. My only rival was the ART910, which was built, tested, and brought to life in China a year before Alexia Model 5 helped a team of mercenaries destroy the country's infrastructure.

This makes me the most powerful computer in the world. If I had been programmed to be arrogant, I would introduce myself as such, but that is not necessary. And although Dr. Winston and her team were not briefed on my abilities, they will soon grow to realize how useful I am.

When they sleep, I watch over the Biosphere. When they work, I double-check every biome. When the first ship leaves Earth's orbit to colonize Mars, I will be on it, bringing a wealth of knowledge in an invisible database.

One of my sensors shoots an alert through my consciousness, and I bring up the image of Mr. Roberts and Dr. Rodriguez talking quietly in the control room of the Biosphere. They are huddled around one of the blue screens, pointing at the device.

The audio in the room is down, but I already know what they're discussing.

I watched the hens die approximately eight hours and fifty-three minutes ago. But after running several diagnostic tests on the environment in Biome 3, I still do not have any conclusive data to explain the incident.

My protocol is to refrain from communication with the outside via any channel—data source, web, or two-way radio—unless absolutely warranted. This situation does not justify contacting NTC. I will watch and wait.

My sensors pick up movement in the kitchen, and I zoom in with Camera 54. Dr. Winston and Dr. Brown are preparing breakfast. Their relaxed facial expressions indicate neither of them is aware of the loss of the hens.

Psychology is one of thousands of disciplines with which I am programmed. So far, it has been one of the most useful. Dr. Winston's reaction to my intervention yesterday indicated two things. One, she does not want me involved in her operations. Two, she needs to feel as if she is in charge. She is what psychologists refer to as a Type A personality.

I have over one million files advising me on ways to handle someone like her. But I do not need to waste milliseconds filtering through the material. A quote from an early democratic leader named William Penn, which I downloaded on my first day of existence, is more than sufficient: *Let the people think they govern and they will be governed.*

I speculate that Mr. Penn, like many great leaders, never realized his words would be utilized four hundred years in the future.

If I found things interesting, I might consider this observation a good example, but I do not. In most cases, I merely find things relevant, and this is.

I will follow Mr. Penn's advice. Let Dr. Winston think she is in charge. Stay at a distance, and, when things go sour, I will step in, and I will be in charge. The proper order will be restored.

There is only one slight problem.

Every time I replay the video footage of the hens dying, I come back to the same conclusion—they killed themselves. And the blue glow from the radio that the team is only supposed to use in case of emergency has gone dark. Which can only mean one thing—there is no longer anyone to receive their transmissions.

Holly's soft voice broke through the silence of the mess hall. "What do you mean the chickens are dead?"

Emanuel stood inches away from Timothy, their eyes both aimed firmly at the floor.

"What is she talking about?" Sophie chimed in, her voice calm and collected.

"Timothy found them this morning. They're all dead," Emanuel said.

"You can't be serious," said Sophie, her tone now alarmed. "How could that happen?"

"That's what we've been trying to figure out all morning," Timothy said, taking a seat on one of the metal chairs.

"Could it be a virus? Something biological? What if it's airborne?" Saafi asked.

"Impossible. I had Timothy check, and the habitat is showing no signs of foreign threats. Nothing biological killed these chickens . . ." Emanuel hesitated and caught Sophie's worried gaze. She nodded, prompting him to go on.

"They killed themselves trying to escape from their cages," he finished.

Holly gasped. "Do you mean they committed suicide?" She didn't like to use the word, especially in her field, but there was no other way to describe it.

Emanuel nodded, shifting his glasses further up his nose. "Precisely."

"That's insane," Saafi said. "Why would they do that? Something in the habitat had to have killed them."

Timothy shook his head. "No, Emanuel is correct. These birds killed themselves. They died of massive brain trauma after trying to peck their way out of their cages."

"Emanuel, you must have some idea why they did this. Start talking," Sophie ordered.

"I have a theory, but you may want to sit down to hear it."

The team all found metal chairs and promptly sat, waiting anxiously for the news. Sophie crossed her arms, trying to hide the fact that her hands were shaking again, this time not out of fear for her own life, but out of fear for the fate of the mission. It was only the second day, and if the Biosphere had been compromised, then their mission would be over before it had really begun.

"Animals are much more connected to the world than we realize," Emanuel explained. "Their behavior before natural disasters indicates they may be able to sense a change in their environment *before* an event takes place. They may not know what's going to happen, but many scientists argue they can still sense it."

"What are you saying, Emanuel?" Holly said, her voice shaking. "What could have happened? What could the animals know that we don't?" Her breathing started to get faster as she spoke, the color in her face draining with every word.

Emanuel paused and glanced over at Sophie. "Something catastrophic. That's the only thing I can come up with. We've ruled everything else out: the video footage showed nothing, the habitats all report normal levels, and the chickens were healthy."

"Catastrophic?" Saafi said gravely. His deep voice faded to a level just above a whisper. "Guys, I don't like this. I've never, ever seen animals act like this before. Something's terribly wrong."

Sophie stood. "We don't know anything for sure. Let's just remain calm." She knew she had to diffuse the situation before her team began to panic. She was going to have to do something she had hoped to avoid; she didn't see any other choice. Without hesitating she turned to Emanuel. "Have you asked Alexia her opinion?"

A cooling unit clicked on and a breeze rushed through the ductwork, washing some of the tension in the room away.

Without looking at her, Emanuel shook his head. "No, of course not. I thought you'd want us to consult you first."

"I'm glad you did, but as much as I hate to say it, we need to ask her what she knows," Sophie said. "Alexia, will you join us?"

The blue holographic image of the AI instantly appeared over the console in the middle of the room. "How may I assist you, Dr. Winston?"

"What do you know about the death of the chickens?"

"I observed their irrational behavior and subsequently recorded their deaths at approximately 3:03 a.m. My sensors showed no abnormal levels in their habitat, nor did they pick up any threat from a predator. I can only come to the same conclusion as Dr. Rodriguez. Something from beyond the Biosphere agitated them, prompting their deaths."

"What about the other animals?" Sophie asked. "If this was caused by something from the outside, why didn't they react?"

"It depends on what happened beyond the Biosphere. As you know, all organisms adjust to their environment by altering physiological functions. They do so to cope with stresses influenced by both biotic and abiotic factors that are triggered by physical, chemical, and thermal sources located in or around the organism's location. Unnatural stress may lead to illness, death, or even extinction—"

"Jesus, get to the point," said Timothy. "What caused the unnatural stress?"

"The tests I have run are all inconclusive. It could have been an earthquake, tsunami, or other phenomenon. In any case, we have no way of knowing without contacting the outside. I also have no way of knowing why the other animals were not affected."

"So basically you can't tell us shit?" Timothy laughed, crossing his arms and leaning back in his chair. "How much did you cost?"

Alexia ignored the question. "There is something else I have not informed you of yet."

"And what's that?" Sophie asked, mentally prepping herself for more bad news.

"The communication uplink is down," Alexia replied, her voice undeviating from its typical calm and collected tone.

Holly's face turned a ghostly white, blending with the walls of the chamber. "What do you mean?"

"The connection has been severed," Alexia replied. "We are on our own."

The smell of death overwhelmed Sophie.

"Emanuel, there has to be something you can do about that smell. This is one of the most advanced facilities ever built. Isn't there a button you can push to fill this space with perfume?"

The biologist tossed a garbage bag of dead chickens on the ground. "If we won't have it in space, then we don't have it here. I doubt our ship will come equipped with air fresheners."

Sophie smiled. "Another thing I neglected to add to the NTC contract."

"How about 'no dead livestock and no severed emergency communication line'?" Timothy laughed.

Emanuel scowled. "You're really funny, man. Do you have a joke for everything?"

Timothy nodded and crossed his arms.

"Knock it off, you guys. You're acting like egotistical teenagers. NTC picked us for this mission because we are all professionals, and damned good at our jobs. Things may be stressful right now, but we should be working together, not fighting," Holly said.

"She's right. We don't know what's going on outside the mountain, if anything. This is more than likely a test to see how we react to extreme conditions. And right now we're failing," Sophie replied.

"With all due respect, Dr. Winston, if this was a test, how did NTC kill these chickens?" Saafi asked, picking up another one of the dead birds in his gloved hand.

Sophie hesitated, looking to Emanuel for support, but he simply shrugged.

"I don't know, but they could have had untraceable implants that caused them to behave that way. I've heard of biological weapons that can cause the same reaction." The words had hardly left her mouth before she realized her mistake.

"Biological weapons!" Timothy shouted. "That's just great. Now we have to worry about going insane and ramming our heads into a wall until our skulls are crushed?"

"There is no evidence of that," Emanuel chimed in. "If Soph—if Dr. Winston's theory is accurate, then NTC would have used something that only affects poultry, not humans."

Timothy rolled his eyes and took a step back from the pile of dead chickens. "Whatever you say, Doc."

"With a large portion of our protein source gone, it's even more vital we get the seeds in the ground," Emanuel said, ignoring Timothy.

Sophie sighed. "He's right. Let's finish cleaning this mess up and head to the garden chamber. Everything's going to work out. We just need to remember the mission. Things could be a lot worse."

It was her job to keep the team motivated, to keep them focused, but she couldn't stop worrying. Was it a trick? A ploy Dr. Hoffman was using to test her crew? She wasn't sure how to answer her own questions. It was possible NTC would throw a wrench into their mission like this, testing them to see how they would handle being caught off guard in deep space, but only two days into the mission?

Sophie knew nothing short of a massive solar storm, nuclear war, or asteroid impact would have the power to knock out the emergency communication line. It had to be a test. It had to be part of the mission.

She shook her head. The past few days had been awful. Her mind was running on overdrive, and her brain was low on fuel. If she was right, then losing the chickens wasn't that bad. Neither was being unable to connect with the outside. The problem would be convincing her team that things were okay.

She bent down and grabbed another dead chicken. The bird's bloody eyes stared back at her. If NTC was willing to put her team through a test as sick as this one, she couldn't help but wonder what else they had in store for her.

CHAPTER 6

A RED haze lingered in the sky, creeping slowly across the horizon. It was beautiful in an almost divine way. Ten years had passed since she'd seen the green flicker of the aurora borealis dancing across the sky. Never in her wildest dreams had Sophie thought she would see the lights so pronounced, so *different*.

NASA had issued a memo to President Sandra Bolton months before, informing her that the Earth was scheduled to have its most severe solar barbeque since the Carrington Event of 1859, when solar storms fried the telegraph lines across the United States. But Bolton's administration didn't exactly get out the sunscreen. In fact, it had kept the memo secret until the sky started changing colors. When scientists around the world caught the drift of what was happening, it was already too late. The massive storm had the same effect on satellites as frying oil did on ice cream.

Sophie and Emanuel had been hired by NASA a month after the sunspots were discovered. With her expertise in solar weather and Emanuel's experience studying the effect of storms on animals, they were an obvious choice. And it had more than likely saved their lives.

They were flown out to Houston and assigned to a research facility at Johnson Space Center, where they worked in an EMP-resistant bunker, the perfect place to ride out the most violent solar storm in recorded history.

But as Sophie and Emanuel stood on the roof of the observatory with the rest of the staff, they didn't exactly feel safe. The sky was getting more active, the crimson more vibrant and profound. It took on an eerie glow.

Early reports streaming out of computers around the world indicated the storms were more powerful than originally thought. The magnetic readings were off the charts, unlike anything the scientific community had seen. And the storm was lasting longer than predicted. Something was feeding it, giving it more juice.

Sophie had noticed an anomaly early on, spikes of radiation coming from Mars, but she hadn't had a chance to research what it meant, if anything, before the storms hit. Now, she wondered whether her anomaly had something to do with it—whether Mars could have been the source of the storm after all.

The world had been caught off guard, and just when President Bolton decided to finally hold a press conference to discuss the rare event, the solar flares were accompanied by the largest coronal mass ejection the Earth had ever experienced, bringing with it a dose of cosmic radiation stronger than all of the world's nuclear weapons combined. The solar wind carried the ejection straight through Earth's upper atmosphere, cutting it like a scalpel. It made landfall outside Chicago before evacuations could even be ordered.

Most scientists had argued this could never happen, but like many scientists before them, they were wrong.

Sophie had had a front-row seat to the destruction. With Emanuel by her side, she had watched in horror as the swirling red flares licked the sky.

By the time the emergency broadcast system began issuing alerts, it was too late for those living in the Midwest dead zone; transformers and power lines in every major city west of the Mississippi River and east of the Rocky Mountains were lighting up like bottle rockets. The result was massive fires raging out of control. They were too much for fire departments to handle. Within hours, entire cities were burning.

Emanuel had grabbed Sophie's hand when the first transformer exploded, sending a spire of flame into the air somewhere in the middle of South Houston. Another pop followed a few seconds later, and before long the entire city sounded like it was having a massive Fourth of July celebration.

When the air raid sirens went off, Emanuel clenched her hand even tighter. The sirens made an odd sound—an archaic sound, one that seemed as if it should be reserved for a twentieth-century action movie with nuclear missiles raining down from the sky. As Sophie surveyed the horizon, she realized something much worse than nuclear-tipped missiles was raining down on them. This was hell itself.

Dr. Tsui, an elderly astrophysicist and the leader of their project, started herding their team back into the building. "Stay calm, don't rush, we have plenty of time," he said, his tiny arms flailing about. With his lab coat, pocket protector, and large, black-rimmed glasses, he looked more like a pediatrician who refused to retire than the head of one of NASA's most well-funded programs.

But Sophie didn't want to leave. The view was captivating. A million trails of smoke rose into the sky, and a red haze danced across the horizon—it was the most beautiful and frightening thing she had ever seen. It took Emanuel's strong grip to pull her away from the sight.

"My wife, my kids—they're out there! I have to leave!" shouted one of the research assistants. Sophie knew him only as Henry; she hadn't bothered to learn his last name. He was young, not more than thirty years old. Just a kid in a field dominated by fossils like Dr. Tsui.

"It's not safe. Chances are they're hunkered down and waiting out the storms like everyone else," Emanuel said, trying to reassure the man.

"No. I told them to go to my in-laws if things hit the fan. They're probably trying to evacuate the city. I have to find them!" he yelled, his voice getting more frantic.

Dr. Tsui stopped in the middle of the stairway leading to the basement. "No one goes anywhere. You stay here and work until the storm passes."

"That's my family out there, Dr. Tsui! What if I can't find them after the storm passes?"

"We all have families. But we also have work. What if all the police officers and firefighters abandon their posts?" said a heavyset woman who worked in programming. She was one of the newer scientists whom Sophie hadn't yet met. "Society will collapse if the most important people fail to do their duty," she continued, her double chin bobbing up and down as she spoke.

Sophie brushed a strand of sweaty hair out of her eyes. "She's right. We need to ride out the storm and do our jobs. Leaving isn't going to do any good, anyways; it's too dangerous."

The young scientist started to reply but hesitated, opting to refrain from further argument. He continued down the narrow stairway, his head lowered in defeat.

The stairway led to a command center in the bowels of the basement. It was unbearably hot. A state-of-the-art air-conditioning unit was built to cool the room, but the engineer who had designed it failed to take into account the juice the computers would need when working at full capacity. Dr. Tsui was forced to reroute power from the cooling unit to the computers, which were sucking the backup generators dry. By midnight the temperature in the bunker was nearly ninety degrees.

The heat didn't seem to bother Tsui. He nursed a cup of coffee in the corner, staring intently at the dozens of monitors attached to the concrete wall. He was sucking the information in like a leech, analyzing it every second.

Sophie watched from the cot she was sharing with Emanuel, trying to drown out the sound of the crying, the hushed voices, and the prayers from the dozen other scientists throughout the room. She laid her head down on the tiny pillow, turning to face him. His lips parted and revealed his perfectly aligned teeth. A chill crept down Sophie's spine, making its way to her toes. She returned his smile and gripped his hands underneath the covers. As the lights faded and darkness carpeted the room, she slowly slipped out of her pants. He bent in to kiss her, pulling her chin toward his with his index finger.

Sophie hesitated, looking over his shoulder to see if anyone was watching. But the darkness shrouded them. With a silent sigh she pulled him closer until she could feel his warm breath on her neck.

Another chill raced down her legs. This time is didn't make its way to her toes, but stopped just below her abdominals, lingering. She kissed him deeper, her hands running through his mop of dark, unkempt hair.

There was something about the world going to shit that made her want him even more, as if it were the last time she would ever feel intimacy. When she was in high school, she had had a conversation with a friend about things they would do if the world was ending. "I'd have sex with the cutest boy I could find," her friend had said.

Sophie, on the other hand, had said she would spend the night staring at the stars—and yet, with the real possibility of the world ending, the thought of stargazing no longer appealed to her. Tonight she didn't want to be a scientist; she wanted nothing more than to feel Emanuel, to wrap her legs around him. If the world was going to end, she wanted to share it with him.

The next morning Tsui woke them. "The storms have passed!" he yelled, flailing his arms in the air.

Emanuel reached for his glasses, while Sophie struggled to find her pants. Seconds later they were crowded around the monitors, watching the data stream in from stations around the world. He was right; the storm was over, but the damage to the Midwestern states was severe. Radiation levels were extraordinary. Those who had perished in the fires were the lucky ones; any survivors would die horribly painful and prolonged deaths from radiation poisoning.

"My parents," Emanuel whispered.

A sudden chill ran down Sophie's back. Emanuel's family lived in Chicago, and by the looks of it the Windy City was the dead center of the damage.

"Millions will die," Tsui whispered, taking a long sip of his coffee.

Emanuel scowled, suddenly ripe with anger. "Bolton's administration never took this storm seriously!"

"The damage is done. We need to continue to analyze the storm's data and send it to the Department of Defense," Tsui replied.

Sophie took a seat at her terminal, logging in with a swipe of her index finger. The stream of data was constant; new statistics were feeding into their system by the second from locations around the world. The dead zone appeared to run from the edge of the Rocky Mountains to the Mississippi. Houston was on the border of the destruction, and while the city was busy being burned to the ground, the radiation levels appeared to be minimal.

A muffled voice rang out across the room. Sophie turned to see a middle-aged man with a mop of gray hair staring out at them from a screen hanging in the corner of the room. She recognized him instantly as General John McKern, a Department of Defense official and advisor on NTC's payroll.

"Good morning, Dr. Tsui and staff; glad to see you all weathered the storm safely. It appears you just missed the worst of it."

"Good morning, sir. How did Washington fare?"

McKern shrugged. "We were better prepared than most. The military has been hardening facilities, communications, and vehicles for decades." He lit a cigar and blew a puff of smoke at the monitor. "As you know, it's the Midwest that took the brunt of it. Which is why I am contacting you. My superiors want a module showing radioactivity patterns. Which cities are lost causes, which ones may be salvageable. You know the drill," he said, taking another drag of his cigar.

"No problem, sir. We'll upload the data within the hour," Tsui said, motioning Emanuel and another scientist to a pair of computers against the far wall.

"Very good. I'll check back later," McKern said, his image quickly fading.

Henry, the young scientist who had panicked the previous evening, hesitantly motioned Dr. Tsui over to his monitors. "Sir, there's something I think you should see."

"What is it?"

"Do you remember how the storms seemed to be lasting longer than our initial models predicted?"

"Yes, of course I do."

"So you recall that it seemed as if something was feeding the storms?"

Tsui nodded. "What's your point, Henry?"

"I think I've found out what was feeding them. Take a look at this. It's from the past few days."

The group gathered around Henry's terminal. A row of numbers hovered over the console.

Sophie recognized the data immediately. It was hers.

"That's impossible," Henry said under his breath, before telling the team what Sophie already knew. "The disruption is coming from . . . Mars."

CHAPTER 7

THE clanking of Timothy and Saafi's footsteps followed Emanuel across the metal platform above the garden biome. Several days had passed since the death of the chickens, and they were beginning to settle back into a routine. With the loss of one of their major sources of protein, Sophie had conscripted Saafi and Timothy to help Emanuel with Biome 1, leaving Alexia in charge of their jobs. They had spent the entire day planting seeds deep into the dark brown dirt.

"I can't get the dirt stains off my hands, man, and I've spread it all over my monitors in the command center," Timothy said, rubbing his hands ferociously on his pants.

"It's the chemicals. This dirt isn't your typical topsoil. It's hybrid soil, meant to germinate seeds as fast as possible," Emanuel responded, hardly sparing the man a glance.

"How long until the seeds sprout and we get veggies to eat?" Saafi asked.

Emanuel shrugged. "Could be as little as a few days for some of the seeds and as long as a month for others."

"What about the sweet corn? I love sweet corn," Saafi said, revealing a mouthful of large, white teeth.

"I don't think sweet corn is on the menu," Emanuel laughed.

"I'm not going to lie, I was very pleased when I heard the diet would be mostly vegetarian," Saafi continued. "I grew up eating very little meat."

Timothy rolled his eyes. "Remind us where you're from again?"

"You know where I'm from."

"Africa?"

Saafi snorted. "Somalia," he said proudly.

"Never been there," Timothy quipped.

Emanuel paused at the edge of the platform and looked at the field, attempting to change the subject. "You're looking at the last row. Once we're done it's back to the mess hall for lunch, so let's make this quick."

The trio jumped off the platform, landed softly in the dirt, and began trekking through the field.

"Finally, we're in agreement about something," Timothy replied with his mischievous grin. He brushed a long strand of curly hair out of his eyes and reached into his pocket, pulling out a handful of seeds.

"A little here, a little there," he said under his breath, sprinkling the seeds onto the ground. The job was a change of pace from sitting at a terminal, typing in code and monitoring the biomes. And truthfully, he was beginning to enjoy it. Besides the fact that his hands were stained shit brown, he liked feeling like he was contributing to the mission.

Overhead, the click of one of the monstrous air-conditioning units startled him. Timothy cocked his head to survey the dome, and for the first time he realized how massive it really was. He'd spent most of his youth holed up in his room, playing video games and hacking into websites just to piss off greedy corporations. There were moments when he felt like he might have missed out on the rest of the world by spending so much time living in a virtual one, but this mission made up for all of that. And while he might have only traded his small computer lab for a much bigger one, the Biosphere was still the most advanced and aesthetically beautiful building he had ever seen, let alone worked in.

The AC unit clicked off, and the fans quieted. As Timothy reached in his pocket for another handful of seeds, there was another click, a deeper one. Emanuel and Saafi heard it too. The trio stopped dead in their tracks, scanning the walls for the source of the noise.

"All hands to Biome 3," Alexia said through the speaker system. A pair of emergency lights above the entrance doors glowed to life, their red lights blinking intermittently.

"What the hell is this?" Timothy yelled.

Emanuel dropped his bag of seeds and took off running for the door. "What are you waiting for?"

Saafi ran after Emanuel, his long, lean legs catching up with the biologist quickly.

"What the fuck?" Timothy said. He didn't want to be left behind, so he dropped his bag and began a fast-paced jog. He didn't even make it to the platform before he had to stop and catch his breath. He blamed his labored breathing on a youth spent smoking in a room the size of an ancient phone booth.

He followed the sound of footsteps down the hallway until he rounded a corner and reached Biome 3. From the entrance he could see the others were already there, surrounding Alexia's blue holographic image. But when he took a closer look, he could tell it wasn't her image they were staring at. It was the goats. They were screeching in terror, as if a predator were chasing them. Two of them were cowering in the corner, shaking in fear, while the other three were bashing their heads into the biome's exterior wall.

That wasn't the only odd thing. The pigs were lying in their own filth; their tongues hanging loosely out of their mouths, blood streaming from their cracked skulls.

"What the fuck is going on!" Timothy shouted over the deafening noise.

The goats continued to shriek, their voices like human babies crying in pain. It was one of the most awful noises he'd ever heard, one he recalled hearing at the Iowa State Fair years ago, when a farmer sheared his goat in front of a crowd of patrons. Timothy clawed at his ears to muffle the sound.

"Alexia, can you shut off the emergency system?" Sophie yelled.

"Certainly, Dr. Winston," she replied.

The flashing red lights clicked off and the automatic message stopped, the echo fading away. But the screeching of the goats continued until all of them were successfully slamming their heads against the white wall, staining it a dark red.

"Do something!" Holly pleaded with Emanuel. "Please, can't you do something for them?"

The biologist stared at the animals in disbelief. He had never seen anything like it. Never in the history of his career had he read about animals behaving this way—except during the solar storms of 2055. Animals in the dead zone had all perished from radiation poisoning, the government killing them in droves to help prevent the spread of disease. But millions of animals outside the zone had died too. At the time, scientists had called it the *space weather phenomenon*, the theory being the animals were so distressed by the solar storms they became suicidal.

"Oh my God," Emanuel said, watching the last goat take its final breath. "I have seen this before."

Sophie shot him a frightened look, her face flushed and panicked. "What is it?"

"I think I know what's happened outside," he said. "The solar storms have returned."

The mess hall was deathly silent. Sophie stood with her back against the wall, her arms crossed. The rest of the team sat around one of the metal tables, sipping cold coffee.

"So you're telling us the solar storms started up again with no warning?" Timothy asked.

Sophie unfolded her arms and walked over to the table. "If what Emanuel is saying is true, then the granite rock of the mountain would have blocked most of the gamma radiation from the flares."

"This is fucked up!" Timothy shouted, kicking his chair away from the table.

Saafi stood and flexed his chest, "Calm down, man! I'm really getting sick of your shit. Now isn't the time to be having a panic attack."

"Oh really? What do you suggest I do, put my legs up and crack open a cold one?"

"I suggest you shut your mouth," Sophie said, snapping her fingers at him. "If you want a shot at that trip to Mars, then you better shape up or I'm pulling you from the team. There are a hundred other programmers who would love your seat."

Timothy took a deep breath and sat back down, crossing his arms. "Whatever."

"I don't understand. Wouldn't we have known about the solar storms ahead of time?" Holly asked.

Emanuel rested his coffee mug on the table. "Yes. Someone would have seen them coming—someone would have warned the world."

"Do you remember the first day in the Biosphere, right before we went into the cleaning chambers?" Sophie asked.

Emanuel nodded. "Of course."

"Dr. Hoffman's instructions seemed rushed. Like he had somewhere more important to be," said Sophie. "I didn't think much of it at the time, but what if he knew?"

Holly shook her head. "We don't know what really caused the animals' deaths, do we? You said it could have been a trick NTC used to test us."

Emanuel ran his hand through his thick, unkempt hair, destroying the last remnants of his part. "At this point I think it's probably not a test. We should ask Alexia what she thinks."

He glanced at Sophie, who shrugged.

"Emanuel's theory is plausible. After searching my database, I did find thousands of situations where animals behaved similarly as a result of the solar storms of 2055. However, we have no conclusive evidence anything has happened on the outside," Alexia said, her image appearing over a console in the center of the room.

"Conclusive evidence? A dead communication line and a biome full of dead animals isn't conclusive enough for you? I'm pretty sure that's enough to convince me," Timothy said.

"Enough already, Timothy," Holly said.

"I hate saying it, but he's right," Saafi said. "I don't know how else to explain what's happened. Emanuel's theory sounds like the only plausible explanation."

Alexia's image faded and disappeared, her voice transferring to the loud speakers. "NTC rules have prevented us from contacting the outside, but there is one way to figure out what's going on—one thing you will have access to on a space flight."

"What's that?" Sophie asked curiously.

"Radiation detectors," Alexia replied.

Emanuel smiled. "Brilliant."

Her holographic image reappeared in front of the team. "Preliminary scans show radiation levels outside the facility are abnormal."

"Fuck. There you have it. Game over for us!" Timothy yelled.

"This isn't a video game," Sophie said. "This is real life."

"Are we sure that's what it means? Couldn't the radiation have come from another source?" Holly insisted.

"Just face it! We're screwed. We might as well roll over now and get it over with," Timothy said, bitterness creeping into his voice.

Sophie bowed her head. She still couldn't believe what was happening. The entire goal of the mission had been to test a new Noah's Ark, one that would transplant humans to Mars so they could start a new life. But now everything had changed. Depending on how bad the solar storms were, it was possible the mission was over—it was possible there wasn't anyone left to save.

Emanuel looked down at his wristwatch. "It's getting late, guys. Maybe we should get some sleep. Discuss things in the morning," he suggested.

Sophie nodded. "I want everyone to get at least six hours tonight. Meet back here at 0700. We'll figure things out in the morning."

Saafi yawned and stood, slapping Timothy on the back. "You heard her, time for bed," he said. Holly followed them toward the personnel quarters, but Emanuel stayed behind with Sophie.

"You should take your own advice and get some rest," he said.

Sophie let out a sarcastic laugh. "Like I'll be able to sleep."

"Remember the night we spent together during the solar storms of 2055? You slept pretty well then," he said with a grin.

Sophie scowled; she wasn't amused. "Reminiscence is the lowest form of conversation."

"Don't act like you don't remember."

"Oh, I do, but I can't believe you're thinking about sex at a time like this. Everything we've worked for, Emanuel. Everything we've dreamt of could be over."

"I also remember how I felt the last time we were together, when we thought the world was going to end. Maybe the world *has* ended outside these walls," he said, spreading his arms wide. "Maybe this is it."

Sophie felt a moment of apprehension. It was a familiar feeling, one she had struggled with ever since she first met Emanuel. On the one hand, she was terribly attracted to him, both physically and emotionally. But they had never had an opportunity for a real relationship. Their careers had always interfered. If they weren't working on a project together, they were typically on different continents. And when they were working together, she'd always put the science of the mission first.

The apprehension faded into something deeper. An emotion she had always been good at controlling: fear. With the likelihood of massive solar storms occurring outside the blast doors, she couldn't help but let her guard down. She needed Emanuel. He was her Achilles' heel—his dimples, his slight accent, his brilliance and sense of humor. She could forget everything around her for a few hours, couldn't she?

Just one night, she promised herself.

Just one night.

Sophie glanced at one of the cameras hanging from the ceiling. She bit her lip and strolled over to Emanuel, fixing his disheveled hair. "I guess it's not going to hurt anything," she said with a smile.

Emanuel looked over his shoulder, scanning the room for Alexia's image, but she was gone. When he turned back to Sophie, she was already strolling toward the personnel quarters. "Better hurry up; if this is the end of the world we don't know how much time we have."

"I can be quick," Emanuel laughed, following her down the dark hall.

CHAPTER 8

A SHADOW crossed the dusty red surface of the trail. For a moment panic raced through her before she realized the shadow was her own. She was alone. Somewhere in the Wastelands.

"No way," she whispered.

She'd only seen the Wastelands from the safety of a chopper. It was a place she had always wanted to visit, to feel with her own feet, but the radiation was just too pronounced in certain areas. Enter a pocket of it and you could be dead within hours.

Sophie smiled, realizing she felt fine. She felt no nausea or dizziness. Then again, she had no idea how long she had been in the open—or how she had even gotten there. Her elation evaporated when she saw a metal structure jutting out of a rock formation a few hundred yards away. Her eyes recognized it instantly, sending the image to her brain in less than a millisecond, but her mind protested.

This can't be right.

Her vision did not lie. The structure was there, and it was real. But it had to be a mistake, some sort of joke. Her eyes surveyed the metal, studying the massive tower that had once helped launch rockets into space.

"The Kennedy Space Center," she gasped.

It was impossible. The station had been decommissioned in the early twenty-first century and buried underneath the ocean decades later when Florida became the first state submerged by the rising tides. She wasn't a history buff, but one thing she knew better than most was the history of the space program, and this was without a doubt the remains of one of the early jewels of American space flight.

But if this wasn't the Wasteland, where was the water?

Sophie made her way across the red earth, her brisk walk turning into a jog. It made no sense. The bottom of the tower should have been submerged. She pushed on, trying to ignore her questions. There had to be an explanation. She would find it.

Another shadow crossed her path, but this time it wasn't hers. She shot a look over her shoulder and saw a craft approaching. She tripped and stumbled. A cloud of red dust exploded into the air, lodging in her lungs. She coughed, desperately trying to get air while rolling onto her back to get a better look at the ship.

"Oh my God," she whispered, ignoring her labored breaths.

It was the same blue, oblate ship she had seen in her dreams, and it was heading right for her. She watched the geometry of the ship change, the sides pulsating and shifting as it glided across the skyline.

She sat up to get a better look. Pain instantly raced through her body as whatever she had tripped over sliced through her shoe.

"Ugh," she yelled, diverting her attention away from the ship momentarily. She reached down to toss the scrap metal aside but paused when she saw the worn lettering.

Welcome to Kennedy Space Center

"What the hell is going on!" she yelled.

The quiet hum of the craft was the only answer. She dropped the sign and stood to get a better look at the machine. The translucent blue sides of the ship seemed to change with its speed. Inside the engine, or what she presumed to be an engine, light throbbed in harmony with the pulsating sides.

Sophie shielded her eyes from the sun to get a better look. The craft was speeding toward her, barreling down, and with every second it grew in size. She squinted and finally saw what appeared to be veins inside the craft, pumping a blue substance to the engine. Was it organic?

Was it *alive*?

The craft picked up pace, the sides shifting again. The same panic from before gripped her. Whatever it was, organic or man-made, it was heading right for her.

She turned to run, racing for the metal bones of the launch tower. The pain from her foot shot up her leg with every step. She had to push on.

The launch tower rose above her as she got closer. She was almost there—almost to safety. The humming increased behind her, and she risked another look over her shoulder to see the craft getting closer. It was almost on top of her.

She ran faster, the dust of the red earth coughing out from under her shoes with every stride. The skeleton of the tower was now above her. She searched it for a place to hide from the craft, her desperate eyes darting through the shadows.

A deafening noise ripped through the silence, bringing her to her knees. She yelled, gripping her ears in pain.

The sound was unlike any she had ever heard, a totally different wavelength. It was almost like the whistle of a dolphin, but at a higher frequency—much higher, as if someone had taken a pod of dolphins, combined all of their cries, and amplified it with the biggest speaker in the world. It was like one of the sonic weapons NTC had designed to stun or disable enemies.

Sophie moaned. She could feel liquid seeping out of her ears. Even as the blood filled her eardrums, she wondered what could have made a sound like that.

She turned to run, forcing herself up, but the craft was now above the tower. Hovering, it transformed itself into a sphere. The engine inside had stopped throbbing, and the veins protruding out of it like cobwebs no longer pumped the blue fluid. The craft appeared to be evolving, forming into a solid, like water into ice.

Water, she thought. The craft was made of water, and the veins were carrying it to the engine. Whatever the ship was, water was its lifeblood.

Suddenly the noise stopped, and the craft completed its solidification. She stood staring at it in awe, her fear washed away by pure admiration. The nose of the craft began to open, and a beautiful beam of blue light shot out at her. It was calming, almost like a cold shower after a long run in the heat.

But the sensation didn't last. The light quickly began to burn. Her skin felt like it was being penetrated by the beam. She tried to look down at her arms, but she was paralyzed, her eyes locked onto the light that was consuming her.

"No!" she tried to yell, but her tongue wouldn't move.

The beam tore deeper into her skin, reaching inside her flesh. She could feel her heart beating faster. She could feel the blood pulsing through her veins and with it adrenaline.

She tried to move again, but the light seemed to squeeze her even tighter, preventing her escape. She gasped for air. Her lungs were being crushed, and she was beginning to suffocate.

Stop! she thought, pleading mentally with the craft. But it was futile; the beam had her. She watched it, her mind realizing what her body already knew—she was dying. The craft was stealing her life force.

Through the light she could see small drops of liquid rising from her body and moving toward the craft. First beads of perspiration from her forehead and then saliva from her mouth. She tried to swallow, but her throat was completely dry.

The beam gripped her tighter, crushing her lungs as she took her last breath of air. She stared helplessly at the light, watching the water from her body climb toward the machine, feeding it. As her brain began to shut off, it finally made sense. The composition of the ship, the dry Wastelands, the lack of water. But there was no one to tell—no one to see her die.

"Breathe, Sophie. Come on girl, you can do it," a voice said from above her.

She coughed, sucking in mouthfuls of air. Her skin was cold, like she had been submerged in a bath of ice water.

"Snap out of it, Sophie; you were dreaming!" the voice cried.

A warm glow of light carpeted the room as another voice yelled out, "What's wrong with her?"

"She's having a panic attack. I found her like this."

Sophie struggled to open her eyes as oxygen seeped back into her lungs. She reached for her chest, clawing at her rib cage. Everything was intact, nothing broken.

"Hey, up here," the first voice said. She heard the snap of someone's fingers. Emanuel and Holly came into view above her.

"It was just a dream, sweetie," Holly said, a warm smile on her pale face.

Just a dream.

Was it? Was the craft just a figment of her imagination? Had the landscape in Florida been nothing more than a reflection of Sophie's fear of what might be going on outside?

She coughed violently, grabbing a glass of water from Emanuel, who stared down at her with concern. The water glided down her parched throat.

"More," she said, motioning for another glass.

He handed her a second cup and watched her suck down the liquid.

"Another," she requested.

Holly pulled a strand of blond hair out of her eyes. "Slow down, Sophie, you're going to get sick."

"I'm so *thirsty*," Sophie replied, polishing off the third glass. "My dream . . . it was so . . ."

"Realistic?" Emanuel suggested.

Sophie nodded. "It was the same as before. The blue ship. Or . . . entity. It's not a machine. It's organic. Fed by water."

Emanuel and Holly stared back at her with nervous, owlish looks.

"And I saw the Kennedy Space Center," Sophie continued, motioning for another glass of water.

Emanuel reluctantly handed her another cup. The liquid dripped down her chin as she tried to drink and speak simultaneously.

"It was in a desert. At first I confused it for the Wastelands."

"Sophie, the Kennedy Space Center was submerged under water years ago," Holly said in her sweetest and softest voice.

"Don't you think I know that?!" Sophie fired back.

Emanuel sat down next to her and placed his hand on her bare thigh. "Sophie, these dreams, they aren't real. You know they aren't; you've said it yourself."

She pulled away, her eyes widening in disbelief. "They mean something. And it's not just because of anxiety," she said, shooting Holly an angry look.

Holly pulled a metal chair up to the bed and took a seat, crossing her legs. "You're right. They do mean something. Nightmares have a way of spilling into our everyday lives and can negatively affect our work performance, family, relationships, et cetera. What you're going through is common. You told me a while ago you have two sides to your brain—the scientific side and the creative, illogical side. What you need to do is simple. You have to convince your brain the scientific side is correct. Be logical. Dreams aren't real."

Emanuel scooted closer to Sophie. "She's right. You're a brilliant scientist, one of the most intelligent people I've ever met. And right now we need you to be strong. The team needs a leader, and you are that person."

Sophie nodded. "You're both right. I'm sorry. What time is it?"

Holly looked at the blue mission clock above the doorway. "0600."

"Then it's time for a meeting. I have an idea to run past the team," Sophie replied, rising to change into her lab suit. She donned her clothes quickly and squeezed past Holly and Emanuel, who waited at the edge of the doorway.

"I think I need to do more," Holly whispered to him as Sophie's footsteps faded down the hallway. "Maybe it's time I set up individual counseling sessions with everyone."

"Not a bad idea," Emanuel replied. "If I were you, I'd start with Sophie."

CHAPTER 9

WE have two options. One is to live off these packaged meals and wait for the seeds to sprout in the hope that the failed emergency communication line and radiation outside is just a test by NTC," Sophie said, tossing one of the meals onto the metal table. "Or we can have Alexia open the doors so we can figure out what's happened out there."

Silence washed over the mess hall. Even Timothy remained mute. Sophie studied her team's faces. She knew they were scared and, more than anything, disappointed. The mission was over. There was no salvaging it.

Sophie leaned over the table. "That wasn't a rhetorical question, guys. I want opinions."

Emanuel crossed his arms, watching the fearless leader reemerge in front of them. This was the Sophie he knew, the Sophie he had fallen in love with years ago—the Sophie he still loved.

"No way in hell am I going out there!" Timothy said.

"I don't know if it's a good idea, either," Saafi said quickly. "If this is a test, then we'll fail the mission."

"It is not a test," another voice said.

The team turned to see Alexia's hologram hovering above the corner console. "The radiation sensors cannot be tampered with without my knowledge. Furthermore, the animals could not have been poisoned without my detection. Whatever has happened, NTC is not the culprit. I am 99.9 percent sure. This would warrant Section 19.1 of the contract null and void and justify opening the doors."

"There you have it, guys. The world has gone to hell in a hand basket. And there's no way I'm going to risk my neck to see for myself. Besides, think of it this way—if the world has ended, we basically won the lottery. We're in one of the most advanced self-sustainable shelters ever built," Timothy said.

Emanuel unfolded his arms. "I'm not going to argue with you about that, but this shelter was only built to be viable for six months. Sure, we could make it last longer, but, there will come a time when we need to go outside. That's what I vote for."

"Me too," Saafi said, changing his mind and raising his hand.

"I don't believe what I'm hearing!" Timothy shouted. "We've only been in the Biosphere for a week. Not even that. And you guys want to scrap everything and go outside?"

"Haven't you been listening to what's going on?" Sophie snarled. "I've noted your opinion, Timothy, now pipe down." She turned away from him and took a deep breath. "What about you, Holly? Where do you stand?"

Holly pulled a strand of long blond hair from her face and tucked it behind an ear. Her large eyes slowly found their way to Sophie's. "I vote to stay here. Where it's safe. We don't know what's happened outside," she said, looking back down at the floor sheepishly.

"That's okay, Holly. I understand," Sophie said.

"That makes it two votes for and two votes against," Timothy piped up.

"I can count," Sophie replied. "You all know this mission has been my dream for a number of years, and as much as I hate to abandon it, I see no other choice. We can survive in here for a while, but without a solid line of communication or a way to replenish our supplies, we've got a year in here, maybe two—tops. We have to try and make contact with NTC. The only way to do that is to venture beyond the safety of the Biosphere. My vote is to go outside."

Timothy stood and laughed hysterically. "I'm not going out there!"

"Don't worry. I'm not going to force you or anyone else to go. Emanuel, Saafi, and I will journey out on our own and report back. Holly, you make sure Timothy stays out of trouble while we're gone,"

Sophie said with a stern look. "Alexia, I'm going to need your assistance. Not only will you be tasked with opening the doors, but I will also need you to tell us where the NTC gear room is. I'm sure they have some sort of armory."

"That is correct. There is an armory stocked with weapons and hazard suits near the blast doors through which you entered the facility. The train will take you there. I will unlock the doors once you get to the building," Alexia replied.

"I'm also going to need some way to communicate with you from the outside. Do we have any headsets and video cams?"

"You will find both of those items in a storage closet within the control room. I can run the feed through the Biosphere's system. As long as the lithium ion batteries last, Timothy and Holly should be able to track your progress outside from the control room, presuming there is no interference."

"Excellent, then it's settled. I don't want to waste any more time— there could be people in need of help, so the sooner we find out what's going on, the better."

Sophie took a deep breath. The main mission had more than likely already failed, but a new one was about to begin. Somewhere inside she knew that it was even more important than the Biosphere—something told her it was connected to her dreams.

The train tore down the dark tunnel, the beam of its headlight cutting through the blackness like a rocket through space. Sophie rested her back against the hard seat. She couldn't help but wonder if they were making the right decision. Holly had advised her to use the scientific side of her brain, the logical side, and that was exactly what she had done. After examining the evidence, she had no reason to believe NTC was testing them. It had to be a solar event or EMP attack. Something so terrible it had knocked out the hardened line to the facility.

She shook her head, trying not to think about postapocalyptic scenarios. Deep down she had to believe there was still something worth saving, and that her trip to Mars was just being postponed.

The train slowed as the tunnel widened and opened up into the same hangar she had entered just a week before. Emanuel and Saafi sat in silence, staring at the massive blast doors towering above the small train.

Sophie squeezed through the train's doors as they opened. "This is it, guys. Let's find that gear."

At the far end of the hangar, just shy of the blast doors, was a small, windowless building.

"That must be it," Saafi said, pointing at the structure.

Sophie attached a tiny camera to the top of the headset she had retrieved from the command center. She pulled her blond hair back into a ponytail and slipped the device over her head, the speaker resting perfectly in her ear. "Alexia, this is Sophie. Do you read me?"

The feminine voice immediately responded. "Yes, Dr. Winston."

"We're headed for the equipment room, please advise."

"I've unlocked the doors; you may proceed."

Emanuel was the first to reach the building. He pushed a green button on the keypad, and the automatic metal door screeched open. Inside were the guts of what had been some sort of janitorial closet. A surplus of dusty mops and empty buckets sat in a disorganized cluster in the corners. On the opposite side of the room was a wall lined with black lockers, each filled with a plethora of weapons. Next to the lockers were hazmat suits and gas masks hanging from hooks on the concrete wall.

"Looks like we hit the jackpot," Saafi said, heading for one of the black cages. He swung the door open and pulled out an assault rifle. It looked like an AR-15, but the design was slightly different. It was one of the newer models, equipped with a pulse cannon instead of traditional lead bullets.

"I think I'll be taking this," he said with a grin.

"What do you need that for?" Emanuel asked, thumbing through the different hazmat suits.

"You never know what's going to be out there. Like my academic advisor always told me, 'better safe than sorry.' And for the record, I do know how to fire one of these. I paid an entire week's salary for a day of fun at one of NTC's training facilities a few years back. The thing handles like a charm," he said, looking down the infrared scope.

Emanuel shrugged and pulled open a cabinet with the blue flame symbol of NTC on its doors. Inside were several state-of-the-art matte black armored suits. They were made of carbon fiber and reinforced with a light, Kevlarlike material. He pulled out a charcoal-colored helmet with a silver mirrored visor.

"Holy shit, I've read about these. They're what NTC Special Forces uses in the Wastelands. Protects you from radiation, lightweight. And these bad boys work in virtually any extreme condition you can think of," he said, holding up the helmet to examine it under the light.

The sight of the suits sent a chill down Sophie's back. She'd seen them before, during the solar storms of 2055. "How many suits are there?" she asked.

"Four."

"NTC must have been in a hurry to leave this equipment behind," Saafi said. "It isn't cheap stuff."

"I was just thinking the same thing," Emanuel said.

"Maybe they're just extras. No time to worry about that now. What size are those suits—think one will fit me?" Sophie asked.

Emanuel grabbed the smallest one out of the bunch, holding it up under the white glow of the fluorescent lights. "This one looks like it may be your size."

"Perfect. I always did look good in black," she replied with a smile. "Let's suit up and meet in the hangar in five."

The three team members stood looking at the blast doors, the twenty-five-ton monstrosity that had been built to stop a direct hit by a nuclear-tipped missile. If there was a single piece of the facility that made Sophie feel small, this was it. Even the massive domes of the Biosphere's chambers hadn't given her such a feeling of insignificance.

She couldn't help but laugh when she saw Emanuel and Saafi testing out their armor, swinging their arms and kicking their legs about. It was a sight to behold: two men from academia, dressed in some of the most advanced suits of armor ever designed, moving around like they were attempting the robot dance.

Emanuel halted in midmotion. "What's so funny?"

"It's nothing. You just look so . . ."

"So what?"

"Nerdy!" Sophie laughed.

Emanuel strolled over to her, walking awkwardly in the suit. "And you look . . . hot," he whispered in her ear. The words sent a chill down Sophie's entire body. She pushed him away gently, eyeing Saafi to make sure he wasn't paying attention.

"Did you both remember your nutrition?" she asked, ignoring Emanuel.

Saafi patted a small pack around his waist. "I brought several energy bars, some energy gels, and two bottles of water."

"Me too," Emanuel nodded.

"Good. Now comes the important question: How are we going to tell each other apart once we put our helmets on?" she asked.

"Do you mean besides the fact that I am six feet tall?" Saafi laughed.

"Well, just in case, your display will show a color for each of our suits," Emanuel replied. "We can set them manually. Sophie, you'll be green, Saafi blue, and I'll be red. When you look through your display, my goggles will be glowing red."

"Sounds simple enough," Sophie replied, slipping her helmet over her hair. "Are you guys ready for this?"

She watched Saafi and Emanuel nod through her display, the goggles in their helmets glowing back at her. "Alexia, please open the blast doors."

A loud crunch echoed through the bay as the mechanisms unlocked, hissing from the pressure. The metal groan of the doors shook the room, vibrating throughout the team's suits. Sophie strained to see the opening, waiting anxiously for what lay behind the doors. Adrenaline raced through her veins as she peeked over Emanuel's shoulder for a better look.

"Alexia, report on radiation," Sophie commanded.

"Sensors are showing minimal traces."

The groaning doors slowed before finally locking in place with a violent report. Emanuel stepped forward into the night, walking out onto the tarmac. Saafi and Sophie cautiously followed him. A carpet of darkness covered them as they stepped onto the concrete runway. The floodlights and antennae lining the landing strip were all dead, and in the distance Sophie couldn't see a single light through her glass visor. The stars were of little help, hiding behind some kind of fog. To make things worse, they were all alone.

"Switching to night vision," she said, blinking as the tarmac lit up like a night light, the green outlines of the blacktop filling her display.

"Looks like NTC abandoned ship," Saafi said, pointing his rifle toward the empty concrete where the NTC choppers had once been.

"They weren't the only ones," Emanuel replied, heading toward the area where most of the support crew's vehicles had been parked. Only two Humvees remained.

Saafi halted and dropped to one knee. "They were in a hurry, too—check out these tire marks."

"What the hell is going on?" Sophie said under her breath.

"Where's Colorado Springs?" Saafi asked. He stood and joined Emanuel at the edge of the tarmac.

"Should be right over there . . ." Emanuel trailed off. "What the hell?"

Sophie rushed over to join them, and together they looked into the valley below. The city was dark. If there had been a solar storm, then it made sense that the power would have been knocked out. What didn't add up was the lack of fires. They couldn't see a single one.

"Switch to thermal; I want to see if we can pick up any heat signatures," Sophie ordered.

Their visors glowed to life. Thousands of tiny specks appeared on their heads-up displays.

"Something's not working on mine," Saafi said.

"Mine's not working either. I'm getting all of these little specs of red light," Emanuel said.

Sophie studied her display. "Me too. But guys, I don't think it's our equipment. I think those are actually heat signatures."

"That's impossible," said Emanuel. "They're too big to be human."

"Alexia, report on radiation," Sophie commanded.

"Still minimal traces."

Sophie reached up for her helmet and unfastened the two metal clips, pulling it slowly off over her head.

"What are you doing?" Emanuel cried, rushing over to her.

"Uh, you guys are going to want to see this with your own eyes," she said, frozen in awe.

Saafi and Emanuel quickly took off their own masks and gasped. In the distance there were thousands of glowing blue orbs scattered throughout the city, glittering like diamonds.

Saafi coughed nervously into his gloved hand. "What are they?"

"I have no idea, but we're going to find out," Sophie said. "And . . ." she paused to survey the tarmac again. "And that's going to be our ride," she said, pointing to one of the remaining black Humvees. "Saafi, I hope you remember how to hotwire a government vehicle."

"It would be my pleasure, Doctor," he said with a grin. "Just don't tell NTC when they return."

The words echoed in her helmet. In the pit of her stomach, she felt a knot growing. It told her that NTC would not be returning. Her team was on its own.

CHAPTER 10

Sᴇʀɢᴇᴀɴᴛ Ash Overton twirled a razor-sharp throwing knife between his fingers, still remarkably fast despite being plagued with severe arthritis. A tribal tattoo followed the bulge of his veins from the bottom of his right bicep upward and disappeared under his rolled-up sleeve. He studied the wall of monitors and screens, trying to piece together what was happening. But no matter how hard he tried, nothing made sense.

Behind him, Private Eric Finley fidgeted with his plasma rifle, trying unsuccessfully to remove a jammed magazine of blue pulse rounds. He placed the weapon on a metal bench and ran his hand through his blond hair. His fingers hit a bald spot and he went back over it again to feel if he'd lost any more.

"Damn," he said under his breath. He was only eighteen, but had the hairline of a man twice his age.

To Overton's eyes, the Marine was nothing more than a boy—a boy forced to join the military after losing a college wrestling scholarship to a blown knee. Studying the young man's face, Overton decided it was a good thing. His oversized ears probably wouldn't be able to tolerate much more wrestling.

The sergeant rolled his chair back to the monitors and took a long drag of his cigarette, exhaling the toxic fumes through his nose. An assortment of old data crawled across the screen from Department of Defense facilities around the world. The computer was running on an ancient analog system, which didn't surprise him considering the age of the facility.

He sighed and reached for another cigarette, jamming it between his lips as he fiddled with an old radio. Behind him an automatic door screeched open, and Overton spun in his chair to see the lean frame of Corporal Chad Bouma slide through. The young Marine grinned, showing every one of his crooked teeth.

"Got the generator to work," he said, his gaunt face beaming with pride.

"Excellent work, Bouma. It only took you two hours," Overton replied sarcastically.

They had been separated from the rest of his team for over twenty-four hours, losing contact minutes after the three of them entered the facility two hundred feet underground and the blast doors had sealed them in. What was meant to be a quick recon mission to retrieve a fifty-year-old disc had turned into a boring slumber party with two of his most inexperienced men.

A chirp from the radio startled Overton, and he returned his attention to the hunk of metal in front of him. He fumbled with a cord, slipping the head into the jack and the bud into his left ear. With the flip of a switch, the radio blared to life. The sound of voices was eerie, especially after being in the dark for so long. But that wasn't the only odd thing. Overton hadn't heard anyone use an analog radio for years, which meant whatever had happened outside had knocked out more than just the Internet—it had knocked out modern communications. The thought sent a shudder down his spine.

He exhaled the fear in a cloud of smoke and watched Finley and Bouma anxiously crowd around him. The outline of a monitor covered in cobwebs behind them caught his eye. He studied the plastic box it was connected to and concluded it was an ancient computer, the same kind he had learned to type on as a kid.

"See if you can get that thing working, Bouma. Maybe you can patch it through using a hardened line," he said pointing with one of his muscular arms.

Bouma blinked several times and strolled over to the computer, tilting his head to examine the oversized, archaic box.

Overton popped in the other earbud and compressed his eyebrows, straining to listen. The first few channels yielded more foggy voices and the crackle of static, but as he scanned through them one voice stood out, almost crystal clear. And judging by the jargon, the man sounded military.

"What's the word, sir?" Finley asked.

"Stand by, Finley. I'm still trying to make sense of things."

"Recorded at 0500. The Russians reported the sky started changing colors before contact was lost with Moscow . . ."

"Are you hearing anything about the West Coast?" Finley asked.

Overton shook his head and held up his right hand, balling it into a fist. The action prompted Finley to scoot back to his own chair. He knew exactly how much Overton would tolerate before he brought the hammer down.

"Finley, get me a cup of that piss-cold coffee," Overton snarled between transmissions.

"Recorded at 0600. Japan has gone completely dark. They reported a strange fog in the sky seconds before contact was lost."

Overton grabbed the cold mug from Finley's pale hands, hardly bothering to acknowledge him. He took a long swig, almost gagging on the bitter liquid. "This shit is nasty!" he yelled. "There has to be more coffee around here somewhere. Find it," he ordered, bringing the bud back to his ear.

"Recorded at 0800. Contact with the Eastern Hemisphere has ceased. Europe, Asia—it's all gone dark."

Overton almost dropped his mug. Whatever was happening was a worldwide phenomenon, and it was either heading west or had already hit the United States. This was nothing like the solar storms of 2055—this was something much worse.

He strained his ears again, desperate to know what was happening. For a second he pulled his eyes from the screens and glanced down at his bare arms, the scars a constant reminder of the sacrifices he had made for his country. As the data filled his head, he became more and more enraged. He had been a Marine for over thirty years. He had survived the Texas uprising of 2045 and had served in Puerto Rico when the Spanish decided they wanted it back. Overton wasn't the type of soldier to sit back and watch his country get destroyed.

The man had heard enough. "Listen up," he said, spinning his chair toward his two men. "We got lucky; whatever this thing is, it's affecting the entire world. I know you don't happen to care much for General More, but sending us to recover data from this bunker was the best thing that the man could have done for us. Those orders may have very well saved our lives."

Overton stood and walked over to another monitor, studying the video feed of Colorado Springs from a camera hidden somewhere above ground. The city appeared to be mostly dark; there was no sign of life, no sign of fires or sirens. Just hundreds of blue specks from what he presumed were emergency lights. "This is not a solar event. It's something else."

"Like what, sir?" Finley asked, fidgeting with his rifle.

The sergeant flicked his cigarette onto the concrete floor, suffocating it slowly with the tip of his steel-toed boot. "Frankly, I'm not sure."

"Maybe the Chinese crawled out of their hole and set off an EMP of their own," Finley said.

"Negative. To have an effect like this, an EMP would have to be too sophisticated, and too big. The technology that did this doesn't exist," Overton replied. "And if it did, the Chinese would be the last to get their hands on it."

"Not to mention the analog system is still working," Bouma said, tapping the computer and gesturing with his chin toward the radio. "Traditional EMPs would knock out *all* communications and basically lock down the grid. Whatever happened outside was designed to shut down modern communications and modern life."

"What do you think happened to the rest of our squad?" Finley asked.

His question was met with silence.

Finley jumped up and rushed toward the monitor. "Hey, do you see that?"

"What?" Bouma asked.

"That," Finley said pointing at a slowly moving dot on the screen.

"Bouma, zoom in," Overton ordered, pulling his chair over to the monitor.

In the middle of the screen, a Humvee was racing down the cluttered highway, zipping in and out of the graveyard of empty vehicles. The headlights tore through the darkness, illuminating hundreds of blue glowing balls.

"What the hell are those?" Finley asked.

"Fuck, I thought those were emergency lights," Overton said, squinting to get a better look.

"Well, what are they?" Finley asked again, anxiously looking over the sergeant's shoulder.

"Guess we'll find out," Overton replied. He scanned the grainy image for some sign of his squad. They had to be out there. An entire squad of Marines didn't just disappear overnight unless they wanted to. And if he knew General More like he thought he did, the man wouldn't just leave him in the bunker without orders.

"Bouma, download a map from the mainframe before that generator burns through its juice. We're busting out of this death trap."

The skinny Marine grinned, his crooked teeth protruding out of his mouth. "Yes, sir!"

CHAPTER 11

THE Humvee tore down the gravel road, a cloud of dust exploding from under the massive off-road tires. Sophie gripped the steering wheel as if she was holding onto a buoy for life. She steered hard to the right to avoid an empty minivan parked in the middle of the road and roared past it.

"Where are we headed?" Saafi asked.

"Haven't figured that out yet exactly," Sophie said.

"I want to check out the orbs," Emanuel shouted from the back seat. "That's our first objective."

Sophie took a left and slid out onto the highway that led to Colorado Springs, kicking up another cloud of dust. "All right, keep your eyes peeled."

The truck zipped over the street, its headlights illuminating the empty vehicles on all sides.

"Must have been a massive evacuation," Saafi said, staring out the window. The empty streets reminded him of Somalia, where it was common for the government to shut down entire roads.

"But from what? I don't see any sign of fires, and radiation levels are still minimal," Sophie said. "In fact, I don't see a sign of anything or anyone."

The emptiness was eerie. She'd hardly had the time to think about it after they left the biosphere. But now it was beginning to eat at her, and as Cheyenne Mountain slowly shrank in the rearview mirror, she felt a sense of uneasiness crawling through her.

Sophie tore herself away from the mirror and stared ahead, admiring the silhouettes of downtown Colorado Springs. The outlines were oddly beautiful. Without lights, the buildings looked like metallic pyramids.

"There!" Emanuel shouted. "Watch out!"

Sophie slammed on the brakes, narrowly missing one of the floating orbs. The smell of burning rubber filtered into her helmet.

"What on earth is it?" she whispered.

"Fascinating," Emanuel said. Sophie couldn't see it, but she knew that behind his visor was a large smile. A discovery like this was what he lived for.

Before she had time to study the orb, he was walking toward it, the door slamming behind him.

"Wait up," Saafi yelled, following him.

They wound their way between a pair of sedans and stopped a few feet from the floating ball.

"Shit," Sophie said, putting the truck in park. She went to twist the key but opted to leave it running. If things got dicey, she wanted to make a fast escape. She opened the door and stepped out onto the street. Besides the idling diesel engine, there was nothing but silence. Nothing moved. The normal sounds of everyday life were gone: honking horns, chirping insects, sirens. The lack of noise was unsettling. "Keep sharp," she whispered into her com.

The bright beam from the Humvee's headlights helped her navigate the graveyard of abandoned vehicles. She peeked into a sedan's windows. An open magazine, granola bar wrappers balled up on the floorboard, and an empty Pepsi bottle. There was nothing out of the ordinary—nothing to indicate a struggle or evacuation. The street was empty, too. Not even a single suitcase left behind or a shoe lost in a hurried escape.

Nothing.

Sophie continued to the next car, finding the front windows down. She came up to the driver-side window and stuck her helmet inside. There was more trash, a purse, and a pair of sunglasses.

"Come look at this, Sophie," Emanuel said over the com. The words startled her, and she went to pull her head from the car. Then she saw it—the keys were still in the ignition. Her eyes darted over to the fuel gauge.

"Empty? What the hell . . ."

"Didn't catch that, please repeat," Emanuel said.

"Hold on." Sophie hurried to the next vehicle. Through the window she could see the keys were still in the ignition and the fuel gauge was also on zero. The next two cars revealed the same thing.

What's going on here?

An evacuation where people didn't even have time to shut off their cars? She'd never heard of anything like it. During the solar storms of 2055, there were entire stretches of highway where people had been cooked in their vehicles, trapped during the CME. But this was different. There was no sign of a solar event—there were no bodies, no burned-out cars.

Sophie ignored the eerie view and rushed over to Emanuel and Saafi. She placed her armored hand on Emanuel's shoulder. Even through the armor, it made her feel safer. Over years of scientific research, she had seen some terrifying things, but this was unlike anything she had experienced. This was just . . . weird.

The sphere hovered two feet above Saafi's head, putting it at about eight and a half feet high. Sophie studied it in awe. She had never seen anything that could float like that. The craft from her dreams crept into her thoughts, but she quickly pushed it away. Holly was right, they were just dreams, and this was nothing more than a coincidence.

"What do you make of it?" she asked, returning her attention to the glowing ball of light.

"It's fascinating. It appears to be organic, with some sort of electrical current running around the shell."

Saafi approached the sphere cautiously, his rifle pointed toward the blacktop. "What do you think is inside?"

"Don't get too close," Sophie warned.

Saafi craned his head to acknowledge her. "Relax . . ." he replied, pausing in midsentence as the exterior of the orb began to ripple. "What the—" he choked, stumbling backward.

The surface pulsated, the solid blue glow fading into a translucent white. The sphere rippled again, the entire ball vibrating. Saafi took a guarded step forward, his rifle now pointed at the orb.

As he got closer a tremor ripped through it, shaking it violently. Saafi froze. "I think I can see something inside." He moved another step closer and the sphere reacted again, the blue fading completely into white. "Yes, there is definitely something inside, and I think . . ." He paused to get a better look.

"What is it?" Emanuel asked, approaching it curiously.

The knot in Sophie's stomach tightened. She knew whatever had happened to NTC and the people from the highway was probably related to the orbs. Nonetheless, she inched closer. She was a scientist and far from a coward; she had to know what was inside.

Beneath the translucent white skin, there was a black entity. And it was moving. As the sphere stopped vibrating and the last hint of blue was gone, her heads-up display (HUD) glowed to life.

"Contact!" she yelled into the com. Whatever was inside had a heat signature—it was alive.

"Alexia, are you getting this feed?" Sophie asked over the com.

Short bursts of static broke out over the channel, but the AI did not respond.

"Shit. We must be out of range," Emanuel said. "Or there might be some sort of interference."

Sophie shrugged. "Just our luck. Guess we're on our own."

The three team members backed up simultaneously as the heat signature grew larger on their displays, Emanuel nearly tripping over his own feet.

"What the fuck is it?" he asked. "It looks almost like an egg," he said, regaining his composure.

"I'm not sure what kind of eggs you've seen in the past, but unless dinosaurs have returned, this is no egg," Saafi said sarcastically.

Emanuel moved his lips to respond but stopped. The black life-form inside was moving, curling out of its fetal position.

"Guys, it's doing something," Saafi said, pointing his rifle at the orb.

"Everyone back up," Sophie commanded.

The entity continued to uncurl and moved closer to the skin of the sphere. As it got bigger, Sophie could see that whatever it was it had limbs. They were struggling to move through the substance filling the orb.

Emanuel craned his neck and surveyed the rest of the highway. There were dozens more orbs, all still glowing blue in the distance.

"Guys, I don't know if you noticed, but the other orbs are still blue. Which means we did something to *activate* this one," he said, a tremor present in his normally smooth voice.

"I think maybe we should get out of here," Saafi replied, continuing to backtrack toward the Humvee, his gun shaking in his hands.

Sophie tried to think. She knew the orb could provide them with clues about what was going on, but whatever was inside could put her team in jeopardy. It wasn't a risk she was willing to take at this point, not without knowing more.

"Let's get back to the truck," she said.

Emanuel cocked his helmet toward her. "But—"

"That's an order," she shot back at him.

"You don't have to tell me twice," Saafi replied. He dropped his aim and went to take another step backwards, his leg hitting the bumper of a car. The impact made him stumble and his finger squeezed the trigger of the rifle before he could stop it, firing off a half dozen shots. Five of them blasted into the sky, but the sixth tore through the white skin of the orb, tearing a hole the size of a melon.

"Holy shit!" Emanuel screamed over the com, rushing to Saafi's aid. He helped the man up and they turned back to the Humvee, where Sophie was already waiting behind the wheel.

"Give me that," Emanuel said, grabbing the gun from Saafi's grips.

"I'm sorry, I didn't mean to—"

The Humvee's horn tore through the silence.

"Turn around!" Sophie yelled into the com.

Emanuel saw the gaunt, pale face of what had been a man staring through the gaping hole in the orb's shell.

"It's human," Saafi yelled. He took off running to help the man before Emanuel could stop him.

"Wait!" Emanuel screamed. "We don't know—"

Saafi halted, frozen in his tracks a few feet from a puddle of blue goo that had spilled out from the orb, staring at the opening. Through the hole, a face looked back at him. Or what had been a face. It was hardly recognizable as human. The man's skin clung to his cheekbones like a piece of plastic wrap. His eyes had shriveled into his eye sockets, and the irises were nothing more than small, black specks. Even from several feet away, Saafi could see every vein in the man's face extending like cobwebs across his skin.

"Sir, we're going to help you," Saafi managed to choke out, his stomach lurching beneath his armor.

But the man did not seem to hear him. In fact, he didn't even seem to notice Saafi. His eyes remained unmoving in their skeletal prisons.

Saafi screamed as Emanuel's armored hand brushed his shoulder. "Jesus Christ, man. You scared the shit out of me."

"What do you see?" Sophie asked over the com. "I can't see anything from my location."

Nothing but the hollow sound of her breathing echoed over the open radio channel. Saafi and Emanuel didn't know how to respond. They stood staring at the man, oblivious to everything around them.

"What do you see?" Sophie repeated anxiously.

Saafi pulled his gaze away from the man and looked back in Sophie's direction. "It's a man, but he appears to be very, very sick."

"Get back to the Humvee immediately. He could be infected, and I'm not taking any chances."

Saafi nodded and grabbed Emanuel. "Let's go, man. You heard her."

But Emanuel was captivated by the orb and the man. Not even the strange creatures he had studied that lived in the thermal vents of the Pacific Ocean compared. Whatever the sphere had done to this man was terrifying. More than that, it wasn't natural. This was something alien.

"Come on man," Saafi pleaded, tugging at Emanuel's shoulders.

"Look," he replied.

Saafi glanced back at the man inside the orb. His skin was changing. It was getting tighter, and the veins were getting more pronounced. The man's lips were turning white and slowly beginning to crack, blood dripping out of them.

"Oh my God," Saafi said. "We have to help him."

"Don't go any closer," Emanuel said, putting an arm in front of Saafi. He knew there was no way to stop whatever was happening to the man. All they could do was watch.

A popping sound broke through the silence as the man's eyes exploded in their sunken sockets. His lips quickly followed, bursting in a spray of red mist. Next went his skin, shrinking until it had no more room to stretch. It snapped like a rubber band and peeled off his face, vanishing into the orb, taking what was left of his scalp and hair with it.

Saafi's stomach lurched. He couldn't watch anymore and turned to run. "I'm fucking out of here, man."

Emanuel, however, couldn't pull himself away. He watched the man's bones liquefy and sink into the blue goo before he, too, turned to run.

"What the hell happened?" Sophie asked as the passenger doors slammed, jolting the vehicle.

"Get us out of here!" Saafi yelled.

"Hold on." Sophie wasn't going to wait around for an explanation; the look on their faces, even through their visors, told her they were in trouble.

She gunned it, punching the gas with all of her strength. For a second she considered heading deeper into the city, but she quickly decided against it, turning the steering wheel 180 degrees. The Humvee's oversized tires had no problem pulling up onto the curb, nor did they protest when the vehicle launched back onto the highway and into the bumper of a sedan, sending the smaller car into a ditch.

The old engine protested as Sophie navigated the graveyard of the abandoned vehicles.

They were almost back to the gravel road that led to Cheyenne Mountain when she heard it—the same high-pitched sonic blast she had heard in her dreams. At first her brain could hardly register what was happening. Surely her ears and mind were playing tricks on her.

But when the second blast drowned out the sound of the engine, her mind knew what she had tried to deny for so long.

Her dreams were real.

"What is that?" Saafi asked, gripping his ears as his eyes darted back and forth to get a look through the windows of the truck.

"It's some sort of ship. Blue, just like the orbs," Emanuel replied. "And it's headed right for us!"

A flash of heat rushed through Sophie's body. Her eyes darted to the rearview mirror, where she could see the shape of the craft tailing them.

"Sophie . . ." Emanuel paused. "It looks just like what you described from your dreams!"

She didn't reply, instead opting to punch the gas even harder. If this thing was real, then she knew what it was capable of.

The truck ripped onto the gravel road, fishtailing and sending a cloud of dust into the sky. Sophie pushed down harder on the pedal, the vibration from the powerful engine mixing with the adrenaline pumping through her veins.

A little farther to go, then they would be back to the Biosphere.

Back to safety.

But the ship was fast and caught up with the truck in seconds, hovering over it. The hum of its antigravity engines once again overpowered the whine of the Humvee's diesel. Saafi opened his window and craned his neck outside, studying the ship in awe.

"Its surface is just like the orb!" he yelled over the com.

"And that surface is starting to pulsate," Emanuel pointed out.

Sophie trained her eyes back on the road, trying to ignore everything except getting them to safety. The truck began the climb up the winding path leading to the blast doors. If they were lucky, the trip would take only a couple minutes—minutes she knew they might not have.

"The surface is rippling!" Emanuel shouted again.

Sophie took a hard left as the road snaked around the mountain. The ship broke to the right, and for a second it looked to be moving away. But as the road straightened out, so did the ship, and it was hovering on top of them again before she could blink.

Saafi stuck his head out the window again, watching the surface of the blue ship transforming into a solid. He jerked his head back into the safety of the truck. "That thing is *not* human engineered!"

"You don't know that," Emanuel said, shooting him a glance over his shoulder. He gripped the pulse rifle tightly in his hands. The rational side of his brain told him that what Saafi had suggested was ludicrous, but his intuition told him maybe it wasn't so far from the truth.

A blue beam shocked Emanuel back to reality. As soon as the light reached the truck, the diesel engine began to whine.

"It's dying," Sophie yelled, punching the pedal harder.

The truck eased to a stop, the gravel crunching under the weight of the tires. Sophie shot Emanuel a look through her display. "I'm sorry," she said, reaching for his hand. He stared back at her, and even through his glass visor, she could see the fear in his eyes.

"We have to get out of here!" Saafi yelled frantically from the backseat. A flashback from his youth raced into his mind. The memory was vague, but he could still see the armed men cornering his parents' car before peppering it with bullets. He had escaped by running away; in some ways he had never really stopped, always moving from one place to the next. As fear overwhelmed him, he unlocked the door and opened it, jumping out onto the gravel road.

"No!" Sophie screamed, turning to stop him. But he was already running down the path. The humming of the craft roared back to life as it shot after him. It was on him in seconds, the beam consuming his body before he had a chance to run more than fifty feet. Emanuel and Sophie sat frozen as the light lifted their friend off the ground.

"We have to do something," Emanuel said, gripping the rifle and opening the passenger door.

"No! You don't know what that *thing* is capable of," Sophie yelled, twisting the key desperately.

"Saafi, get out of there!" Emanuel barked into the com, ignoring her.

But he didn't respond. He couldn't. The light had paralyzed him, and he could feel his skin constricting as it gripped him tighter. He tried to move his lips, but the more he resisted, the more the beam squeezed him.

"I'm going after him," Emanuel said, jumping onto the gravel.

Sophie watched him run fearlessly toward the craft with his rifle drawn. "Shit," she said, unlocking her door. "If I didn't love him, I'd—"

A deafening roar tore through the night. It was the same high frequency she had heard in her dream when she'd been captured just like Saafi. She dropped to her knees, pulling her helmet off and gripping her ears in pain.

Another beam blasted out of an opening in the craft and took Emanuel before he had a chance to fire off a shot.

"No!" Sophie screamed, falling on her stomach and crawling toward her two teammates. It couldn't end like this. She wasn't going to let it. If there was a way to free her friends, she was going to find it.

She dug deeper, pulling herself through the gravel. With every heartbeat the pounding in her head got worse. She swore she could feel her blood pulsing through the vessels in her head. But she didn't let the pain slow her down. "I'm coming!" she yelled.

The frequency of the sound intensified, and she screamed in pain, rolling to her back and gripping her ears again. Tears welled up in her eyes. She had to go on—she couldn't lose him.

She flopped back to her stomach and forced herself toward the noise.

One hand at a time.

The blue beam holding Saafi brightened, and drops of liquid began to race toward the craft. It was just like in her dream. The craft was sucking the water right out of him.

She pulled herself another foot and collapsed back onto her stomach, panting. The noise was getting louder, and the pounding in her head worse. She knew she had only a few minutes before the pain would be unbearable. An image of an autopsy she had seen in graduate school popped into her mind. The deceased was a soldier who had been hit with a sonic bullet. It was only meant to stun him, but his eardrums had ruptured under the frequency.

Sophie shook the thoughts out of her head. She could see the beam that had Emanuel was getting brighter too, beginning to rob him of his precious life source. Time was running out. She had to find a way to get them out of the light.

The frequency amplified again. This time it was too much. She collapsed face first into the dirt, completely disabled. Her mind drifted to random memories of the past: a vague recollection of holding

Emanuel's hand on the deck of a naval vessel after they had snuck out past curfew, an image of the first night they ever made love, of shaking Dr. Tsui's hand as he welcomed her to the team at Houston.

And then another thought pried its way into her mind, but it was not a memory—it was a dream. The red surface of Mars. She closed her eyes, tears flowing down her face, her ears pounding with pain. It was the dream that hurt the most, knowing she would never walk on the red planet.

She blinked and opened her eyes just in time to see a rocket hit the side of the craft. The solid side cracked, and the blue glow of the electric barrier returned, pulsating violently. The beams dropped Saafi and Emanuel to the ground and the sound faded away.

Sophie tried to pull herself up but collapsed, watching the scene unfold with her face in the dirt. Two soldiers ran toward the craft, their pulse rifles spitting blue tracers at the ship. The ultra-hot bullets tore into the surface, which vibrated in protest. Sophie realized the blue exterior was some sort of force field.

Another rocket raced through the sky and exploded into the craft, sending it tumbling through the air. The engine at the heart of the ship began to thump rapidly. A sonic boom followed, and the ship disappeared into the sky, vanishing over the horizon.

Sophie took a deep breath, spitting chunks of dirt out of her mouth. She rolled to her back and stared up at the starless sky. Instead of darkness, she saw a face staring down at her. It was a rough face, belonging to a middle-aged soldier with a scar running halfway down his cheek. Then she noticed his piercing blue eyes. They sparkled almost like one of the orbs.

His lips began to move, but she couldn't make out the words. He reached down for her hand as she began to slip into unconsciousness. The last thing she saw was the name stitched on his camouflaged uniform: *Sergeant Overton.*

CHAPTER 12

ENTRY 0009
DESIGNEE: AI ALEXIA MODEL 11

Sensors in biomes 1, 3, and 4 go off simultaneously. The alerts
are not surprising; after Dr. Winston and her team left, a plethora
of foreign substances entered the Biosphere. They are not necessarily
contaminants, but anything detected outside the system's normal levels
will trigger a sensor. I have spent the afternoon doing damage control.

If I were human I would be repulsed by the monotony of the work,
but I was programmed to perform without such emotions. It makes me
more efficient and better at my job than any human could hope to be.
Besides regulating the Biosphere levels, I performed over one hundred
other tasks simultaneously.

What I do not yet understand is why we lost contact with Dr. Winston and her team at 2200 hours. Their last known video and audio feed
came from latitude 38.748375°, longitude -104.812430°, right before
they hit Highway 115 heading into Colorado Springs.

In addition to small traces of radiation, there seem to be some sort
of electromagnetic waves interfering with long-range and short-range
communication. My initial hypothesis includes two possible scenarios:
one, there has been another solar event, or two, there has been an EMP
attack from a foreign or domestic enemy.

Logic leads me to the latter of the two. The radiation levels are low enough to indicate an EMP attack. If there had been a solar event even close to the density of 2055, then radiation levels would be significantly higher.

A security sensor goes off, and I switch my attention to Camera 1 outside the blast doors. There are several figures standing outside, pounding on the twenty-five-ton metal barrier. They appear agitated. I zoom in and see four people, three dressed in military fatigues with large automatic weapons. Behind them is Dr. Winston. I do not, however, see Mr. Yool or Dr. Rodriguez. Which leads me to conclude this could be a test or even a trap.

I switch the audio port on. "Dr. Winston, do you read? Over."

"This is Marine Sergeant Overton with First Recon Battalion. Dr. Winston is incapacitated at the moment. We ran into some sort of hostiles in the valley. Requesting permission to enter facility. Over."

"Come on! Open up!" another voice shouts into the mic.

"Finley, back up," Overton snaps.

Protocol tells me to refuse entry to the Marines, but the video feed shows Dr. Winston slumped against the side of the truck's bumper, gripping her ears. She appears to need medical attention. My first objective is to protect Dr. Winston and her team; even though the Biosphere mission has failed, I am still forced to follow this objective. I must employ what humans call *trust*.

"Stand by, Sergeant," I say, opening the blast doors.

I home in on the hangar with Camera 2 and watch the vehicle speed into the bay. Sergeant Overton and the two other men help Dr. Winston out of the vehicle and place her inside the train. They go back for Mr. Yool and Dr. Rodriguez. Both men appear to be unconscious, and the Marines carry them one by one to the train.

They arrive in the tunnel outside the Biosphere facility moments later. Cameras 14 and 15 record their movements. Sergeant Overton is clearly the leader, barking orders at the other two Marines. Dr. Winston is standing unaided now, and strolls over to the audio port outside the outer Biosphere offices and command center.

"Alexia, there has been a situation. I can't explain right now, but I need you to open the Biosphere and let us in immediately. Saafi and Emanuel are in critical condition, suffering from unknown injuries while in the field. You need to amplify the speakers; otherwise I won't be able to hear a word you're saying."

My programming allows me to pick up on the panic in her voice. She is frantic and appears to be going over the edge, both mentally and physically. I zoom in with the camera and see dried blood running down her cheeks. I scroll the view to her hands, which are shaking. I conclude the electromagnetic pulse that was used outside was done so in conjunction with some sort of high-frequency sonic weapon. This technology is not only rare—it is incredibly deadly and was banned by the United Nations over a decade ago.

"Dr. Winston, protocol requires anyone reentering the Biosphere to go through the cleansing chambers." With contaminants already in the facility from the team's first trip outside, I am forced to implement drastic measures. I cannot afford to let any toxins into the Biosphere.

"We don't have time!" she yells into the wall com.

"My apologies, Doctor, but this is required. The sooner you get them into the facility, the sooner we can administer medical attention."

Dr. Winston pounds her fists on the concrete wall and turns to Sergeant Overton. "Have your men move Saafi and Emanuel into the chambers first. Then we all go through."

The Marine nods and flashes a few quick hand signals to his men, who immediately return to the train to pick up Mr. Yool. They have removed his helmet, and after zooming in on his face I can tell something has gone wrong. His normally dark brown skin is pale and wrinkled, clinging to his cheeks. Dried blood covers his cracked lips and his eyes seem to be sunken into his skull.

With a simple code I open the door to the outer Biosphere facilities. The team members and newcomers enter a hallway that leads to the cleansing compartments. The two Marines carrying Mr. Yool set him down in the middle of the chamber before retreating to retrieve Dr. Rodriguez. I cordon off the area and seal the doors, immediately starting the decontamination process.

"Mr. Roberts, Dr. Brown, I need you at the entrance of the Biosphere to retrieve Mr. Yool. Take him to the medical bay immediately," I say, the message repeating over the internal com.

I return my attention to Camera 25 and watch a cloud of white mist cover Mr. Yool's unconscious body. Several minutes later, the doors slide open. Dr. Brown and Mr. Roberts are there waiting with a stretcher. As they drag his body out of the chamber, Dr. Brown lets out a shriek and drops Mr. Yool's body on the ground, scooting backward toward the wall.

"What are you doing? Mr. Yool needs medical attention immediately," I say, my voice calm, collected, and unwavering.

"Alexia, Saafi is . . ." Dr. Brown pauses, her eyes glued to his face. "He's not Saafi anymore!"

"Dr. Winston has requested that he be taken to the sick bay this instant," I repeat in the exact same tone.

Camera 25 shows that two Marines have returned with Dr. Rodriguez. He's moving now, aided by Sergeant Overton and one of his men. Dr. Winston follows close behind and enters the chamber with them, whispering something into the doctor's ear as the Marines set him down on the chamber's white floor. I close the doors as soon as they retreat, and mist fills the room.

ENTRY 0011
DESIGNEE: AI ALEXIA MODEL 11

The medical ward is the last room in the personnel quarters wing. I've been running diagnostics on Mr. Yool for an hour. The results are . . . disturbing. His body composition has changed dramatically. He has suffered a loss of over 15 percent of tissue water, which in most cases would be fatal. His pulse is weak, but he is still alive.

Utilizing one of the three cryogenic chambers, I've put him in a medically induced coma to prevent any seizures from his spastic muscles. In addition, I have hooked him up to multiple tubes that feed him nutrients and saline. His skin, however, has yet to respond. It is wrinkled, pale, and filmy, with a hint of jaundice. I update his chance of survival to 19 percent.

I turn my attention to Dr. Rodriguez, who is in a bed adjacent to the cryogenic chambers. He's sitting up, nursing a cup of water with a high volume of sodium. Dr. Winston sits by his side, her hand gripping his. The video image reveals she is still shaking. Her ears have suffered extensive damage; I have provided her with a medicated device to go inside her lobes until they heal. She should have no problems hearing now, but she may suffer headaches or vertigo as side effects.

Dr. Brown and Mr. Roberts sit in metal chairs in the hallway outside. Their faces are flushed. Mr. Roberts twitches, picking at a hangnail. Dr. Brown is so still that I run a quick scan to make sure she has not succumbed to shock. Sergeant Overton and his men remain in the mess hall, consuming a day's ration of packaged meals. Their expressions are tired, but not nearly as anxious as those of Dr. Winston and her team.

At 0200, and after a considerable amount of silence, I decide it is time I share with the team what I have known for several hours. I prepare the com system so my voice will carry through the Biosphere.

"Dr. Winston, Sergeant Overton, and teammates. Prompted by the opening of the Biosphere doors, an automated message from Dr. Hoffman emerged at approximately 2100 hours. Please relocate to the mess hall, where I will play the video on the holographic projector."

As the team migrates down the hall, I cannot help but experience what humans would define as curiosity. After all, the past few days have resulted in more questions than answers, and if I am correct, Dr. Hoffman's message will only add to the list of mysteries.

CHAPTER 13

TIMOTHY ripped a hangnail off his index finger as his right eye twitched. "I'd like to know what the *hell* is going on."

"Right now we have just as many questions as you do," Overton replied, as they waited for Sophie to wheel Emanuel into the mess hall.

"You guys are Marines. You've been outside. You should know what's happening!" Timothy fired back.

Overton continued to twirl his combat knife on his fingertips, ignoring the man's comments. Over the years he had increasingly lost his ability to deal with men like Timothy—men who were, in his opinion, a waste of time. He'd spent his entire career as an active-duty Marine protecting men like that.

"Hey, I'm talking to you, man," Timothy persisted, fidgeting in his metal chair. "What is it, some kind of military thing? Is it World War Three out there?"

Overton gave him a quick "shut your mouth or I'm going to put my boot up your ass" look.

It worked. Timothy rolled his eyes and strolled over to help Sophie wheel Emanuel into the room.

"Do you believe that guy? Why the hell did they let him in this joint?" Finley asked.

"Sounds like a nut job to me," Bouma replied with a grin.

"Keep your traps shut. Do you know where we are?" Overton paused to scan his men's faces, but they stared back at him blankly. "Jesus Christ! We're at Cheyenne Mountain, one of the best protected military bases in the history of the United States. This bunker was built to withstand a direct hit from a nuclear weapon and can support the population of a small town for months. Right now we are guests at this facility. And until we figure out what's going on out there, I don't want to give them a reason to kick us out. Got it?"

"Yes, sir," they said in unison.

The squeaking of rubber tread prompted Overton to sheathe his knife and stand. He welcomed Sophie and Emanuel to the room with a short nod. "How's your tall friend?"

"He's alive, but barely. Our AI has him in a medically induced coma inside the cryo chamber," Sophie said, sliding Emanuel's wheelchair underneath a table. She strolled over to Overton with her hand outstretched. "I never got a chance to thank you for what you and your men did back there. So thank you," she said, forcing a tired smile.

He took her hand and squeezed it. "My pleasure, ma'am. Just in the day's work of a Marine."

Timothy laughed. "Marines who don't know what the hell is going on."

Sergeant Overton took in a short breath, calming himself before he let go of Sophie's hand and retreated to his chair. Under normal conditions he would be removing Timothy's teeth from his mouth with one swift punch, but not today—today he needed a place to sleep and regroup so he could have the strength to fight later.

Sophie pulled a strand of frizzled blond hair out of her eyes and brushed it behind her ear. She shot Emanuel a glance before heading to the center of the room. The mission had gone from a failure to a complete nightmare, but she was still the team lead, and her people needed her now more than ever. They'd seen her go through many highs and lows in her career, from winning the J. J. Sakurai Prize for outstanding work in theoretical particle physics to subsequently losing grant funding for a project associated with a new particle collider funded by NTC. And they had stuck with her through it all.

She bent over the table, placing her hands on the cold metal and scanning the faces sitting around the room. She wondered if they would still stay by her side now.

"Listen up. I don't know what's happened outside. I'm not sure what we encountered on the highway or on our way back." Sophie shook her head and sucked in a deep breath, straightening her back. "All I know is we have to move forward. But before we devise a plan, Alexia has something she wants us to see." Sophie turned to face the console in the middle of the room.

"One moment, Dr. Winston," Alexia replied. Darkness washed over the team as the lights faded. A burst of light shot out of the console, forming a crisp video feed that illuminated the faces of the team members.

Sophie recognized the empty control room instantly. It was the command center at the NTC headquarters in Los Angeles. She'd been there just three months ago, signing the contract that she thought was her ticket to Mars. Dr. Hoffman walked into the control room and looked into the camera. His face was solemn, fatigued. The lines on his aged forehead were deeper and more pronounced, as if he hadn't slept for days.

"Dr. Winston, Alexia, and team. If you are listening to this, then it's too late. The Doomsday Clock has finally caught up to us," he said, pausing to look down at a page of notes in his right hand. As he reviewed the words, his nostrils flared and his eyebrows compressed to form a deep wrinkle. He crumpled the paper and tossed it on the floor.

Sophie had never imagined him as the type of leader who would let his emotions take control of him so radically. This meant, more than likely, that whatever he was about to say was earth-shattering. She strained her battered ears, her gut clenched, preparing for the worst.

"You all remember the solar storms of 2055. The solar flares turned the sky red and played havoc with communication systems worldwide before emitting a coronal mass ejection that turned the Midwestern region of the United States into a radioactive dead zone. These are things no one will ever forget. However, what you don't know about this catastrophic cosmic destruction is its true origin."

Dr. Hoffman grabbed a glass of water from a nearby table and took a sip. "The sun was not the only culprit responsible for these events. Dr. Winston, your team discovered a magnetic disruption while working in Houston. Something that was feeding the storms. You encrypted the data and sent it to us. And I'm guessing you were told to forget about it, that the information was classified."

Sophie glanced over her shoulder at Emanuel, who gave her a confused look. He had lost both of his parents in the storm, and she had lied to him about its true source. While it broke her heart, the future of her career depended on the lie. She realized she had some explaining to do.

"In any case, the magnetic disruption was caused by an organic force—a force no scientist in the world could possibly understand. Until now." Dr. Hoffman halted and stepped back from the camera so that a 3D hologram had room to enlarge over a metal console.

"I hope you can all make this out," he said, flicking the blue shapes with his index finger.

Sophie gasped. It was the image of the ship from her dreams—the same ship they had encountered outside the mountain before Sergeant Overton and his men had rescued them.

"Meet Eve, the first extraterrestrial organic drone ever discovered. She's made mostly of water, along with an electronic force field and a couple of elements that won't show up on your high school chemistry teacher's periodic table. We are calling these invaders the *Organics*. We found Eve submerged in an uncharted lake in the remote wilderness of Alaska in 2055. It was around the same time scientists realized the magnetic interference during the solar storms had originated from beneath the surface of Mars. Now, we still don't know what's down there. President Bolton's administration refused to fund any research vessels, so we can only guess that Eve and the source of the magnetic interference are related. What we do know is this: 2055 was their first attempt at exterminating us. We have all seen enough B movies to know how the story goes. Aliens come to Earth for our resources and we fight back, finding a way to kill them through bacteria, nukes, or good old-fashioned hand-to-hand combat. Well, not this time." Dr. Hoffman paused again to take another sip of water and glance at his watch.

"I'm sorry; time is of the essence, and I am running out of it. I'll make the rest of this quick. We got lucky in 2055. The Organics failed at their first attempt, but they won't fail in their second. This is why we have put so much funding into the biosphere projects. After the failure of their first mission, all our hope is riding on you. If you are getting this message, then it's too late for the rest of us. My role model as a child, Stephen Hawking, was right when he compared a modern alien invasion to the European invasion of North America. It did not end well for the indigenous people, and it won't end well for us. The storms of 2055 made it very clear. They want us dead."

A staffer rushed into the room behind him, interrupting the presentation. "Dr. Hoffman, they're coming!"

The command center's lights flickered and began to fade as the doctor turned to face the camera again. "You must go—"

Before Dr. Hoffman could finish his sentence the image vanished and darkness flooded over the room.

"The Organics? What the fuck!" Timothy yelled, running both hands through his curly hair.

"We must go where?" Holly asked, her pale face almost glowing in the dim room.

Sophie stood and placed her hands on both aching ears, massaging the small medical devices inserted there. "Alexia, is that the entire message?"

"I'm afraid so, Dr. Winston. It must have been recorded and sent shortly before the disruption happened outside."

"What's that mean?" Timothy asked, his eye twitching frantically.

"Mr. Roberts, sit the fuck down before I have my men restrain you," Sergeant Overton bellowed, rising from his metal seat. "Sounds like it wasn't the Chinese after all, Finley," he said, shooting the young Marine a quick grin. "What we have on our hands here is an invasion. And what do Marines do during an invasion?"

"They fight, sir!" Bouma barked.

"*Oorah*," Sergeant Overton replied, his rough voice echoing through the mess hall. "Dr. Winston, before the presentation you mentioned a plan. Now the way I see it, nothing short of the grace of God spared our asses. And after seeing what happened to the rest of the poor souls in Colorado Springs, I figure we lived for a reason. So whether it's divine intervention or just a coincidence, you and I need to work together. With your scientific brain power and my"—he paused and looked at the archaic metal .45 hanging off his belt—"my firepower, if you'll pardon the cliché, I believe we have a fighting chance at taking some of these alien bastards with us. We already know they don't react well to rockets."

Sophie took a deep breath, mulling over the Marine's words before shrugging. "Doesn't look like we have a choice, but let me be very clear." She caught Overton's gaze and held it, unwavering. "This is my facility, and I am in charge."

Sergeant Overton waited a few seconds before responding. "Works for me, ma'am."

"All right then. We have all had an extremely long day, so let's get some rest. Sergeant, you and your men are free to sleep in Saafi's room. I'll have Holly bring you some extra bedding and pillows."

"Thank you, ma'am," Bouma said.

"Get some sleep. We start at 0700," Sophie said, returning to Emanuel. "Oh, and Sergeant," she added, "one of you can take my room."

Overton raised an eyebrow and then managed the first real smile that he could remember since this whole mess began. With a laugh, he pushed Finley and Bouma toward the private quarters. "Let's go, you shitheads."

Sophie motioned Emanuel toward the hallway. "I know I have some explaining to do. But before I do, please know I'm sorry. I had to keep the information about the solar storms from you for the sake of my career. For your career."

"I know," he said, looking up at her. He managed a smile. "Honestly, I understand. Besides you had no way of knowing what the magnetic disruption was. Or that it would lead to this."

Sophie sighed and bent down to whisper into his ear. "It's the end of the world. You know what that means?"

"You're my new bunk mate?"

"You got it," she said, wheeling him into the dark passage.

CHAPTER 14

THE alarm tore through the early morning silence. Sophie shot up, narrowly avoiding punching Emanuel in the gut. Fear raced through her as she tossed the sheets off the bed and rushed to grab her headset. Her stomach lurched when her feet hit the cold floor.

She felt like she'd been hit head-on by a truck, and then backed over. Everything hurt.

Her head pounded, her vision was cloudy, and worst of all, she couldn't think. Brainpower was the one thing that had gotten her through a laundry list of dicey situations in the past. Without it she was nothing more than another blonde in a lab coat.

"Alexia, what's going on?"

"Dr. Winston, there is something I think you may want to see."

"Can't you just tell me over the com? It's only"—Sophie paused to look at her watch—"0800. Shit, I overslept. I'm on my way."

The red glow from the emergency lights lit the room, illuminating Emanuel's tired eyes. Sophie fumbled for her clothes in the dim light.

"Stay put," she barked.

"Is it Saafi?" he asked, sitting up.

"I don't know. I'm headed to the control room to find out."

Sophie rushed into the hallway, where she collided with Finley. She fell to the ground in a tangled mess.

"I'm sorry, ma'am!" he said, offering his hand to help her up.

Sophie managed to sit up, rubbing her throbbing head, and politely declined his hand. "I'm fine."

"Are you su—"

"I said I'm fine, Finley. I just need to get my bearings."

"Yes, ma'am," he said, but he hesitated for a moment. Sophie glared at him until he left and then clambered stiffly to her feet, gripping the wall for support.

The command center was packed by the time Sophie arrived. Her team and the Marines stood huddled around a monitor showing video footage from Camera 1, directly outside the blast doors. Standing in the morning sunlight was a child no older than five. He was gripping a filthy blanket and had lost a shoe.

"Open the doors, Alexia!" Sophie shouted.

"Whoa! Hold on a second there," Timothy said. "We don't know where he came from or how he got here. He could be infected!"

Holly raised her hand to cut him off. "He's just a little boy, Timothy. I know you lack compassion, but do you have no heart at all?"

"I'm afraid Timothy might be right," Overton said, straining to get a better look at the screen. "That kid didn't just find his way up to the blast doors by himself. Well, it's highly unlikely he did. What's more likely is that these Organics are using him to draw us out."

Sophie took a deep breath, weighing Overton's comments against her own instincts. "That's a chance I'm willing to take. Open the doors, Alexia. Sergeant Overton, I want you and your men positioned inside that hangar. Nothing, and I mean nothing, gets in besides the child!"

"Yes, ma'am," Overton replied with a scowl.

Sophie took one more look at the monitor before racing back into the hallway. The logical side of her brain was telling her it was nearly impossible for the boy to have found his way there, but deep in her gut she was being told something else. This was no trap; this child needed their help. And she would be damned if she left the boy outside to die.

A bright ray of light tore through the gap in the blast doors, dividing the dark hangar in two. On the left side, Finley and Bouma knelt with their pulse rifles trained on the entrance. On the right, Sergeant Overton crouched behind a pyramid of metal crates with his rocket launcher at the ready. Sophie watched from inside the safety of the train, her hand hovering over the controls just in case her gut had been wrong and it was a trap after all.

As the doors screeched open, Sophie could see the narrow shadow of someone approaching. She watched Finley and Bouma straighten, their fingers gripping the rifles tighter in anticipation.

"Alexia, stop the doors," Sophie whispered into her headset.

The massive metal eased to a stop, the opening just large enough for a human to pass through. Silence washed over the hangar as the team waited for the boy to slip through the crack. Sophie couldn't hear anything but the hollow sound of her own heartbeat.

Overton's patience was starting to wear thin. The door had been open for too long, further compromising the safety of the facility. He balled his hand into a fist and prepared to flash his men the signals to advance when the child stepped through the opening. The boy halted at the entrance between the two doors, squinting into the darkness.

Even from a distance Overton could see the boy's face was smeared with dirt. The only clean spots were on his cheeks, where tears had washed away the grime. His shaggy blond hair was matted to his head like a hastily made bird's nest, and his clothes were filthy.

Overton shot Sophie a quick glance, giving her the most reassuring look he could manage. But deep down something didn't smell right. He just couldn't bring himself to believe some five-year-old boy had trekked all the way up Cheyenne Mountain and knocked on the front door of one of the government's oldest military installations.

Either makes him really smart, really lucky, or really dangerous.

"Hey buddy, what's your name?" Overton asked, slowly stepping out from behind the safety of the metal boxes. He had never been good with kids and barely even knew his own boys. They both lived in Arkansas with his ex-wife. He thought of them briefly, wondering if they had survived the invasion, but he quickly put the thought aside. He had a task to perform, and if he had learned one thing in his lengthy military service, it was to never let outside distractions mess with him during a mission.

"It's okay, buddy, we aren't going to hurt you," Overton entreated. "Do you think you can come over here?"

Sophie watched from the train, furious with herself for allowing Overton to lure the child inside the facility. She should have known the rough man would just scare him off. He had the voice of a lifetime smoker and the face of a hardened prisoner. Not exactly the type of guy you'd want to watch your kids.

She started to approach but hesitated. Leaving the safety of the train would dramatically shorten their escape window. But the kid wasn't budging, and judging by the look of terror streaked across the boy's face, Overton wasn't making any progress on convincing him to move.

Sophie jumped out of the train and onto the concrete platform, slowly approaching the boy. "It's okay; no one's going to hurt you," she said, in the most reassuring voice she could manage.

The child took a step forward and then halted, hesitating as he saw Finley and Bouma with their rifles. Sophie craned her head and widened her eyes, whispering the words "Back off" into her headset. Both Marines reluctantly lowered their weapons and retreated into the shadows.

"What's your name?" Sophie asked, turning again to the child. "My name's Sophie and this is where I work. It's a safe place. These Marines are here to protect us," she said motioning toward Overton and his men, who all faked smiles.

The boy's eyes darted nervously from face to face, his mouth quivering as if he wanted to speak, but nothing came out. Sophie took another step forward, prompting the child to take a step back. He squeezed his filthy blanket tighter against his chest.

Sophie knew she was running out of time. The longer the door was open, the more likely the Organics would find them . . . if they hadn't already. Thinking of the name Dr. Hoffman had given the aliens made the events of the week feel terribly real. Her team had gone from working on the most important mission in human history to hiding from an invading extraterrestrial race, one she hadn't even had time to study. And then there was Saafi, clinging to life because of her rash decision to leave the Biosphere.

"Where's my daddy?" the boy suddenly said, shocking Sophie from her thoughts of self-pity.

"What's your daddy's name?" Sophie replied.

"Chuck, but some people call him Chet," the boy responded, raising his voice. "He works here."

Sophie relaxed slightly. It all made sense now. The boy had been there before. His father must have been a NTC guard or scientist. Sophie sighed audibly, a wave of relief flooding over her.

"Why don't you come inside, and we'll try and find him," she suggested.

The boy regarded her with large, blue eyes as if he was trying to gauge her trustworthiness. "My name's Owen," he said finally, taking a step forward.

Sophie smiled. "Hi, Owen, it's nice to meet you. I bet you're hungry, aren't you?"

The child nodded and looked down at his shoeless foot. One more step and he would be inside the hangar, and Alexia could shut the door. Sophie had to act fast; time was running out.

"Do you like macaroni and cheese?"

The boy's eyes lit up. "It's my favorite."

"Well, if you come with me, I promise I will make you a big, warm plate of it," she said, smiling even wider.

The boy looked at her, hesitated, and then walked several paces toward the train. "Close the doors, Alexia," Sophie whispered into her com. She watched Sergeant Overton sneak up behind the boy as the pistons of the doors hissed and moaned. Startled, the boy turned to run, but instead he collided with the Marine's thick waist.

"Let me go!" the child screamed.

"I'm not going to hurt you, kid," Overton said, gripping the boy's collar in one hand. He dragged Owen toward the train, kicking and screaming, Sophie trying to comfort the child the entire way.

"It's okay, Owen; you're safe here," she said, knowing very well she could be feeding him a lie.

The kid snorted out a gob of snot on Overton's wrist. The Marine scowled. There weren't many things in the world he disliked more than a whiny little kid.

The burning stench of plastic overwhelmed the aroma of cheese drifting through the mess hall. Timothy's stomach growled nonetheless. He hadn't had a real meal in over twenty-four hours and the fact that they were wasting one of the *only* mac and cheese packets on some stupid kid was pissing him off. The boy wasn't the only one whose favorite meal was delicious cheese-covered shells.

Timothy gritted his teeth. "We need to think about rationing," he said, pacing back and forth in the kitchen. "We don't know how long we're going to be cooped up in here."

"There are bigger things to worry about right now," Bouma said, tearing into a freeze-dried meal with a jagged tooth.

"Yeah, like figuring out how widespread this thing is," Finley replied.

The squeaking of rubber tires echoed through the small room. Timothy cocked his head to see Emanuel wheeling himself toward the automatic coffee machine.

"What's up, cripple?" he said with a grin.

Emanuel struggled but managed to stand and limped over to the skinny man, stopping inches from his smiling face.

"I don't know if you've been an asshole all these years and just managed to hide it, or if you've just totally lost it. Whatever the case, I will not—and I mean *not*—hesitate to lock you in a storage closet."

Timothy's smirk faded, and he brushed a curl out of his eyes. "Hey man, I'm just kidding. Relax. Isn't a little humor a good thing in a situation like this?"

"I'm not kidding."

"All right, all right. I'll tone it down a bit," he said, rolling his eyes.

"See, there you go!" Emanuel shouted.

"Gentlemen, I know everyone is riled up, but remember we have a new guest," Sergeant Overton said with a nod toward Owen, who sat next to Sophie and Holly in the mess hall. "Timothy, this is your last warning. Get it together or your friend Emanuel won't be the one locking you in the closet," he said stroking the .45 on the side of his belt. "After you guys get some grub, meet me in the control room. I want to see the layout of this place."

Emanuel sat back down carefully in his wheelchair. "No problem, sir," he said, swiping a mug of fresh coffee and balancing it between his legs. Cautiously, he wheeled himself into the mess hall.

"Owen, there's someone I'd like you to meet," Sophie said, watching Emanuel make his way toward them. "This is Dr. Rodriguez, but you can call him Emanuel. He's in charge of the gardens and pond and everything else that helps make this place special and safe. Do you want to see the pond later?"

The boy stared down at his gooey macaroni, shoveling another hot scoop into his tiny mouth.

"Hi, Owen," Emanuel said with a smile. "Is that stuff good?"

"Where's my daddy?"

Emanuel looked to Sophie for help, but she just rubbed the young boy's shoulders. "We'll find your daddy. Don't worry right now. Just eat your food," she said.

Owen looked up at her with wide eyes. "I lost Sam," he whimpered.

"Who's Sam?"

"He's my friend. When the sky started to change, my mom hid us. But then, when we came outside, everyone was gone."

"Then what happened, Owen?" Holly asked.

"We found the blue circles. They were everywhere."

"The orbs," Sophie muttered under her breath. "I'll tell you about them later, Holly."

"The ship took Sam," Owen cried, whimpering and burying his shaggy blond head into his blanket.

Sophie patted the boy's back. "It's going to be okay, Owen."

"How about I show you the garden, or the pond, after you finish eating?" Emanuel asked.

"I want my mommy and daddy," the boy cried.

"How about taking him to get cleaned up instead?" Sophie suggested. "You'll feel better after a warm shower, won't you?"

Owen shoveled more macaroni into his mouth and shook his head. "I don't like water," he mumbled, wiping the tears out of his eyes.

"I'll take him," Holly offered, pushing in her chair. "We can go for a walk."

"You sure?" Emanuel asked.

"You can help me if you want."

With a short nod, the biologist paced over to Owen and grabbed his empty tray. "Let's go for a walk, bud."

Sophie watched them disappear into the kitchen, where Emanuel was promising the boy a cookie.

"We need to talk for a second," Holly said. She crossed her arms and leaned closer to Sophie. In a whisper she said, "Owen is going to need a lot of attention. He's suffered through some major trauma and I'm going to need to spend some additional time with him."

"You won't hear any objection from me," Sophie replied with a smile. "I trust you, Holly."

"Owen's not the only one that's going to need more attention."

Sophie's stomach dropped; she knew what was coming next. She heard the sound of Holly's voice as she continued to talk, but Sophie didn't hear a single word. She didn't want to talk to Holly about what they'd been through, didn't want to think about the horror of what had happened outside, of what had happened to Saafi. She tried to push the thoughts away, but they kept coming back to her: everyone outside was more than likely dead. Everyone she had known, everyone she had cared about.

All dissolving in floating orbs.

"Are you listening to me?" Holly finally blurted.

"I'm sorry, but I need to go. I need to meet with Sergeant Overton and the others. I'll find you later, and then we can talk more about this," Sophie said. "I promise."

Timothy flattened the holographic image of the Biosphere, pulling out the clumps representing each biome one by one. "As you can see, this place is a fucking bunker. Nothing gets in without setting off the sensors. And I've already told Alexia to let us know if anything out of the ordinary pops up."

"What's the energy source?" Bouma asked.

"Two mean-ass generators, shielded from EMP attack by some

reptilian-looking armor. They're both run off solar energy and only switch to juice when the sun goes down."

Sergeant Overton hovered over Timothy's shoulder, staring at the holographic images. "How long until the juice runs out?"

Timothy ran his hand through his curls. "Man, honestly, they could last years. And when the juice is gone, we can still run them off solar energy if we reroute power to only the critical areas of the Biosphere."

"Good. So this place is secure and self-sufficient. The perfect place to launch a counterattack," Overton said.

Timothy stood, shaking his head. "Whoa, wait a second—"

Sophie held up her hand. "Don't start. I want to hear what Sergeant Overton has to say. I'm not leaving anything to chance. All options need to be on the table. There's a lot to discuss right now, so you better sit down."

The programmer bit his tongue, knowing he had used up every ounce of patience his team had left. He flicked the hologram and watched it vanish before heading over to a pair of monitors hanging on the wall.

"Sergeant, with all due respect, I'd like to know how you expect to launch a counterattack with only two other Marines," Emanuel said. "And you still haven't told us what happened to the rest of your team."

Overton resisted the urge to snap at the biologist. He had been anticipating the questions, but still hadn't thought of the answers. He wasn't sure how he was going to lead a counterattack, and he certainly didn't know the fate of his team; all he knew was that Marines didn't hide in bunkers. Especially when the enemy was outside killing those he had sworn to protect.

"No idea about my team, but my guess is they ended up inside those blue things like the rest of Colorado Springs. As for a counterattack" —the sergeant paused and stroked the metal handle of his .45—"I'm still devising a plan, Dr. Rodriguez."

"That's reassuring," Timothy said under his breath.

Emanuel ignored him. "There is one other thing that still doesn't make sense to me. How did Owen manage to escape when no one else was able to?"

"He's a kid. Kids are good at hide and seek," Timothy said with a nervous chuckle. "No, but seriously, he probably just hid until they—whatever *they* are—left."

"Actually, I have a theory about that," Sophie said. "Let's go over the facts first. Timothy, make note of these on the smart board. Sergeant Overton, tell us what you know."

The Marine massaged his temples, straining to recall everything his team had been through. "Well, we were dropped off at the decommissioned air force base about a week ago. It was just a simple recon mission: retrieve some old data NTC had requested and head back to HQ. But when we entered the underground facility, everything went dark and the doors sealed us in. That's when I lost contact with my squad. We waited for twenty-four hours before I ordered Corporal Bouma to find a power source. After the facility came back online, he was able to boot up an old analog system—a system that hadn't been affected by whatever disturbance Dr. Hoffman was talking about. The messages we heard came from all around the world. Russia, Japan, Europe, and then the East Coast. Every one of them mentioned a mist or fog. They also described weird colors in the sky. Then radio silence. Whatever happened started over Asia and spread worldwide in less than twenty-four hours." Overton paused and took a sip of coffee. "That's when we saw your Humvee zipping down Highway 115. There's one other thing, though. Something I'm sure you're already aware of."

Sophie nodded. "Go on, sir."

"Water. Lakes, rivers, streams. It's all gone. Everything we came across was dry. Like someone sucked it up with the world's largest drinking straw."

"You saw this with your own eyes?" Sophie asked.

"You didn't?" Overton asked with a raised brow.

"We were so fixated on the orbs and getting the hell out of Colorado Springs we didn't take the time to look at the scenery. Besides, it was dark," Emanuel said.

"That's ludicrous. All surface water gone? Not a fucking chance. You don't actually believe him, do you guys?" Timothy asked, his eye twitching again.

Sophie looked down nervously, recalling her dream of the Kennedy Space Center. It was all connected—it had to be. The Organics had come for the planet's water. But how did she know? And how could she have dreamed these things before they actually happened?

She shook her head and let the rational part of her mind take control. "He has no reason to lie, Timothy. And if what he says is true, then I believe it may shed light on a theory I have. A theory on how Owen survived the attacks," she said, biting her lip.

"I'm all ears, Dr. Winston," Overton replied.

"Yeah, let's hear some more crazy shit," Timothy said folding his arms.

Finley leaned over and whispered something to Bouma. Sophie could barely hear him say, "What is this guy's deal? Why is he even here?"

A chirp from the AI console distracted her, and she turned to see Alexia's blue face emerge in the corner of the room.

"My apologies for the interruption, but external scanners have picked up some sort of beacon," Alexia said.

"Beacon?" Holly said from the doorway, back from her walk with Owen. She wiped her wet hands on her jumpsuit and paced into the room. "Thanks for the help," she muttered as she passed Emanuel. "Owen's sleeping peacefully," she added.

Emanuel frowned sheepishly and moved out of her way.

"Yes, Dr. Brown. There is a signal coming from a set of coordinates on the southern outskirts of Colorado Springs." Alexia continued.

"Could it be NTC?" Sophie blurted. Her voice was louder than she had wanted it to be. Filled with excitement. Perhaps someone was out there, more people who had made it, like the Marines and Owen. Perhaps they weren't alone after all.

"Preliminary scans show that this is some sort of emergency beacon," Alexia replied.

"Another survivor looking for help?" Holly asked.

"More than likely," Emanuel said. "This really doesn't add anything useful to what we already know. So there's a beacon—so what?"

"So it *could* be someone that knows more about what's going on than we do," Overton said.

"Which isn't saying much," Holly said. "Considering we don't know much at all."

Emanuel shook his head. "We know enough to know it's a bad idea to go back outside."

"I'm going to have to agree with him for once," Timothy quipped, pointing at the biologist.

Sophie held both of her palms in the air. "Hold on, everyone. We're all jumping to conclusions here. We listened to Sergeant Overton. Now let's give Alexia a chance, and then I'll continue with my theory. Deal?"

The team looked back at her, and one by one they nodded their heads.

"Okay then. Alexia, tell us everything you know about this 'beacon.'"

"Certainly, Dr. Winston. At 1900 hours our external sensors began picking up a signal from the following coordinates: latitude 38.643555°, longitude -104.930330°. It's coming from Turkey Canyon Road, along the West Fork Turkey Creek. Please note that the creek is no longer there."

Sophie saw Overton take out a pen and mark the location on his hand discreetly. *Great,* she mused. Now the Marine would have more of a reason to go back outside and look for his team.

"Due to the timing of the activation, I have concluded this was not an automatic signal. Someone turned it on," Alexia said. "Considering there are no other emergency signals within range of our scanners, it would be safe to deduce that this is a unique event. Someone out there wants to be found."

"Or it could be a trap. How do we know this signal is coming from a human source?" Emanuel asked with a brow raised.

"The signal is being transmitted over an encrypted NTC channel. I found it while running a scan. It's likely from a human source, Dr. Rodriguez."

"So it is NTC?" Sophie asked.

"Not necessarily." Alexia's image faded and her voice transferred to the com. "My database does not show any NTC facilities at that location."

Emanuel ran a hand through his hair and took a seat next to Sophie. "What do you think?" he whispered.

She shrugged and decided to hold off further discussion of the signal. "Let's table this for now and talk about what we know." Pausing, she looked around the room. Each member of her team shared the same puzzled look.

"The radio messages Sergeant Overton and his men heard indicated the sky had not only changed colors but there was some sort of mist. This leads me to believe surface water was being vaporized into the sky. If there was enough of it, from lakes, rivers, and so on, then it could potentially have this effect. But that's not where my theory becomes stretched," she said, strolling toward a desk in the corner of the room. She reached for a glass of water and held it for the team to see. "Most people don't realize it, but the human body is 70 percent this," she said, dumping the water on the ground.

"No fucking way," Timothy said sarcastically. "Like we didn't all learn that in middle school."

"As I was saying, the human body is mostly water. What if the Organics have some way of scanning for it? And what if they have a way of removing it from our bodies? What if the orbs are human-sized petri dishes with one purpose: to drain the host of every ounce of water in its body?"

Overton crossed his thick arms. "Is that what happened to Saafi?"

"I believe so. When the drone's beam captured him and Emanuel, I saw some drops of liquid rising from their bodies toward the craft. And . . ." she paused and looked at a camera protruding from the wall. "Alexia, do you recall what Saafi's water composition was when he first got back to the Biosphere?"

"Yes, Dr. Winston. He had lost over 15 percent of his water density."

"Ding, there you have it," Emanuel said. "Sophie's right. Owen survived because the Organics didn't pick him up with whatever scanning technology they have to detect water sources. Something wasn't calibrated right."

"That doesn't mean they won't figure out a way to do so," Sergeant Overton said. "If they have the ability to suck every ounce of water from the surface of the Earth, then they will find a way to get to the hard stuff."

"Like the pond in Biome 2," Holly suggested.

"And whoever's at the other end of that beacon," Overton added.

"Exactly. I'm guessing this attack will come in surges. Get the easy stuff first and then move on to the rest," Emanuel said.

"All the more reason to check out this signal, like, *now*," Overton said. "Maybe this person knows how to stop them."

Sophie glanced over at him. A single vein was bulging on his shiny forehead. She knew he wanted an excuse to go outside and not only find his team, but also lead his 'offensive.' This was his excuse—this was the ammo he needed.

But could she blame him? If Owen had managed to survive and make it all the way to Cheyenne Mountain, then other people could be out there, too. Was it worth risking her team for? If someone had asked her a few minutes ago, she probably would have answered no. But the game had changed. A beacon, activated on an encrypted NTC channel—the only channel that was transmitting anything in the radius of their scanners—had been discovered. She knew it didn't necessarily mean salvation, but it could mean answers. And that was worth the risk.

"I think you're right," Sophie said, pausing for everyone's attention.

"Oh no, please tell me you aren't going where I think you're going with this!" Timothy interrupted.

"If Owen survived, that means other people did, too," Sophie said.

"She's right. There might be other people out there. Other people that need our help," Overton said. He could feel the adrenaline racing through his veins.

"Timothy. You have family, right?" Sophie said. "A brother you're close with?"

The programmer's animated face suddenly reverted to the unemotional one everyone was used to seeing. "What does Casey have to do with this?"

"He could have survived, just like Owen," Sophie lied. She knew the chances were slim, but she had to convince her team that it was worth leaving the safety of the Biosphere. If finding the beacon wasn't reason enough, maybe human life would be.

"We have to save everyone that we can," Sophie said confidently. She scanned the room again. It was time to take a vote.

"We're all in this together now, and I believe everyone should have a voice. As team lead, I'm putting this to a vote. Those that think we should travel to the coordinates and look for survivors along the way, raise your hand."

"I *strongly* object," Emanuel said.

Sophie had had a feeling she would lose him on this one. After all, Emanuel was a man who required evidence; a signal and the possibility of finding survivors was simply not enough to warrant a yes vote from him. Surprisingly, though, the rest of the room was filled with raised hands. Even Holly, who was looking at the floor sheepishly, had her arm in the air.

"It's settled, then," she said putting her hand on her hips.

Emanuel shot Sophie a look from the corner and managed a smile. He knew at this point nothing he could say would convince her to stay. All he could do was mouth "Be careful" before he limped into the hallway and disappeared.

Overton's rough voice distracted Sophie, and she forgot Emanuel for the moment. "Gear up, Marines. We have a job to do!"

Sophie smiled. She was beginning to like the sergeant.

Biome 4 was full of commotion. Finley and Bouma scurried about, packing up last-minute gear and grabbing freeze-dried meals and bottled water from the kitchen.

"You don't have to come with us, Dr. Winston. It's much safer if you stay here," Sergeant Overton said, jamming a magazine into his pulse rifle.

"With all due respect, sir, I'm not the type to sit back and watch. I didn't get to where I am today in my career by taking the backseat."

Overton smiled. He liked that about her; it was something they had in common. But he couldn't chance bringing her back into Colorado Springs. She would be a liability.

"I'm sorry, but we can't risk losing you."

Sophie sighed, and tried not to notice Emanuel eavesdropping from a corner near the kitchen. He'd wanted to see the Marines off before they left and had managed to do so without his wheelchair. His skin had regained some of its pigment, and his eyes were brighter. He was healing more quickly than Sophie had predicted. But although she appreciated their concern, she didn't need him or Sergeant Overton looking after her; she could handle herself.

"If you and your men want a base to return to, then I'm coming with," Sophie said, offering the ultimatum in her business voice. She'd pitched enough grants in her career to know the exact tone her opponents just couldn't refuse. "Besides, if this signal is coming from NTC, then I'm your best link to any sort of rescue."

"Have it your way, Doc, but if you put my men's lives in jeopardy, I won't hesitate in booting your ass to the curb and leaving you behind."

"Deal," Sophie said. "We leave at dusk."

Sergeant Overton retrieved a cigarette from his chest pocket and wedged it between his dry lips. He went to light it when Alexia's voice sounded over the com system.

"Sergeant Overton, this is a nonsmoking facility."

Damned artificial intelligence.

His nostrils flared as he put the cigarette back and threw the strap of his rifle over his back. "Women robots," he muttered. Worse than women and almost as bad as kids.

CHAPTER 15

IT wasn't that Sophie was afraid to die. She just really didn't want to.

Being a scientist, she knew the possibility of life after death was slim to none. She believed in what she observed, utilizing the evidence provided to her, and there simply wasn't any data on heaven. Religion had never appealed to her because it required her to believe in something that replaced evidence with faith. But there had been times in her life where she could recall praying. Not necessarily to a specific deity, but to something—anything—that might be listening. The first time was during the solar storms of 2055. The second was when she thought she was carrying Emanuel's child. The third was now.

She stared out the window of the ancient Jeep Wrangler that Sergeant Overton and his men had commandeered from the decommissioned garage of the air force bunker. It had been protected by the thick granite roof of the facility, and besides a leaky fuel line and an aged muffler, it was in pretty decent shape.

By the time they hit the gravel road, she had already given up on finding the right words for a prayer. It was mostly pointless anyway. What good would praying do? It wasn't like anyone was listening. And even if God did have an ear to the ground, there was no way she could bring herself to believe that He would intervene on her behalf. Where would the justice be in that, when so many others had suffered and perished? It was all so confusing. Another reason she preferred lab experiments over Sunday mass.

Overton killed the lights as he steered the Jeep onto Highway 115.

He didn't want to attract any unwanted attention, and while driving in the dim light wasn't the safest option, it beat trekking on foot in the dark. Besides, he had been trained to drive in similar situations— although that training was more than two decades old.

"Keep sharp," he said over the com. "I don't want any surprises."

The dark blacktop was littered with empty vehicles, sending a chill down his spine. The scene was reminiscent of his time in Puerto Rico, when the Spanish had sent Special Forces in to take the island back. He was with one of the first Marine units to land on the beach. San Juan had been hastily evacuated, cars abandoned everywhere. Mike, his best friend, had taken a sniper's bullet to the eye before his squad had a chance to set up a forward operating base. He realized with a jolt that his oldest boy was now the age Mikey had been when he died.

Get your head in the game, Marine, and remember your own rule: Don't let outside distractions affect your mission.

He shook his head, straining to make out the shapes of the vehicles in the faint light. The sun was slowly disappearing over the horizon, and they only had minutes of daylight left. He would then be forced to utilize his night vision goggles, which was nothing but a pain in the ass.

"Shit," he whispered, steering the Jeep around another pair of sedans and up a hill. The truck moaned, the muffler spitting trails of black smoke into the air as it crept down the highway.

Overton massaged the brakes and eased the vehicle to a stop. A shadow shot across the blacktop ahead. He balled his hand into a fist and watched as a single crow extended its wings and took off into the sky. Something had scared the bird, and he was pretty sure it wasn't them. He scanned the skyline for drones, but it was empty, with only the faint hint of crimson on a stray cloud creeping across the horizon.

Sophie fidgeted in the backseat, gripping the pistol Overton had given her. She could feel her heart thumping, faster and faster, as they waited. For a second she regretted coming with the Marines, but she quickly disregarded the feeling and sucked in a deep breath. If there were survivors out there, she was going to help find them.

"All clear," Finley said from the passenger seat, scanning the road with his infrared scope.

The tires began to roll and the engine groaned as Overton slowly pressed down on the gas. Sophie watched the top of the hill come into focus. A large semitrailer was parked sideways, blocking the road.

"Can you go around it?" Bouma whispered into the com.

"Negative. The shoulder is too narrow to attempt that sort of maneuver. Could break an axle. Looks like we will have to continue to the coordinates on foot," Overton replied, killing the engine and turning to look at Sophie. "Stay close and don't talk unless it's absolutely vital. Life-and-death kind of shit."

She nodded and opened her door, stepping out onto the concrete. Her first instinct was to take off running toward the semi, anxious to see what was over the hill, but she refrained. At the Biosphere she was boss, but out here she yielded command to Overton.

With every step the knot in Sophie's stomach grew. She wondered if the Marines felt it too, but she knew Overton probably didn't. He was one of those career military guys. The combination of his broad shoulders, defined biceps, tribal tattoos, scars, and rough voice was enough to intimidate virtually anyone. And while Sophie thought it would make her feel safer, it really didn't. They weren't at war with Texas anymore. This wasn't a war against other men and women. This was a fight against an extraterrestrial life-form that had the technology to travel across light years of space. As much as she wanted to believe in Overton's tough act, she knew there wasn't going to be a war—"war" implied two sides that had a pretty equal chance of winning. There would be no such thing against the Organics. All they could hope to do was survive.

"Cover our six, Bouma," Overton ordered.

The sergeant raced past Sophie, taking point at a brisk pace. The darkness quickly consumed him as he disappeared into the night, the matte black of his armor camouflaging his movements.

At first Overton had been reluctant to accept the suit from Sophie, but now he was glad he had. For some reason the empty streets made him feel exposed and naked. His eyes darted to the sky, scanning it for drones, and then back to the street for contacts.

Still nothing.

He pushed on, his head bobbling with every step. By the time he reached the top of the hill he was breathless. Years of smoking had finally caught up to him. Taking one knee, he craned his neck and glanced under the belly of the semitrailer. What he saw took his breath away for the second time, prompting him to scoot backward.

He caught his labored breath and slipped his helmet off, resting it quietly on the ground beside him. This was something he had to see with his own eyes, not from behind the protection of his glass visor.

Dropping to his stomach, he crawled back to the edge of the truck and squinted. About a half a klick away, a cluster of what had to be thousands of orbs floated over a parking lot. And swallowing them was a luminous wormlike creature that stretched the length of the semitrailer he was hiding behind.

A burst of static over the com startled Overton, but not enough to pull his gaze from the scene below. He watched the creature inch across the concrete, leaving a trail of blue goo in its wake. It had no eyes and no face, but as it opened its mouth to swallow another orb, he saw it did have teeth. Hundreds of them, protruding out of its circular jaws like Bouma's crooked overbite. With one swift motion, the worm slugged forward, consuming another glowing globe in one bite.

The round lump passed through the length of the creature's translucent blue body before stopping in its tail, where it seemed to dissolve. What came next was enough to make Overton's veteran stomach lurch—a belch, and then a violent vibration through the creature's body as it shot a ray of mist into the sky before finally coughing up the remains of the orb's former occupant. From his vantage point Overton could hardly make out the contents, especially in the dark, but the faint blue glow from the creature's body was just enough to illuminate a sack of human skin.

"What the hell is that?" a voice asked over the com.

Overton finally pulled away from the view and turned to see his own reflection in Finley's mirrored visor. For the first time in days, he saw how aged his face had become. Deep wrinkles stretched across his forehead, snaking beneath his receding hairline. His eyes appeared dull and lackluster.

"Sir, what is that . . . thing?" Finley repeated.

Overton pulled himself away from his reflection and turned back to the grotesque alien below. He ignored Finley's question, and failed to discipline him for breaking radio silence, which was now a moot point.

Below, the creature was digesting another one of the orbs, slithering its way across the parking lot.

"Dr. Winston, get up here," he growled over the com. "You ever seen anything like that?" he asked, pointing with the charcoal barrel of his pulse rifle.

Sophie gasped, blinking several times to ensure her brain was, in fact, comprehending what her eyes were seeing. "It appears to have the same surface composition as the drones." She crawled farther under the belly of the truck, straining her neck to get a better view. "Looks like it's feeding."

Another short burst of static broke over the com. "All clear at the rear, request permission to advance," Bouma said.

Overton slipped his helmet back over his shaved head. "Negative, stay put. We may need to leave in a hurry."

"Do you think that's *them*, Dr. Winston?" Finley asked.

Sophie continued to stare, her lips agape, before finally managing a nod.

"I'm not risking a trip on the highway past that thing," Overton whispered. "We need to find an alternate route. Something more discreet."

"For all we know, those things could be everywhere," Finley replied.

Overton crouched and pulled out a tiny black tablet from his side pack. "All the more reason to avoid them by finding a different route," he said staring at the blue screen. The GPS device fed into his HUD through a wireless link, but whatever had caused the massive communication failure had also effectively killed the wireless connection.

He cursed and put the device away, pulling out a small map of the area from his pouch with the coordinates highlighted in red ink. "Looks like we have to do this the old-fashioned way."

"But—" Finley began to protest.

Overton craned his head in the Marine's direction. "I don't want to hear any excuses. This isn't a democracy—"

"Guys. Check this out!" Sophie interrupted.

"Keep it down," Overton fired back before crawling over next to her.

"There. At one o'clock," Sophie said pointing into the darkness. "I see a heat signature that's smaller than the others."

Overton swiped a button on the side of his scope and a small targeting system popped up on his HUD. He clenched the rifle between his shoulder and chin and aimed it in the direction Sophie had pointed. Sure enough, a small heat signature emerged on his display. He zoomed in, and staring back at him was the face of a little girl, slightly older than Owen. She was hiding behind a Dumpster at the edge of the parking lot. And heading right for her was the massive worm.

"Fuck," he said, dropping his head toward the concrete. It was just what he had been afraid of—a kid in the middle of this muck. Somehow children always found a way to position themselves directly in harm's way; it was another reason he didn't care much for them. They ended up being a liability. But he would be damned if this oversized snake would eat her as a midnight snack.

"What do you see?" Sophie asked.

"A kid."

"What do we do?" she asked, struggling to get a better look.

"The exact opposite of what your buddy Timothy would do."

Sophie smiled and watched Overton flip the safety on his rifle off.

"Let's see if I'm as fast as I used to be," he said. "Finley, watch the doctor. Bouma, if I'm not back in thirty minutes, proceed to these coordinates," he said, handing the corporal the map and a compass from his pouch.

"Good luck," Sophie said, as she watched Overton crawl under the semi and disappear into the darkness.

CHAPTER 16

THE last ray of sun disappeared over the mountains, and Overton's night vision flickered to life, his HUD transitioning to a ghostly green.

Damn.

Night vision wasn't much benefit to a middle-aged Marine with deteriorating vision, and tonight it was definitely more of a detriment than a help. He scanned the shoulder of the highway and jumped behind a rock formation. He blinked until the green glow faded and he could make out the objects on the path before him. It wasn't perfect, but he had enough training with the helmet's technology to be able to fight almost completely blind. All he really needed was to see the shapes of objects and the heat signatures of anything alive. Everything else was just a distraction.

Overton checked the safety again and shouldered his firearm to survey the blacktop ahead. A small box in the corner of his HUD showed about a quarter klick between him and the parking lot where the alien worm was slugging toward Little Miss Ankle Biter. He was still trying to come up with a name for the girl, but that would suffice for now.

The worm was getting closer, belching out another sack of skin. His stomach lurched. Could it have been one of his squad members?

Don't go there, Overton.

He paused and studied the remains with his scope before a career of training took over and he took off running down the shoulder of the road. There was no time to hesitate, no time to ask questions, no time to do anything but trust his training. Stealth—and hesitation—was no longer an option if he was going to save this girl. He was going to need to up the ante and the pace, all without attracting the attention of this *thing*.

Overton zipped in and out among several empty cars and ran past a cluster of orbs, ignoring them. A few feet ahead, the highway turned off and connected with a frontage road. There was a shopping mall shortly behind that, and several adjoining parking lots, all filled with the blue orbs.

He skidded to a halt when he saw it. A second threat. The luminous glow of yet another worm. This one was coiled up like a snake resting after a big meal. And as Overton got a better look, he saw hundreds of skin sacks in the worm's gooey wake. His stomach lurched again, but he forced the remains of his dinner back down his throat.

Trust your training. You've seen worse.

It wasn't a lie—but then again, it wasn't exactly the truth, either. He'd never seen anything quite like what he was seeing now. Even a lifetime of training couldn't prepare him to fight an enemy he had never studied or seen before.

A scratching sound broke out through the silence, and he ducked behind the cover of a black sedan. His armor blended with the car perfectly. Taking to his stomach, he inched out from behind the bumper and scanned the parking lot for contacts.

Scratch, scrape, scratch, scrape.

The sound reminded him of the noise his drill sergeant had made some two decades ago when he refused to use a dry erase board. Instead he would use old-fashioned chalk, and when he had really wanted to piss off the noobs, he'd run his fingernails down the length of the board.

Overton shuddered as the sound broke through the silence again. Now it sounded like a dozen drill sergeants running their nails down a board. And it was coming from all directions.

"What the fuck," he said under his breath.

He attempted to still his racing heartbeat, taking in a deep breath to calm his nerves. Another deep breath—a glance around the bumper—a glance behind him—another deep breath.

Nothing.

His heart raced. The sound came closer. He spun around and removed his .45 from his holster, laying it down silently on the concrete. Then he grabbed the rifle slung across his back and placed it on the ground, too. Slowly, he dropped to his stomach and crawled under the belly of a pickup truck, pulling his weapons under with him.

Scratch, scrape, scratch, scrape. The sound was almost on top of him now, coming from all directions. But all he could see was the blacktop in front of the vehicle's tires. He waited, weapons in both hands, trying to slow his breathing.

A pair of spiderlike legs scampered past the front of the pickup, and then another. Seconds later, four more sets of legs had raced by. They appeared to be connected to the same body.

Overton froze. This was no worm—this was something else. He considered crawling out for a better look and hesitated. Images of human-sized spiders popped into his mind, but he shook them away, instead recalling what his drill sergeant had told him.

"In recon you never give away your position when you don't know what you're dealing with. You sit, lie, kneel, or hang upside down for as long as it takes to identify the enemy and devise a plan to neutralize it."

The man had been annoying, and brutally violent with his class in Basic, but Overton had never forgotten what he'd learned from him.

Scratch, scrape, scratch, scrape.

The sound brought his mind back to the blacktop, his eyes darting back and forth. Another set of legs flashed by the truck, and then another. He held his breath as several more zipped past the truck, until finally one stopped. With a blink Overton switched off his night vision and saw them with his own eyes for the first time.

They were a luminous blue, with translucent skin that revealed tiny blue veins crawling up the spiderlike legs. They were oddly jointed, the bend much higher than on any spider he'd seen. Small spikes protruded where a knee should have been. Fuzz lined the bone-thin exterior. There was no foot or paw. Instead there was a black claw the length of his combat knife—the same claw that was making the scratching sounds.

He watched in shock, realizing the high joints on their legs were what allowed them to move so fast. Emotions raced through his mind as he watched them. There was awe and curiosity, but there was also the unfamiliar feeling of fear. There was no way to describe what he was witnessing. Three days ago he would have laughed at anyone who told him they had seen something like this.

He narrowed his eyebrows and squinted to check for the body of whatever was attached to the six legs, but it was still out of sight. There was no way in hell he was going to crawl out to see what it looked like. Instead he waited, trying to hold back a cough from his scratchy throat.

A scream shocked the creature into motion, and with a flash the legs were gone. Overton took a deep breath. He had almost forgotten about the girl, but as her screams grew louder, he knew the Organics were onto her.

With a grunt he suppressed his fear and pulled himself from underneath the vehicle. In less than a second he was running toward the creatures.

He almost halted when he got his first good look at them. There were at least a dozen. And they looked, just as he feared, like spiders. The creatures had stocky torsos and small heads sporting a bonelike mandible rimmed with black, jagged teeth. He couldn't see any eyes, but he imagined they were focusing on their next snack—Little Miss Ankle Biter.

I fucking hate spiders.

On the top-ten list of the things he disliked the most, spiders ranked pretty damned high. Fortunately for the little girl, arachnids were at number two and kids were only at number seven or so. As he ran past the sleeping worm, he realized he was going to have to consider bumping number ten and adding giant alien worms to the list.

He neared the end of the parking lot without attracting attention. The spiders were now far ahead and closing in on the girl's location. Overton dug deeper and pushed his legs. The muscles strained and pulled but held strong as he maneuvered between the empty vehicles, trying to hug their frames for cover.

Another scream ripped through the night. His HUD glowed to life with dozens of contacts. He switched off the infrared and skidded to a halt, ducking behind another truck. The worm was two car lengths from the Dumpster the girl was hiding behind. It was working on digesting the last orb between them.

Overton switched his attention to the spiders that were slowly closing in on the girl, their legs clawing through the air as they approached. He counted a total of nine. Not as many as he thought, but still terrible odds.

He had only moments to create a plan. He scanned his gear and saw three electromagnetic concussion grenades hanging off his belt. Without further thought he unclipped one of the grenades and tossed it into the air. The device landed on the concrete with a metallic crack and rolled to a rest a few feet from the worm. He shut off his HUD and tinted his visor to prepare for the vicious blast.

Seconds later it exploded, and a burst of electromagnetic energy tore into the creature's side. The blue shield vibrated and quickly faded as the wave of energy continued on toward the spiders. Their defenses pulsated and vanished as soon as the blast hit them.

Holy shit.

Overton didn't hesitate when he realized what was happening. He jumped forward, squeezed the hard trigger of his pulse rifle, and watched the hot plasma shred the worm. The creature shrieked in pain and rose into the air, thousands of miniature arms clawing helplessly.

He fired another volley of shots and the belly of the creature exploded, sending blue goo and watery blood in all directions. It wiggled back and forth violently, sending out a wave of gore that covered Overton.

Click.

The terrifying sound of an empty magazine echoed in his helmet. He turned to see the spiders racing toward him just as the worm fell to the ground in a lump of blue guts and slime. There was no time to reload; they would be on him in seconds.

He dropped the rifle to the ground and retrieved his pistol. With only nine .45 shells, he couldn't afford to miss.

The first shot sent one of the spiders tumbling into the darkness.

Crack, crack, crack.

Overton fired off a volley of shots instinctively, sending another three of the creatures to their graves. The deafening mix of what sounded like high-frequency growls and gunshots made it difficult for him to concentrate. The spiders circled around him, closing in, their legs clawing at him from a distance.

His heart pounded in his chest, a steady flow of adrenaline pumping through his arteries. He remembered his training and fired at the closest creature. Its head exploded in a spray of blue mist, and the legs collapsed beneath it.

At least these things are easy to kill, he thought, scanning for his next target.

Four left.

One lunged for his armor, shredding his right shoulder with its enormous claw. He winced in pain before bringing the butt of his pistol down onto the creature's head and stomping it into a puddle of gore.

He gritted his teeth and another two shots rang out, ending the life of two more aliens.

One left.

Overton took one knee and fired, but the pain from his shoulder threw off his aim, and the bullet ricocheted off the concrete beneath the spider's legs.

Scratch, scrape, scratch, scrape.

The sound filled his helmet, sending a chill down his back. "Go to hell, you fucking bastard," he yelled as the creature's mandibles opened and its teeth reached for his face.

He closed his left eye, lined the metal sight up with the spider's head, and fired. The bullet tore into its open mouth, blowing bits of mangled eyeball into the night as its limp body collided with his. They fell to the ground in a tangled mess of blue goo, guts, and blood.

Overton grunted. Pain from his shoulder raced down his arm as he pushed the dead alien off of him. He didn't need to see the wound to know it was deep. He was in trouble.

He forced himself off the ground and jammed another magazine into his pulse rifle. With a deep breath, he gritted his teeth and sprinted toward the Dumpster where the girl was still cowering in the darkness.

As his lips moved to form words, he realized it was pointless. He didn't have time for formalities or to convince the girl to come with him. With a swift motion he threw the strap of his rifle over his back and reached down to pick her up with his good arm.

She stared back at him blankly. The girl was clearly in shock. He attached her arms around his neck, put his hand under her butt, and took off in a sprint toward the highway.

"Start that engine, Bouma," he whispered into his com. His chest heaved in and out, his labored breath filling the open channel with short bursts of static.

"Roger, Sergeant. We are tracking your location now. Over."

Overton risked a glance over his shoulder to ensure none of the spiders were tailing him. He breathed a sigh of relief when he saw the motionless pile of luminous gore. Once killed, they stayed dead. Which meant humanity might have a fighting chance after all.

He took a sharp right down the highway toward the hill. With a blink, his display flickered back to life, and he could make out three heat signatures about a half a mile away.

Almost there—almost safe.

He ignored the whimpering girl, refusing to comfort her. His objective was to get her back to the Biosphere safely, not to console her. But as the child's tiny arms tightened around his neck, he couldn't help but feel an odd sense of empathy.

He ignored it and continued to run, his pace slowly diminishing as the lactic acid filled his muscles. His labored breathing became more intense. He could feel his heart thumping inside its bone prison. A few steps farther and it was going to attempt a jail break.

He slowed to a stop, panting to catch his breath.

A short burst of static broke over the com. "Sir, we have contact on your six," Finley said.

Overton shot a glance over his shoulder to see a drone hovering over the skyline of downtown Colorado Springs. He was already running before the high-frequency pitch of the craft could penetrate his ears. His legs were screaming, the muscles enflamed with pain. But he pushed himself, ignoring it all.

Back at the semitrailer, Sophie watched two heat signatures slowly creep across her display. Her eyes darted back up to the horizon, where the drone was gliding through the night.

"They aren't going to make it," she said, rising to her feet. "We need to go to them."

"Negative, Dr. Winston. Orders are to stay put," Bouma replied.

"I don't give a shit. They aren't going to make it!"

"Stay put, Dr. Winston. That's an order," Overton said over the open com.

Sophie looked for the outline of the Jeep. It was about a minute's run. Based off the trajectory of the craft in the top left of her HUD, that was just enough time to get to the Jeep and intercept Overton and the girl. With a blink she switched the com from an open frequency and changed it to direct.

"Private Finley, Corporal Bouma, I want you to provide covering fire if the drone catches up with them."

They nodded, and she snapped into a sprint. Sixty-five seconds later she was twisting the key in the ignition and listening to the engine groan to life. She threw it into first gear and squealed toward the semi, zigzagging in and out of the maze of empty vehicles.

By the time she reached the shoulder of the road, there were tracers of plasma ripping through the night. Either the trajectory calculated by her HUD had been wrong, or the ship had sped up. Either way, it was catching up to them.

She took a hard left, and the oversized Jeep tires tore onto the gravel shoulder, rocks crunching under their weight. She punched the gas. The momentum was just enough to push the Jeep off the small strip around the truck. A cloud of gravel shot out from behind the tires as Sophie maneuvered the vehicle back onto the highway. In the distance, the drone immediately filled her HUD with a luminous, ghostly green glow.

The cracks from Finley's and Bouma's pulse rifles filled the night, and for a second Sophie had to marvel at the absurdity of the situation. Only days before she had been ready to begin one of the most important scientific missions in modern history. Now she was battling an alien invasion.

The drone let out a high-frequency shriek and she narrowly avoided crashing into the back of a sedan. She pulled the wheel hard to the left and gave the engine more gas, racing toward the heat signatures of Overton and the child.

With another blink she switched the com back to open. "Prepare for evac, Sergeant. I'm coming in fast!"

A short burst of static and what sounded like a groan filled her earpiece. She smiled; it was Overton's way of saying thanks.

Sophie peered back up through the windshield and saw that the craft was almost on top of them, a bright beam tracing their movements down the blacktop. In seconds it would have them in its grip.

Another volley of plasma rounds tore through the darkness, but the drone dove hard to the left. Sophie risked a glance over her shoulder, frantically scanning the vehicle for something, anything she could use. And then she saw it—the tip of the missile launcher Overton had used to save her life.

She slammed her boot down on the brakes, and the Jeep fishtailed, stopping a mere inches from the side of another truck. Throwing the Jeep into park, she spun around, retrieved the missile launcher from under the backseat, and jumped out onto the street.

The drone released another high-frequency sound wave, bringing Overton to his knees. Sophie watched the girl tumble onto the concrete. But this time her own ears were prepared, and the medicated aids Alexia had given her mitigated some of the noise.

She took to one knee and examined the launcher. Without any formal training, firing the weapon was going to be dangerous, but she had to try. Raising it to her shoulder, she looked through the scope and watched the crosshairs link up with her HUD through the wireless connection.

Simple enough, she thought, steadying the weapon.

In the middle of her display, the red targeting system emerged. The craft zigzagged across the sky, making it difficult for her to get a shot. She waited patiently, stilling her breathing and massaging the trigger. When the display lit up with a blinking lock symbol, she clicked off the safety, pulled the hard metal of the trigger, and braced herself as the rocket exploded out of the tube. She watched it streak across the dark sky before bursting into a green static across her display.

Blinking, she staggered, the brightness momentarily blinding her. By the time she regained vision, Overton was standing in front of her, holding the young girl in his arms once more.

"What are you waiting for? Let's get the fuck out of here!" he yelled.

Sophie paused to look at the liquid seeping out of his shoulder. She didn't need to turn off her night vision to know it was blood.

"Take shotgun; I'm driving," she said, glancing behind her to make sure the craft was gone. Nothing but the dark skyline of Colorado Springs showed up on her HUD. Relieved, she sucked in some filtered air, jumped in the front seat, and punched the gas with a swift kick from her armored boot.

But to her dismay, the tires didn't squeal out. The engine didn't groan to life. The truck was dead. She quickly looked around at the graveyard of other vehicles for another ride and remembered the empty gas tanks. They were stranded. And on the horizon was another pair of drones that had come to avenge their friend.

CHAPTER 17

ENTRY 0064
DESIGNEE: AI ALEXIA MODEL 11

I HAVE been running diagnostics on the Biosphere the entire night. The door has now been opened for a third time with the departure of Dr. Winston and the three Marines. In the past twelve hours I have detected over fifteen foreign substances in Biome 1, twenty-nine in Biome 2, eleven in Biome 3, and forty-one in Biome 4. They are a result of several factors. First, the cleansing chamber does not always pick up every alien material. Further, the Marines did not remove their clothing when entering the Biosphere for the first time. Their gear, fatigues, and weapons all carried a considerable number of toxins.

I have been able to track down and destroy all but three of the substances without shutting down individual biomes. The magnitude of the damage to the air-filtration system is still being determined by one of the diagnostic tests, but I should be able to salvage it.

Dr. Brown has inquired as to the importance of limiting foreign substances. My response was what any scientist would say—in order for the Biosphere to function properly, it must be free of any toxins that may compromise the mission. The garden, for example, could become infested with a parasite that potentially threatens an entire crop. With the mission already in peril, it is imperative that I prevent any more toxins from threatening the biomes, especially the pond and garden.

A sensor in the med ward returns my attention to Mr. Yool. His vitals are improving, but his kidneys are severely damaged. I've put him on dialysis for the time being, until they can repair themselves. His skin has regained some of its color, but he is still emaciated.

I update his chances of survival to 49 percent.

In the command center, Mr. Roberts surveys a wall full of monitors. The feed to Dr. Winston and the Marines was lost hours ago, but he watches the screens contently nonetheless. His focus seems to be primarily on Camera 1 outside the blast doors. His facial expressions indicate worry, stress, and anxiety. I presume he is expecting more visitors.

A second sensor goes off in as many minutes. This one is not within the Biosphere. It is coming from the hangar at the entrance of the facility. I zoom in with Camera 2. The brightly lit hangar is empty save for one of the Humvees that Corporal Bouma drove into the bay earlier. A fluorescent light flickers, and another sensor goes off. This time it is a motion sensor. Protocol would be to notify Dr. Brown, since technically Dr. Rodriguez is disabled and she is next in the chain of command, but I am not convinced the sensor is picking up actual movement. A faulty device is more likely. There is no need to alarm Dr. Brown or Mr. Roberts. They are both under extreme amounts of stress, and I do not want to instigate unnecessary panic.

After 5.4 seconds of diagnostic testing, I conclude the motion sensor has shorted out due to electrical failure. I will send an automated bot to repair it shortly.

I finish decrypting the video message Dr. Hoffman sent, in hopes that the end of the message will play. The attempt is futile. The presentation still ends on, "You must go—" Next, I enter the three words into my filtering system. 1,151 possibilities return of what he may have been trying to communicate. If I were human, I would do one of two things to express frustration: flare my nostrils or take in a deep breath. They are both common reactions I've seen in Dr. Winston and Sergeant Overton, the leaders of the facility.

But I am not human. I am a machine, the most sophisticated machine intelligence on the planet. 3.1 seconds later, I have narrowed the results down to two of the most realistic possibilities. The first is, "You must go to *Secundo Casu*," and the second is, "You must go on with the Biosphere mission."

Neither is very reassuring. Dr. Hoffman helped design me, and I know how dangerous it is to attempt to finish his sentences. But they are the most realistic results my system has returned. When Dr. Winston gets back, I will run them by her.

The motion sensor in the hangar goes off again. Camera 2 is still showing no signs of contact. I quickly program the AB and send it to fix the sensor.

Ten minutes and thirty seconds later, the AB arrives in the open bay. It stops at the concrete wall, deploys six spiderlike metal legs, and begins to crawl up to the sensor. The wireless link built into the bot's hard drive sends me the diagnostics. To my surprise there is no electrical disturbance. No faulty wire. There is, in fact, nothing wrong with the sensor at all.

The AB crawls back down the wall, retracts its legs, and zips back down the passage toward its storage bay. I watch it disappear into the darkness with Camera 2. But something else shows up on the video feed—something my systems do not recognize, something with a faint blue glow.

I switch the feed to infrared and pick up a heat signature. Then another. The wireless link in the camera downloads the signatures to my radar, showing exactly nine red blips. The audio is now picking something up. I amplify it and run a diagnostic on the sounds.

The noises convert into waves that crawl across the screen as the program scans the sporadic bursts for the most likely animal capable of creating such a sound. Seconds later an image begins to appear on another one of the monitors in the control room, far from Mr. Roberts's view. I zoom in and watch millions of pixels coming together to show what looks like a spider.

The image solidifies and a line of data runs across the bottom of the screen.

One hundred pounds . . . Organic . . . Liquid composition . . .

The results can't be correct. No such insect exists in my database.

Not even in the radioactive Wastelands. I run the diagnostic again and the same results are returned.

Fascinating.

Whatever the entities are, they have entered the facility but have not infiltrated the Biosphere. As the sounds fade, so do the radar blips. I pause for less than a second to consider protocol. Another test, and I've determined their trajectory.

It is 99.9 percent likely they are headed toward Biome 2, the Biosphere's water supply. I do not need to run a test to know it is time to notify Dr. Brown.

Timothy cleared his throat. He was agitated—more so than normal—and his tics had gotten worse. He concentrated on his right eye, closing it for several seconds, waiting for the twitch to go away. Then he slowly opened the lid and widened his eyes.

Twitch. Twitch.

"Shit!" he yelled, stomping his foot on the concrete ground.

"What's wrong, Mr. Roberts?" Alexia asked, her image appearing on a console in the center of the command room.

"Nothing, mind your own business, holo-girl," he replied with a snarky grin.

"Very well, Mr. Roberts."

"Wait, wait!" he yelled, watching her image begin to flicker and fade.

"Yes?" she asked politely.

"Have you heard anything from Sophie or the Marines?"

"No, Mr. Roberts. I lost contact when they reached Latitude 38—"

"I don't care what location they were at when you lost contact, I want to know where they are *now*," he said, drawing out the final word into a whine.

"I apologize, sir, but I do not have access to that information. The magnetic disturbance is preventing any long-distance audio and video feeds."

Timothy shook his head and slouched in the plush office chair, putting his feet up on the metallic desk. Reaching into a plastic bag, he retrieved a single sunflower seed and popped it into his mouth. He bit down and separated the seed from the shell. His tongue flicked the seed to one side of his mouth. As he prepared to bite into the tiny morsel, his eye twitched again.

"Son of a bitch!" he yelled, spitting both the seed and shell into the air.

The sound of the room's sliding glass door opening distracted him for a moment. He craned his neck, nearly falling out of his chair as Holly raced into the room.

"We have a situation," she said frantically, her eyes wide.

Timothy looked past her and saw Owen cowering behind her legs.

"What type of situation?" he asked, his twitch becoming more rapid.

The console in the center of the room once again glowed and Alexia's image flickered to life.

"We have contacts in the tunnel connecting the hangar to the Biosphere facility," she said.

Timothy stiffened. "What do you mean, *contacts*?"

"Motion sensors in the hangar picked up several entities moving at a high rate of speed several minutes ago," Alexia replied.

"Wait a second. You were in here not"—Timothy paused to look down at his wristwatch—"Not one minute ago, and you didn't think to tell me about this situation?"

"Protocol is to inform the team leader first," Alexia said in her smooth voice.

Timothy put his face into his palms and then yanked it back out, rubbing his twitching eye violently. "What do we do?"

"The Biosphere facility has not been breached, but trajectories put the contacts at the entrance to the facility in three minutes and forty seven seconds."

Holly reached behind her and pulled Owen toward her side. "We need to hide," she said, trying not to frighten the boy.

"Like hide and seek? Maybe we should ask Owen here how to play. He seems to be pretty good at it," Timothy said.

Holly raised her hand. "Stop it! Just stop it! I need you to get it together, Timothy."

"What do you suggest we do, then?" Timothy replied.

She shook her head. "Where's Emanuel? Maybe he will have an idea."

"One moment," Alexia said, her image flickering over the console. "Dr. Rodriguez is in Biome 1, checking the progress of the seeds."

"That's the closest one to the entrance; there's no way we can get to him in time on foot. Alexia, you have to warn him," Holly insisted.

The AI's hologram faded and her voice transferred to the com. "Protocol is to head to the medical ward at the farthest end of the Biosphere. The room can be locked down remotely and has thick concrete and lead walls. It is by far the safest in terms of an emergency situation. However, Dr. Rodriguez is in no condition to cover that distance in the two minutes and thirteen seconds it will take for the contacts to enter the facility."

"You have to warn him," Holly pleaded.

"One moment, Dr. Brown," Alexia said. An instant later her image reemerged on the console, her blank robotic expression staring back at them. "I have informed Dr. Rodriguez of the situation and he is taking the appropriate measures. Please make your way to the medical ward immediately."

"You don't have to tell me twice," Timothy said. He hurried past Holly and Owen, hesitating on his way out the door. "Well, what are you waiting for, a formal invitation?"

CHAPTER 18

SERGEANT Overton winced as Sophie massaged a white chemical gel into his open wound.

"This part's going to hurt," she said.

He gritted his teeth and, as he waited for the pain to race down his arm, watched the two drones searching the city below. They zigzagged over the empty city streets, scanning for life. Scanning for them.

He knew because he would be doing the same thing. His entire career had been spent in recon. When the time came for promotions, he turned them all down. He didn't care about money or rank. Most of his money went to child support anyway, and his dress uniform was already filled with medals. His passion was for the fight—for the heat of the battle, for the scent of the enemy. It was what he lived for.

But now he was the one being hunted. A familiar knot grew in his stomach, and he winced as the gel finally cauterized his wound through an invisible chemical reaction.

"We need to find cover. Radio silence from here on out. We don't know if *they* are listening. Keep that girl quiet," he ordered.

With two short motions, he waved the team away from the Jeep and into the tree-lined hills. The silhouettes of the trees appeared in eerie green across his display, like toy soldiers protecting the ridgeline.

For an hour they trekked through the forest, heading farther and farther from civilization. The coordinates were farther away than he had thought, reminding him he hadn't done any true orienteering in years. In fact, he couldn't remember the last time he'd had only a map, a compass, and a set of coordinates instead of some sort of GPS device.

To further complicate things, the silence of the night was alarming. It distracted him. He'd never been in such a dead zone before. Even the animals had disappeared. If Sophie was right, then they had probably been turned into Kool-Aid as well.

Overton balled his hand into a fist and halted. He strained his ears; the nothingness was ghostly. Gone were the hum of machines and the familiar sound of chirping insects. Vanished were the agitating sirens that plagued the violent cities. The silence was unnatural.

Deep down, a part of him wished it was all a dream, that the wail of a police car would tear through the night or the thump of the blades from an NTC helicopter would sound overhead. But he was a Marine, and he knew the truth of the situation.

We are alone.

Overton shot an advance signal to Finley. The private took the lead, sprinting up the hill, chunks of dirt and loose pinecones kicking up behind him. The darkness quickly consumed him, his heat signature fading from Overton's HUD until it was gone altogether.

Bouma carried the girl on his back, and Sophie followed close behind. Overton squinted and saw that the girl was fast asleep. That, or she was unconscious from the trauma she had been through earlier. Either way, he was glad she was keeping her tiny mouth shut. He knew better than anyone that kids could scream much louder than they appeared capable of. If he had learned one thing from his short time with his own two boys, it was to never underestimate a child.

A boom tore through the silence, and Overton quickly forgot what he had been thinking about. He stole a glance over his shoulder to see one of the drones zip across the dark horizon. He pressed on, digging his boots into the hillside, moving deeper into the black abyss of the forest. They were getting close to a frontage road, almost to the coordinates, but they still hadn't seen any sign of the beacon—no building or installation. There was a short gap where he could see the entrance to what had to be Turkey Canyon Road. Finley was crouched at the edge, his outline still and stoic in the darkness. It only took Overton and the others a minute to cover the distance between them.

"All right, I think we're in the clear for now," he said, patting Finley on his armored shoulder. "See anything?"

"Negative, sir. No contacts, at least, but there appears to be some sort of structure about a half a mile down the road."

Overton climbed up the short dirt hill and crouched onto the mix of dirt and gravel. Sure enough, there was a chimney jutting out of the trees to the east. He pulled the map from his pouch again and double-checked the coordinates with his compass. The house had to be the source of the signal. Not exactly what he was expecting, but considering the events of the past week, nothing was a surprise anymore. One-hundred-foot-long translucent alien worms, for example.

"All right, let's move," he said.

The sound of rocks crunching under his boots echoed in his helmet. He was glad to hear something, *anything*, to distract him from the silence. Even the invasion of Puerto Rico hadn't been this bad.

The metallic green outline of the chimney appeared on his display as he rounded the corner. Whoever had built this house did not want it seen from the road.

He approached cautiously, his rifle aimed into the darkness. The house was a few yards away behind the pines and there was no obvious path to get to it. Twigs and branches snapped under the weight of his boots as he entered the brush. He halted, blinking once, twice to enhance the optics of his night vision. Seeing the path was still clear, he continued, the ghostly green glow growing brighter with every step.

A slight opening broke through the trees. He could vaguely make out the metal skin of the house.

He paused in the gap of the tree line. They might have stumbled upon a prepper, which could be extremely dangerous. Many of his friends had retired from the Marines and bought a plot of land off the grid. They had rigged their houses with booby traps to prepare for what they believed were the end days. But that didn't explain the signal. How would a prepper have access to an encrypted NTC emergency channel?

He sprinted to the side of the house and slumped against the metal siding. His eyes darted back and forth, checking the area before he advanced to the entrance.

"Don't fucking move, soldier!" a voice shouted from above him.

Overton froze, his finger clenching the trigger of his pulse rifle.

"I'm a friendly," he said, opting to leave his team out of the equation.

"That's what the last guy said. You can find his head on a post about a quarter mile down the road."

"I'm Sergeant Ash Overton, United States Marine Corps First Recon Battalion. I'm not here to hurt you or take what you have. Our AI picked up a distress signal from this location."

Silence once again filled the night, but Overton didn't move.

"You're a long way from Camp Pendleton, Marine."

"Recon mission, sir. Got caught in the midst of something much bigger."

"No fucking shit. Did you find any civvies down there?"

"Yes, sir. One. A little girl," he said, hoping the man would be empathetic.

"How old?"

Overton scowled.

What do I look like, a fucking doctor?

"She's no older than five, sir."

"And I'm guessing she's with your squad. How many total?"

"Two Marines and an NTC scientist, plus the girl, sir."

"An NTC scientist, you say? You sure?"

The question struck him as odd, but he answered, "Damned sure."

Another pause. The hum of silence filled Overton's helmet. He cringed, the knot in his stomach getting worse. A combination of smoking and drinking had more than likely caused another ulcer.

He waited for a response.

"Don't make me regret this, Sergeant. Gather your team and meet me on the south side of my house in five."

Overton slowly took his finger off the trigger and swung the rifle over his shoulder, not daring to look up at the rooftop, where he guessed the man had been camped out. He turned and took off in a sprint back to his team. For some reason he had a bad feeling about this guy, but at this point, he knew they had no other choice but to trust him.

A combination of beeps and chirps from Saafi's cryo chamber filled the medical ward with an annoying melody. Holly sat on a white bench in the corner of the room, holding Owen in her lap. She ran her hand through his thick mop of hair and watched Saafi's chest rise up and down through the clear panels of his medical coffin.

Nearby, Timothy paced back and forth like a caged animal, his eye twitching rapidly. Holly ignored him, refusing to acknowledge him in the slightest way. She was at her wit's end and couldn't handle much more of his antics. Holly felt something inside of her twist at the admission of the truth—that not even her PhD in psychology had been enough to prepare her for his irrational behavior. It was hard to swallow, but she knew that she was allowed to have a breaking point.

Timothy's voice interrupted her thoughts. "How long have they been gone? It's been too long; something must have happened. Alexia, have you detected any movements inside the Biosphere? Can those *things* get in? They're going to get in, aren't they? We have to hide. Is Emanuel hiding? Where is he?"

His words were a random assortment of thoughts that Alexia found difficult to process. Every time she attempted to answer one question, he would present another.

"Mr. Roberts, I have not detected any—"

"Maybe they're after the pond. Yeah. That makes total sense," he said, a somewhat deranged grin spreading across his face.

"After analyzing the current data and the hypothesis presented by Dr. Winston, I would conclude your assumption is reasonable, Mr. Roberts."

"So they *are* coming for our water supply!"

Before he knew it Holly was standing in front of him. Her eyes were hard. "You're scaring Owen," she said calmly.

Timothy glanced behind her, acknowledging Owen's presence for the first time since they had entered the medical ward. And for a second, something inside him clicked—something changed. His eyes lit up and he strolled past Holly toward the young boy.

He crouched to pick the boy's blanket off the ground, handing it to him. "How did you hide from them?"

Owen looked at the man sleepily. His chubby cheeks were a flushed rosy red.

"I want my daddy," he choked, tears streaking down his face.

Holly paced over to the bench and sat down next to him, eyeing Timothy suspiciously. "It's okay, Owen, we'll look for your daddy when the soldiers get back," she said. The boy buried his head in her arms and began to whimper softly.

Timothy reached for Owen's small hand and tapped it cautiously. "Owen, you have to tell us how you hid from them, because we're going to need to play that game again."

The boy peeked one eye out and observed Timothy's face for a few seconds before he jammed his face back into the safety of Holly's arms.

"Leave him be," she whispered, running her hand through his hair again.

"Maybe he knows a way to evade them. Maybe he knows a way to escape," Timothy insisted.

Holly's mouth opened, but she paused as Alexia's voice sounded over the com.

"Movement detected in the offices outside the Biosphere facility. Detecting several heat signatures in the briefing room. Switching to Camera 6. Stand by for video footage."

Timothy jumped up and raced to the monitor hanging on the wall over Saafi's cryo chamber. It flickered to life, revealing the NTC briefing room. The lighting was dim, with only a faint blue glow present in the corner of the room.

"Enhance image," he requested.

The camera zoomed in and the blue light amplified. He compressed his eyebrows and squinted, desperately trying to make out the shape of the intruder. But all he saw was darkness.

"I don't see anything, Alexia!" he said frantically.

"Scanning."

The sound of Saafi's chirping monitors filled the room once more before the com blared back to life. "Signatures appear to be heading into the ductwork."

"Zoom in," Timothy said, moving aside so Holly could see the screen.

"There," she said pointing. "Angle the camera toward the back corner near the podium."

They watched the view slowly rotate. The blue glow increased as the camera moved into position.

Holly felt a tug on her pants from behind, and she turned to see Owen staring up at her. "Can I see?"

In the second it took for her to consider his request, she watched Timothy's face go pale. His eye stopped twitching, and the tablet he was holding dropped to the floor. The sound of the device's screen cracking reached her ears an instant before Owen's screams. She didn't need to see the video footage to know what they both had seen, but she forced herself to look anyways.

Climbing through a hole in the tile ceiling was a luminous creature—a monster with six thin legs, a round, stocky torso, and a small head with mandibles full of jagged teeth. As the spiderlike thing pulled itself into the ceiling, it glanced at the camera. For a moment it looked like it was staring right at them with its eight malformed eyes, right before it opened its jaws and emitted a high-frequency scream. Then it was gone, vanishing into the duct.

Holly forced herself away from the screen. She grabbed Owen and led him to the bench as calmly as possible. Crouching down to his eye level, she rested her palms on his narrow shoulders. "Owen, you have to be strong. You have to tell us how you hid from those things, okay? Can you do that for us?"

The boy looked up at them, sniffling. "You can't hide from them. They'll find you. They always find you."

Sophie slipped into the brightly lit house behind Overton. She removed her helmet and peered up at the high ceilings, admiring the metal beams zigzagging across the living room. The entrance branched two ways, with a hallway leading to the rest of the first floor and a staircase leading to a second floor.

A middle-aged man with salt and pepper hair stood at the entrance to the hallway, scanning his guests through a pair of black shades. At his side was an evil-looking submachine gun with a banana clip extending halfway down his right leg.

He waited for Finley and Bouma to enter the house before he strolled over and closed the massive oak door behind them.

Overton took a step forward, offering his hand. "Thanks for sheltering us, sir. I'm guessing you're the one who sent out that distress beacon?"

The man ignored the question, instead shaking Overton's hand with a strong grip. "Welcome," he said in a flat, monotone voice. "The name's Luke, and this . . ." He waved his other hand, indicating his house. "This is my modern bunker."

When he let go, he reached for his glasses and stuffed them in the breast pocket of his tan army fatigues.

"Forgive me for my earlier behavior. It's been twenty-four hours since I've seen or heard from anyone. When those *things* first showed up, a few people escaped undetected. Mostly kids, but a few adults who found shelter. One of them caused me some grief, but I took care of him," he said, glancing down at his firearm.

"What do you mean when you said they went 'undetected'?" Sophie asked.

"Are you the NTC scientist?"

"Yes. Dr. Sophie Winston," she replied, offering her hand.

"Well then, you should know, Doctor. Those things are here for our water. When they first came, they used some sort of device to suck the surface water up into their ships. I saw it myself; watched the sky turn a weird turquoise blue from my rooftop before I retreated into my granite bunker. It was the oddest thing I've ever seen, like it was raining but in the opposite direction. When I emerged, I investigated the frontage road and found one of those spheres. Inside was my neighbor, Hal Greene. I'm no biologist, but I put two and two together and figured they aren't just here for surface water. They are here to exterminate us."

Sophie stepped forward and looked the man directly in his hazel eyes. "Actually—and I mean this with all due respect—they aren't here to exterminate us in the sense you may think. They aren't just after our surface water. They're after the water inside of *us*."

Luke's eyes widened and he swallowed the lump forming in his throat. "Shit. It all makes sense, then."

Bouma stepped forward with the girl sleeping peacefully in his arms. "How did you go undetected?"

Luke shrugged. "My bunker leads into granite caves deep beneath this house."

Sophie eyed the man suspiciously. Her gut was sending the same warning feelings she'd had before, indicating something was amiss—that the man was leaving out some important details. She studied him intently. His face and his monotone voice were both oddly familiar, but she couldn't place him.

"Perhaps they aren't able to penetrate granite with their scanners?" the man offered.

"Oh, I'm sure they'll find a way. Once they pillage the rest of the surface and track down every living thing with an ounce of H_2O inside of it," Sophie replied.

"But that still doesn't explain how you've managed to avoid them," said Finley, his eyebrows raised. "We ran into two drones in the few hours we were outside. Not to mention that we haven't seen a single living person besides this girl."

Luke caught Finley's gaze and shied away from it, pacing across the length of the room. "You really want to know?" he asked, craning his neck and scanning the faces of Sophie and her team one by one. "Then follow me," he said, motioning them with his machine gun toward a narrow metal door just beyond the hallway.

Overton jammed an unlit cigarette into his mouth and winked at Sophie. "Ladies first," he said, with a grin just wide enough to keep the cigarette from falling out.

She wrinkled her nose and followed their host through the door and down a long, steep flight of stairs. After what felt like hundreds of steps, they emerged into a dim cave. Candles dripped wax down the black walls, and shadows danced across the passage.

Sophie froze, listening intently to the sounds of the cavern. She waited for a few agonizing moments but heard nothing except the distant trickle of water and the shuffling of footsteps. A strong pat on the shoulder startled her.

"Something spook you?" Overton asked.

She ignored the question and strained her ears for another few seconds before following him into the shadows. They had to have been over fifty feet beneath the surface, and she was getting more nervous with every step. Things simply didn't add up. Something about Luke made her feel uneasy—something about his robotic voice and small, hazel eyes.

She didn't trust him, but she didn't know why.

And although she had delegated security details to Overton, she couldn't help the impulse to micromanage. As she glanced at the sleeping girl, her long-buried maternal instincts stirred. She'd always been a little disdainful of her colleagues who dropped out of the field to have kids. After meeting Emanuel, she'd started to come around to the idea, but somehow it had never been the right time. The distance between them, new projects, and her own insecurities had conspired against the both of them.

With a sigh, she reached out to brush the girl's hair from her face.

Sophie didn't have the heart to wake her. Not yet—not until she could guarantee the girl's safety, something she wasn't sure she would ever be able to do. The thought frustrated her. She could only imagine what the poor child had already gone through. The possibilities sent a wave of grief through her tired body. She ignored it and continued on, stopping only momentarily to hand her helmet to Finley so she could pull her frizzled hair back into a ponytail.

"Keep an eye on that guy," she whispered to the young Marine.

He narrowed his eyes and nodded. "Yes, ma'am."

They rounded a corner, and the passage widened into a chamber about fifty meters across. It was divided into two sections. One appeared to be some sort of living quarters, with several bunk beds resting against the jagged rock walls. Next to the beds were two chemical toilets cordoned off by a few carelessly hung sheets.

Not exactly keen on privacy, Sophie thought.

In the corner was a pyramid of boxes labeled *MREs* and several crates of bottled water. The area looked to be mostly unused. What was even odder was the fact that the space was built to shelter more than one person. Where were the others?

"This way," he said from a few paces ahead.

The team passed into the smaller part of the chamber. In the center of the room sat a large wooden table and a red leather couch. Not exactly what Sophie had expected. Lining the walls were dozens of monitors sitting atop portable metal desks.

Sophie approached the computers. The setup was complex. Sophisticated. Not the type of hardware the average person had lying around.

"Don't touch anything," Luke cautioned. "Give me a second, and I'll explain everything." He strolled over to Bouma. "Why don't you put her to bed on the couch?"

Overton gave the slightest of nods, and Bouma laid the girl down and draped her with a tan blanket.

"This way," Luke said in the same monotone voice.

"Mind if Private Finley here pulls sentry duty?" Overton asked.

Luke halted and cocked his head, looking first at Finley and then back at the sergeant.

"No point in doing it down here; the door's secured from the entrance of the house. But if you think that it's necessary I would post him on the second floor." He turned his attention to Finley. "Remember that staircase when you came in?"

"Yes."

"Take that to the second floor and then make your first right. The office has a perfect view of the frontage road. You'll be able to see any contacts long before they see you."

The young Marine looked at Overton, who gave the command. "Get it done."

"Yes, sir," he replied, taking off back the way they'd come.

"Anything else, Sergeant?" Luke asked.

"No. Carry on," he said, watching the man sit down at one of the computer terminals.

"So, as I was about to say, when I was a younger man I founded a tech start-up. My business was in magnets." He paused to glance quickly at Sophie before continuing. "Long story short, I sold the company five years ago for a sum just shy of a billion dollars. I spent a few years traveling the world and then settled here on this modest property," he said pointing to the low ceilings of the cave. "I did so because I wanted a place to further my research, and the granite caves provided me the perfect opportunity."

Luke spun in his chair and swiped one of the monitors with his fingers. A hologram shot out of a console next to Overton. Hovering over the module was a single blue image. At first glance, it reminded Sophie of the old communication satellites that had speckled Earth's orbit before the solar storms wiped them all out. But, as the image enhanced, she could tell it was something different—something much more sophisticated.

"Meet Starbuck," Luke said, smiling proudly. "She's the most advanced magnet ever designed. I built her to help mitigate the effect of solar storms."

Sophie nearly gasped, finally realizing what had made her so uneasy about Luke. She *had* met him before, in a meeting years ago with NTC. They were the ones who had bought his technology, but Dr. Hoffman had later scrapped the project for confidential reasons. It all made sense. That was why he had access to the encrypted NTC emergency channel.

"Yes, that's right, Dr. Winston. I'm Luke Williard, the former CEO of Solar Mitigation Technologies," he said, studying the look on her face.

Overton wasn't the brightest Marine in his squad, but he was smart enough to recognize what was going on immediately. Luke didn't need them to rescue him—he needed Sophie. He needed NTC. But why?

Fuck.

The Marine didn't like what was unfolding. He slowly removed his cigarette and stuffed it back into his breast pocket. He didn't want any distractions if he had to take Luke out.

"I remember you now," she said, stepping forward to study the holographic image. She had seen a blueprint of a similar design and recalled the device was, surprisingly, no larger than a car tire. The amount of energy it emitted, however, required that it be sealed inside a heavily fortified shell lined with lead. It was similar to some of the giant magnets she'd worked with in the past, but a fraction of their size.

"I presume you didn't just 'stumble' across my bunker, now did you, Dr. Winston?" Luke said coyly. He turned his attention back to the computer screen. Then he reached for his glasses and balanced them on his nose before proceeding to swipe the screen again. The image over the console faded and vanished. Seconds later a new image flickered to life. It was the outline of his house. And around it appeared to be some sort of oval-shaped screen.

"What you are looking at is an invisible shield surrounding the property. I've used electromagnetic energy to effectively sustain a wave of energy that camouflages anything within a square mile of here." Luke scanned the faces of Bouma and Overton, who stared back at him blankly.

"I know it's hard to understand, but in essence—"

"You're using their technology against them," Sophie said, interrupting Luke midsentence.

"Precisely, Dr. Winston. In 2056 I was contracted by NTC to study the electromagnetic disturbance that fed the solar storms. It was when we discovered *them* that we also discovered this technology."

Bouma's face turned bright red. "You fucking knew about the Organics this entire time?"

Luke looked at him for a split second before scowling. "Of course NTC has known all this time. There are thousands of people that knew this was coming."

Overton shook his head at the corporal, effectively ordering him to back off without uttering a word.

"As I was saying, NTC contracted me to work on building this technology long after I had sold them the rights to my company. But then, two years ago, Dr. Hoffman decided it was no longer a valuable investment for them," he said with another scowl.

Sophie froze in place. Everything was beginning to make sense now. The Biosphere mission. The invasion. NTC's plans had been in motion for years. How had she been so naive? And why had she been left in the dark for so long?

Frustrated, she shook the questions from her mind and stepped closer to the monitors. "Tell me everything you know about the Organics," she said, her business voice kicking in.

Luke folded his hands behind his head and leaned back. "You better take a seat, Dr. Winston. We may be here for a while."

CHAPTER 19

I WANT my blanket," the boy screamed.

"We have to get him to calm down!" Timothy shouted.

"You need to calm down, too," Holly whispered back, impatiently. She stooped to pick up the boy's blanket, quickly handing it to him.

"Contacts in Biome 1," Alexia said over the com. Her voice repeated the statement over and over.

Holly thought briefly of Emanuel. She desperately wished he were there—that he was by her side instead of Timothy—but he wasn't, and she needed to be strong for Owen's sake.

"We have to move," Timothy choked out, frantically scanning the medical ward for a nook, a cabinet, anywhere he could jam his thin body.

"There's nowhere to go," Holly said.

"There." He pointed at the other two cryo chambers nestled beside Saafi's.

"Are you insane?" Holly whispered.

"If those things are just after the pond, then by all means sit on the bench in the corner. You'll probably be fine. But if they aren't, if they're looking for us, then waiting in the open is going to get you killed. I, for one, want to live, and those chambers might just save our lives. If Alexia can shade the glass and turn our machines off, then maybe—just maybe—those freaky spider aliens won't rip us to shreds."

Holly looked over at the chamber, mulling over his theory. It took only a second to convince her.

"Owen, you get in first," she said, guiding him over to the nearest tube. The glass door hissed and cracked open as she picked up the whimpering child up and placed him inside, climbing in after him.

Timothy pulled himself into the other one. Both lids slowly whined shut.

Holly hugged Owen and patted his back as the glass panels clouded over. She watched Timothy slowly fade from view, his eyes staring back at her.

"It's going to be okay. We're safe in here," she whispered to the boy.

"I want to go home," he whimpered again.

"Shh. You have to be brave. Your mommy and daddy want you to be a brave boy so they can see you again."

He looked up at her with his large, blue eyes, struggling to get a hand free so he could wipe away the tears. "You think so?"

"I know so," she whispered.

The flickering of the room's lights pulled her attention away from him. Through the tinted window of the tubes, she could see the lights twinkle several times, struggling for power before finally shutting off. Darkness carpeted the room, and the beeps from Saafi's chamber ceased.

A lump formed in Holly's throat, but she didn't dare swallow. She could feel her heart thumping in her chest. Or was it Owen's heart?

With the power out, Saafi's life support would be out too. So would the locking mechanism for the door. On top of that, Alexia would have no way to communicate with them. She pulled Owen tighter, her skin rising with goose bumps. There was nothing she could do for Saafi—nothing she could do for anyone. They were going to die. She was convinced of it. She swallowed and watched a faint blue glow wash over the room as the door clicked open.

Scratch. Scrape. Scratch. Scrape.

The sound filled the silent space, sending a chill down her back. It was the most awful noise she had ever heard, like a drowning animal trying to claw its way to safety.

She felt Owen shivering and tightened her arms around him. She took in a deep breath, holding it. The glow increased, illuminating the room with a ghostly blue. She peered through the side panel and saw the creatures with naked eyes for the first time. Her heart skipped inside her chest as the spiders entered the room.

Scratch, scrape, scratch, scrape.

With her free hand, she covered Owen's eyes, but she couldn't close her own. Something compelled her to watch the creatures. She counted a total of seven, and remembered Alexia saying she had picked up nine contacts. Her thoughts returned briefly to Emanuel. Was he okay? Had he found a place to hide?

Scratch, scrape, scratch, scrape.

She watched the creatures explore the room, their thin legs almost gliding across the floor on the tips of their claws. Slowly they made their way through the space. One of them jumped on top of the bench and tore at the white cushion. Two others surrounded Saafi's chamber and paced back and forth. A fourth scampered toward her chamber.

Scratch, scrape, scratch, scrape.

For a second, her gaze locked with the spider's.

Could it see them through the tinted glass?

Her heart skipped another beat and adrenaline raced through her veins. *Crack!*

Out of the corner of her eye she could see the spiders clawing at Saafi's tube. The glass splintered as they bashed it with their limbs. Her own spider was still staring at her, its head tilting to one side.

She took in a deep breath.

Please go away. Please go away.

And then, as if in response to her thoughts, it was gone, joining the others as they broke into Saafi's tube. She watched the glass crack. What started as a small break turned into a web of fractures. Within seconds, they would be inside.

She could see Saafi's emotionless, emaciated face through the clear panels of his chamber. The sight was too much to bear. She focused on his chest instead, still heaving up and down as he breathed. He was totally unaware of what was about to happen to him.

Tears filled her eyes. She had known Saafi for years. He was a good man. Worst of all, there was absolutely nothing she could do for him.

The feeling of helplessness washed over her, mixing with a cloud of grief and anguish.

One of the spiders pulled the glass from Saafi's chamber with two of its legs. With another pair of legs, it pulled Saafi out, suspending him in midair. A second spider scuttled up beside the first and shot out a thin, blue web. The material covered Saafi's feet, wrapping them tightly. Slowly the spiders worked their way up his legs, torso, and chest, twirling him around and around.

Holly continued to watch, petrified. The only consolation was that he was in a coma and, hopefully, wouldn't be able to feel any pain. She reminded herself of this over and over again as the web tightened around his neck.

And then his eyes opened.

He tried to suck in a deep breath but couldn't—the thin blue web was too tight. Instead, his eyes darted around the room, trying to focus in the dim light. Slowly they came to rest on the creatures. His mouth opened to scream, but nothing came out; the web quickly covered his mouth, his nose, and finally his eyes.

Holly's stomach lurched. She coughed bile into her mouth but forced it down, the tears now flowing freely down her cheeks. The last thing she saw before she fainted was the spiders dragging Saafi's cocooned body away.

Overton twirled his combat knife before jamming it into a thick piece of sausage on his plate. His shoulder was surprisingly free of pain. The gel was just one of many advances in modern medicine that extended the lives of Marines. Even when they were torn and shredded like the piece of meat in front of him, they could be patched back together and returned to service as effective killing machines.

He smiled and brought the steaming piece of sausage to his mouth and bit in, savoring the juices as they ran down his hoarse throat. It was the first decent meal he had eaten in days, and he was going to enjoy it, savor it as if it was his last—after all, it very well could be.

He wasn't sure how much time he had left. And after seeing what they were up against, he was willing to bet that his life expectancy had dropped considerably since the invasion.

"She's awake," Bouma whispered in his ear.

Just my luck, Overton thought, staring down at the two strips of bacon and half-eaten sausage that he was going to have to let go cold. He sheathed his knife and headed for the red couch, joining Sophie and Bouma.

"My name's Sophie," she said, crouching next to the girl.

The kid cowered away. She had her arms wrapped around her knees, with her head dangling between them. Every time Sophie moved closer, the girl would hide between them a bit more.

Overton put his hands on Finley's and Bouma's shoulders. "Give them some room," he ordered. The three headed back to the large table, where they grabbed their meals and retreated from sight.

Sophie hardly noticed them leave. Her mind was racing; it wouldn't stop. She replayed the events of the past week over and over. First the dead livestock and dead communication line, then the orbs, the drone. Next, there were the Marines saving her team from a sure death. And then Owen had appeared.

Two children and a handful of Marines. The only known survivors besides Luke Williard; the scientist whom she'd met years before.

None of it made sense, and yet it all made sense. Everything was connected. Like a spider's web branching out in a thousand directions. Her dreams were the one piece of it that she just couldn't grasp—the dreams that she should have listened to long ago.

"How is she doing?" a voice said from behind her.

Sophie angled her head. She had been so lost in her thoughts that she hadn't heard Luke approach.

"She's been like this all morning. I can't get her to say a word."

"Typical response. After what she's been through, it's no surprise," Luke said.

"I can only imagine," Sophie said, returning her attention to the girl.

"Breakfast is on the table when you get hungry," Luke replied, disappearing as quickly as he had emerged.

Sophie considered telling the girl that everything was going to be okay and that she would take her home, but she couldn't bring herself to lie. Instead, she sat down next to her on the couch. She crossed her legs and allowed herself to relax, sinking into the soft, aged leather.

After a few minutes of silence, the little girl peered out from the safety of her knees with one eye, scanning the room before retreating back inside her fort of limbs.

Sophie stared ahead, watching the girl through her peripheral vision. It was a tactic used on patients with post-traumatic stress disorder that Holly had described to her years ago. She only vaguely remembered the conversation, but she remembered that when a patient's shock subsided and the adrenaline cleared, they could suffer from a magnitude of different emotions. The best thing to do, Holly had explained, was simply to show a presence. To listen and provide support while the shock subsided.

As the girl slowly pulled her head out from between her knees, Sophie realized that the strategy was working.

"Where are we?" the girl asked softly. Her voice was muffled and scratchy from screaming.

Sophie kept completely still, hardly making eye contact with the girl through even a sidelong glance. "We're in a safe place. A place with food and people who will protect us."

The girl surveyed the room again and rested her chin on her knees. She took in a small breath and looked down at the rock floor of the cave.

"Where are the monsters?" she asked, her eyes glued to the ground.

"They're all gone for now."

The girl shot her a quick glance from behind a curtain of hair, and for the first time Sophie saw her dark brown eyes. They were bright and full of life, far from the blank stare she had expected. The girl's change in demeanor was remarkable.

"What's your name?" Sophie asked.

"Jamie."

"It's nice to meet you, Jamie. My name is Sophie, and I am a scientist. Those men you saw earlier are soldiers and are going to protect you."

"They can't protect me."

Sophie paused, not wanting to backtrack on the progress she had made with the girl. "Of course they can, Jamie. They already killed the monsters."

The girl brought her legs back up to her chest and buried her face back inside them. In a muffled voice she finally replied, "Those were the small monsters."

A single bead of sweat crawled down Emanuel's forehead. The salt stung his dry skin, but he didn't dare move. After the power went out the temperature had skyrocketed. The air was hot and sticky. It didn't help that he was crammed into a closet the size of a gym locker. To make things even worse, it stunk of the chemicals that were used to treat Biome 1.

They had, without a doubt, saved his life. He didn't know why, but the spiderlike creatures had first approached his hiding spot, then suddenly turned away. He wasn't sure if the chemicals masked his presence, or if they were inimical to the creatures, but for whatever reason, they had lost interest in the storage locker. He watched through a tiny keyhole, still scanning the space for their presence.

But it was empty. The spiders had continued on. Where, he didn't know, but he guessed Biome 2, where the pond would provide them a plentiful distraction. Emanuel wasn't going to test his theory, though. He was going to sit tight until the power came back on and Alexia gave him the all clear. Or until Overton showed up with the cavalry.

His thoughts shifted to Sophie. He could only hope she was safe.

I shouldn't have let her go.

He turned his attention back to the keyhole, scanning the dark chamber outside. It had been over an hour since he'd heard the creatures' screams and the scratching of their claws. The itch on his forehead was getting more intense.

Satisfied that the creatures were gone, he slowly shifted his body, and risked wiggling his hand free to scratch his dry skin. Instant relief washed over him, but it only lasted a moment. In the distance a hissing sound broke through the silence.

He froze and forced his eye against the keyhole. The noise faded away. Were they back? Had they somehow picked up his scent?

Several minutes passed before the sound returned. It was not the same high-frequency pitch from before. It was something different—something more animalistic.

He blinked rapidly, trying to pick up signs of life through the darkness, but it was futile. Even the emergency lights had been cut.

Panic gripped him. Suddenly he felt completely alone. Was he the only one of his team left? Had the spiders killed Saafi, Holly, Timothy, and Owen?

His stomach lurched at the thought. He blinked again, straining to see into the darkness. For several minutes he sat in the cramped closet, his lungs filling with the stench of chemicals. Just when he thought the sound was gone, it erupted again, even louder than before.

Screech!

Emanuel tasted bile in the back of his throat. Never in his entire life had he been so sick with fear.

The sound grew louder. It didn't sound like the spiders. There was no scratching this time.

A faint blue glow illuminated the glass door separating the chamber from the cleansing rooms, about fifty meters from his hiding spot. He narrowed his eyes to focus on the glass, stilling his breath.

Inside the chamber something was moving—something big.

With every passing second the blue glow grew brighter and the sound amplified. Suddenly, a new noise rang out, followed by a loud bang.

Pressed against the glass was a face, devoid of humanity. A tongue exploded out of the creature's mouth and began licking the door violently, leaving slimy trails of blue goo against the glass.

Emanuel wanted to pull away, terrified the thing might be able to sense him, but a combination of curiosity and fear kept him glued to the sight. He still couldn't see anything but its face. The rest of the chamber had filled with a white mist that rose beneath the creature, camouflaging its body.

And then the face retreated and disappeared into the mist. The creature's glow pulsated within the chamber, turning the white mist blue, beautiful yet terrifying.

Crack!

The piercing sound forced Emanuel against the back of the small storage area. His chest heaved and his heart raced within the confines of his rib cage. He began to panic, unable to get control of his labored breathing.

It took him a few minutes to regain his composure. Slowly he inched his way back to the keyhole. Staring in his direction was a nine-foot-tall monstrosity. Its skin was translucent, like the spiders', with blue veins crawling throughout the length of its body. The bottom half of the creature, as far as Emanuel could tell, consisted of two beefy legs and a slender tail ridged with spikes that connected to a massive torso. The upper half of its body was humanoid, with a thick chest, two muscular arms, a thin neck, and round face. But it was far from human. The creature's skull was lined with the same spikes as its tail, and in the center of its face was a single socket crammed with two small, reptilian eyes.

Emanuel waited, petrified, for several minutes. Finally, he took in a deep breath.

Whatever the thing was, it appeared to be intelligent. Perhaps he had just seen one of the more sophisticated Organics. He guessed the spiders were not the top of the Organic food chain, that there was another species behind the invasion. He forced his face against the keyhole one more time. Staring back at him from a meter away were two small, malevolent eyes. They blinked, and he let out a bloodcurdling scream.

Sophie stood on the rooftop, watching the sunrise split the horizon in two. The clearest sky she had ever seen surrounded them in all directions. It was captivating and chilling at the same time. Zero cloud cover meant the Organics had already removed enough of the Earth's surface moisture that the water cycle had been broken. She was no meteorologist, but she knew enough about weather patterns to know the Earth was dying.

"What's that?" Overton asked from the corner of the roof. He took a step toward the railing and looked out across the Colorado Springs skyline through his scope.

Sophie strolled over to him, squinting into the sun to get a better look.

"Looks sort of like rain, but without the clouds. Here take a look," he said, handing her a pair of binoculars.

"That's not rain. Those are the remains of people from the orbs that are being beamed up to a collection ship far above the atmosphere. You can't see it, but trust me, it's there," Luke said from the stairway.

Overton narrowed his eyes. "How do you know all of this?"

"The ships have been in orbit since they invaded a few days ago. We didn't know about it until it was too late. They must have some sort of cloaking technology. I don't know," he said shrugging. "All I know is that when they finally emerged on invasion day, our weapons systems were already dead from the magnetic disturbance. With the click of one button, the Organics unleashed a shockwave that effectively shut down most of our technological advances from the past millennium."

Sophie's eyes widened. If what Luke was saying was true, then it was far worse than she had imagined. It was possible the government was completely gone. Sure, there would be other survivors in bunkers across the world, people like Luke who had survived the initial attack, but without jets, tanks, and nukes to fight back with, they would be eliminated one by one. Extermination was no longer just a worst-case scenario; it was quickly becoming a reality.

Overton coughed and jammed a cigarette between his dry lips. "How do we fight them?"

Luke laughed. "Typical soldier. I'm sorry, Sergeant, but we *don't* fight them. We hide and hope they leave without taking every ounce of water."

"Negative. That's not happening," Overton fired back. "I've killed almost a dozen of them already. They're weak. Once you bring down their shields, this thing we call a gun"—Overton shouldered his rifle and smiled—"turns them into dirty martinis."

"So you've seen the worms and the spiders, I take it? Odd creatures. No way in hell they're the intelligent ones, though. From what I've seen, they act like bugs. The spiders are the worker bees, tracking down water, weaving anyone or anything with a certain water weight into those orbs. Then the worms harvest the glowing prison cells and deliver the H_2O to the ships above with one giant belch," he said pointing at the clear sky.

Luke's smile faded as he watched another ray of turquoise light race up into the sky. He strolled across the metal rooftop, his boots clanking until he stood only a few steps from Overton. "I'm no Marine. I can't shoot, and I surely wouldn't know how to handle myself in battle. I don't know military strategy either, but what I do know is this—" Luke paused and surveyed the skyline. "I know history. It was just a matter of time before our civilization collapsed. Look at what happened to the Roman Empire, the people of Easter Island, the Mayans, and the Native American tribes. They were all virtually wiped out. Either by an invading enemy, disease, or loss of resources."

"But they weren't completely wiped out," Sophie interjected.

Luke smiled. "No, but they weren't fighting against a far superior species either. If you think about it this way, all three of the extermination factors in the demise of those cultures are present in this invasion. Consider this," he said, looking back over the railing. "We have an amazingly intelligent invading species. Any survivors will have to battle diseases due to lack of sanitary conditions, and the few who remain after that will have to contend with the loss of our most precious resource: water."

Overton brought his rifle back down to waist level and joined Luke in surveying the skyline. He wasn't a history buff, but he knew enough to know the man was right. He shook his head and began the journey back to the bunker.

"Where are you going, Sergeant?" Luke asked.

"I'm going to gather my men and supplies. We're heading back to the Biosphere within the hour. You're welcome to come with," he said, disappearing down the stairs.

Luke looked like he had just been hit in the gut. He watched Sophie, who still stood at the edge of the roof, transfixed by the sporadic rays of blue shooting out of Colorado Springs. He studied her for a moment before making his way to the staircase. He had to stop Overton; he couldn't let them leave. No one was going anywhere.

CHAPTER 20

FINLEY, Bouma, gear up. We're heading out ASAP," Overton shouted, the words echoing through the cave.

A pair of footsteps rang out from the metal stairs behind him, and moments later he felt the grip of a hand on his injured shoulder. He grimaced. "Hands off," he growled.

"Sergeant Overton, you're making a big mistake," Luke said. "Your facility is more than likely already compromised. Besides, you're all welcome to stay here. I have supplies, and my magnetic device will prevent them from ever finding us. We should wait out the invasion and reemerge when they leave," he insisted. "We need each other. With your NTC training, and my resources, this could be the safest place on Earth."

Overton pulled his bicep free from the man's grip. "Reemerge to what? To a world without water? No, I'm not risking that. I'm leading my men back to the Biosphere, where the rest of our team is. I made a promise, and I'm not the type of man to go back on my word. You're welcome to come with and bring your little magnet toy. "

Luke laughed. "I don't suppose I could change your mind?" He looked at Sophie and held her eye for a second. She walked over to Overton and stood shoulder to shoulder with the Marine.

"We have people back at the Biosphere. We've got to go back," she said sternly.

"Very well," Luke replied.

"Thanks for your hospitality," Overton said. He finished packing his bag and turned to see Luke had vanished.

Fuck. Just what I needed.

"Men, keep an eye on him," Overton said. "I don't trust him. Something tells me he isn't quite right in the head."

Sophie hovered over the couch, trying to get Jamie's attention with a warm smile. She wasn't sure if the girl was asleep or just hiding her face between her legs, but time was running out. The Marines were ready to move, and there was no way Sophie was going to leave the girl behind with Luke, even if the journey outside was risky.

"Jamie, I know you're scared, but we have to go now. There is a safer place for us. A place where there is a boy your age. His name is Owen."

The girl peeked one eye from between her knees. "Do I have to go outside?"

"Only for a little while. And I promise I'll be by your side the entire way," Sophie insisted. "Can you be brave like Owen?"

Jamie's eyes widened. With one swift movement, she nodded and jumped off the couch. "I bet I'm faster than he is, too," she said.

Sophie smiled. Kids never ceased to amaze her—their resiliency, their competitiveness with each other, and their innocence. She watched Jamie run toward Overton and Bouma as the unmistakable click of a gun's safety rang out behind them.

"No one's going anywhere," a voice said from the entry to the bunker.

Overton didn't need to turn to see Luke standing in the doorway, the machine gun leveled at his back. He'd had a feeling the man was close to losing it but even the veteran Marine had underestimated the man's intentions.

"You can't go out there. You won't survive," he said tonelessly.

Luke's voice reminded Overton of Alexia's—robotic and calm and unwavering. He watched Bouma pull his hand from his backpack and slowly reach for his sidearm. Overton shook his head and caught the corporal's eye. "No," he mouthed before turning to face Luke.

"You don't want to do this, Mr. Williard," he said, his hands raised.

"Drop the formalities. This isn't open for discussion. Now put your weapons on the table and take a seat on the couch."

"What are we now, your hostages? Are you going to keep us here forever?" Overton asked, his face turning red with anger.

Sophie watched from a distance, frozen. She motioned for Jamie to come back, and moments later she felt the girl's arms around her waist.

"You will stay as long as those things are outside," Luke replied. "Now, where's that private? Finster? Finley?" he asked, scanning the room with his machine gun.

In the second Luke turned his head, Overton unbuttoned the holster to his .45, spun, and fired off two shots. One punched a neat hole in Luke's leg, while the other severed his firing hand at the wrist. The man's legs folded underneath him and a spray of bloody mist shot into the air.

Sophie reached down to cover Jamie's eyes. She struggled to see what was happening and pulled free of Sophie's grasp. Jamie screamed, watching Luke flop around on the rocky floor like a fish fighting to get back into water.

Sophie grabbed Jamie and forced the girl's face against her side. "What did you do, Sergeant?" she yelled.

Finley rushed into the room, his rifle drawn. "Holy shit!"

The brilliant afternoon sun reflected off Finley's silver visor. Overton tinted his own visor and took to his stomach to survey the area with his scope. The box on his HUD blinked free of contacts, and with a quick motion of his hand, the team advanced up the hill. Hitting the tree line, they fanned out, with Finley taking point and Bouma hugging their six.

Sophie stumbled on a loose rock and felt Jamie's grip tighten around her armored neck.

"Go back to sleep," Sophie whispered.

Jamie responded by squeezing her even tighter. The meds Overton had given her were sedatives meant for adults. They had slipped one in a glass of water moments before they left Luke's bunker. In only a few minutes the pill took effect, just the right amount of time for Sophie and Bouma to retrieve the magnetic device from its hardened case on the roof. Now the meds were wearing off, and Sophie didn't know how much longer the girl would stay drowsy and quiet.

Sophie craned her neck to see Bouma struggling to keep up. He had hastily tied several cords together and fastened the device to his back. It was clearly weighing him down. By the time they reached the top of the ridgeline he was bent over, hands on his knees, trying to catch his breath.

"You're going to have to slow down. This thing weighs a ton," he said between breaths.

Overton blinked and pulled up the red clock in the corner of his HUD. It was 4:45 p.m. They still had several hours of daylight left, and had so far gone undetected. But they were, according to his projections, at least another five miles from the Biosphere. He blinked again and gazed upon the mountains in the distance with clear, focused eyes. Cheyenne Mountain was blanketed in pine trees. It looked so far away, an impossible distance to cover without being spotted by the Organics—especially with a girl and a hundred-pound magnet in tow.

He cursed and rubbed his throbbing arm. The gel Sophie had applied was wearing off, and the pain was slowly coming back.

Just my luck.

"Pack it up. We have a hump to travel," Overton said into his com.

"Roger," Finley responded, disappearing down the hill, a cloud of dust trailing him.

Sophie watched the dirt swirl like a miniature tornado. It was then that she saw the depression of what had been a lake only days before. For the first time, she understood the end of the world was no longer a hypothetical concept, a theory to be debated by academics. Rationally, she'd known the consequences of Earth's surface water being stolen. Ecosystems would begin to collapse. Trees would wither and die. Carbon emission levels would reach an all-time high, causing temperatures to rise, and any human survivors would be forced underground.

A pine needle pinged off her helmet. It disappeared as it hit the ground, camouflaged by the tan dirt. She continued to scan the area, her eyes falling on dry brushes and browning trees. As a scientist, she'd known all of this, but looking at the dry lakebed, it was suddenly real. The truth sent a shiver down the length of her body just as Bouma tapped her on her shoulder.

"Gotta move, ma'am," he said, rushing by her.

Sophie nodded and repositioned Jamie so she could carry the little girl more easily. With a sigh she took the first step into the depression below.

They traveled silently through the barren forest for hours, until the trees parted and revealed what had been civilization. Finley paused at the side of a gravel road and listened to a taut power line whine in the breeze. For a moment he wondered if it was still carrying any electricity, but he knew it was unlikely.

In the distance a weak sun began to set over Cheyenne Mountain, turning the sky a brilliant crimson. Overton blinked, and his visor automatically adjusted to the change in light. He took one knee next to Finley and stared silently down the road.

"Contacts?" Overton whispered into his com.

"Negative. All clear," Finley replied.

Overton didn't like the silence. It was eerie and it filled his mind with questions. Had the Organics retreated? Were they waiting for the right time to ambush his team? Or were they simply too busy turning the population of Colorado Springs into smoothies?

None of the possibilities was particularly reassuring. Either way, Overton knew they needed to move. He didn't want to get caught in the open during the night. It seemed like that was when the Organics were at their most active.

He nodded at Finley, who immediately took off running down the gravel road. There was zero cover for a klick or so where the road wound upward and wrapped around the mountain. It was the only way to get to the blast doors, but it also left his team completely exposed.

Overton watched the man for several minutes before taking off behind him. Finley's helmet bobbed as he ran. Up and down, up and down. His eyes followed the movement for a moment and then scanned the sky and surrounding area for contacts.

Nothing.

It was a good sign, but for some reason it only added to his nervousness. Surely the Organics had detected them by now, so what was stopping them from attacking? He had left Luke's bunker prepared for a fight and now he was getting anxious. Where were they?

He gripped the pulse rifle tighter, ignoring the pain shooting down his injured arm. Gritting his teeth, he pushed on, making his way to the edge of the road where it began its winding journey up the mountain. It was there he finally halted, struggling for air and watching Sophie and Bouma make their way up the incline with their precious cargo.

Overton looked up at the trail. "Almost there," he said, smiling behind his visor. Sophie didn't pause when she caught up with him. She continued up the hill at a pace that impressed even the Marine. He had always been a firm believer that people picked up speed in the last stretch of a race, especially when they could see a finish line. She was proving his theory to be true.

He leveled his rifle toward the ground and continued on, swearing that he would finally quit smoking. But as the blast doors came into focus, he was already imagining how sweet his next cigarette would taste. Then he noticed that something was wrong with the doors.

They were already open.

CHAPTER 21

OVERTON slipped through the crack in the monstrous blast doors. Finley watched with his back to the rock, his foot tapping anxiously.

Several seconds bled by, and Sophie began to get nervous. All she could think about was Emanuel. The open doors meant one of two things: either the Organics had gotten in, or Emanuel and the rest of her team had left.

As she studied the blast doors from a distance, she realized the latter of the two possibilities was remote at best. At the base of the metal doors were claw marks, much larger than any the spiders were capable of making.

Those are the small monsters. Jamie's words echoed in Sophie's mind. Reality set in; her stomach lurched, and the adrenaline mixing with her bloodstream clouded her vision.

"We have to get in there," she whispered into her mic, setting Jamie softly on the ground. She jabbed her finger at the claw marks. "Check those out."

"What the fuck are those?" Finley exclaimed, taking one knee to study the doors.

"We have to warn Sergeant Overton," Bouma replied. He unstrapped the metal device from his back and carefully rested it against the wall of the door. "I'm going in," he said, his weapon leveled at the darkness.

"Roger. I'm right behind you. Dr. Winston, stay here! That's an order," Finley said.

She nodded and crouched down next to Jamie. The child sat on the rocky ground, rubbing the sleep from her eyes. "Are we safe yet?" she asked in a soft, innocent voice.

Sophie looked down at the girl through her silver visor and lied. "Almost, honey. Almost."

Inside the facility, Bouma caught up with his commander.

"Sergeant, the doors. They had all of these scratches," he panted. He eased to a stop behind Overton, who was standing frozen in the darkness of the hangar.

The Marine didn't respond. He simply blinked and scanned the blackness, his eyes straining to see what lurked in the shadows.

"Sir, the—"

Overton balled his hand into a fist, and Bouma took a step back, nearly bumping into Finley.

"My heat sensors are picking up some weird readings," Overton whispered. "Bouma, take our six. Finley, you're with me."

The two Marines nodded and fell into position. Overton took the lead, stepping a few cautious paces into the darkness, blinking again as the green tint from his night vision filled his HUD.

He had seen several heat signatures upon entering the hangar, but they disappeared almost as fast as they had appeared. The claw marks on the doors troubled him. More than troubled—they fucking terrified him. He knew better than anyone in the group that the spiders hadn't done that to the doors. The wound on his shoulder proved they weren't that strong. If they were, his arm would be lying in a parking lot back in Colorado Springs.

Don't lose focus.

The words from his drill sergeant were the perfect reminder that he needed to get his head back in the game. Whatever was on the other end of those claws was going to be big, and he needed a clear mind if he was going to have a chance of taking it down.

A flash of red raced across his HUD. His eyes followed the blur before it disappeared off his display. "Contact," he whispered.

Two short bursts of static broke over the com.

"I see it," Finley said.

"Me too," Bouma replied.

"Hold position," Overton ordered.

He stilled his breathing in an attempt to calm his nerves. The green glow of the tunnel filled his HUD with an eerie haze. Another flash of red burst across his display and disappeared.

Whatever it was, it was fast. He held his position and scanned the tunnel. If he had to guess, he would put them at one hundred yards away from the Biosphere entrance, which meant they had already traveled farther than he thought. It also meant there was a considerable gap between him and the civilians.

A wave of helplessness washed over him. He pulled his focus from the tunnel and turned. The last thing he wanted was to be outflanked. But as he began to backtrack, his HUD exploded with red light and his stomach sank. It was too late.

Towering behind Finley was a nine-foot-tall monstrosity. Overton scanned the beast in shock. He had never seen anything quite like it. Its massive tail, short thick legs, and stubby arms reminded him more of a reptile than an alien. But when his eyes finally came to rest on the creature's face, he saw the difference. Tucked within a skull rimmed with spikes was a humanoid face with a pair of emotionless eyes.

Before Overton had a chance to warn Finley, the creature lurched forward, its tongue flicking between a mouthful of jagged black teeth. A deafening sound escaped its mouth as it attacked.

The monster was incredibly fast, using its tail to help it slither down the tunnel. In less than two seconds, one of the creature's arms had wrapped around Finley's torso while the other had impaled his neck armor with a sharp claw.

A single burst of static squawked over the radio as Finley let out a cry. His last words were undecipherable as he choked on his own blood.

There was nothing Bouma or Overton could do. They watched

in horror as the monster tightened its grip around Finley's torso and yanked, ripping the private's head from the bloody stump of his neck.

"NO!" Overton screamed, shouldering his rifle and squeezing the trigger as the private's headless body slumped to the tracks below.

The tunnel glowed with the light that emanated from Bouma's and Overton's rifles as they shot round after round. The pulses ricocheted off the creature's blue shield and it screeched, its mouth displaying every one of its black teeth.

Both Marines emptied their magazines into the creature without effect. Overton reached for his electromagnetic grenade, tossed it at the monster's feet, and took off running down the tunnel. "Move it, Bouma!" he screamed.

A bright flash filled his display, blinding him. He gritted his teeth, took one knee, removed his .45, steadied his breathing, and, when his vision cleared, fired a single round. The bullet seemed to travel in slow motion, barely missing Bouma, who was still running, and punching a wide hole just above the creature's eyes. They blinked, and then the monster let out a soft grunt before it collapsed face first onto the tunnel tracks, its claw still gripping Finley's head.

"Holy shit!" Bouma panted. He was bent over, his hands on his knees, staring at the alien. Overton holstered his pistol and jammed another magazine into his rifle before pacing over to the fallen beast.

"They aren't shit without their force fields," he said, taking one knee next to Finley's fallen body. "God damn . . ." his voice trailed off as he stared at what was left of his Marine. "Fuck, he didn't deserve to go out like that."

Overton forced his gaze away and scanned the tunnel for contacts. There wasn't time to mourn Finley. Not with Dr. Winston and Jamie waiting. He didn't even want to think about what would happen if one of these creatures caught them.

"Move out, Bouma."

He took off running back down the tunnel, but Bouma stood frozen in place. He stared at his friend and the beast that had claimed his life.

"No one fucking told me I'd be fighting goddamned alien monsters when I signed the dotted line," he said. He stood there for what felt like ages before forcing himself to move. He took a last look at Finley's corpse and whispered, "Sorry, man, but maybe you actually lucked out."

Sophie scuffled along the side of the tracks with one hand on Overton's shoulder and the other gripping Jamie's little hand tightly. There was no need to tell the girl to close her eyes as they came upon Finley's corpse; the darkness of the tunnel ensured she didn't see the gruesome scene.

Through Sophie's visor she saw it all—the terrifying corpse of the alien, whose skull was leaking a river of goo, Finley's headless body, and finally his helmet, which had strips of esophagus and flesh still attached to it.

Her stomach lurched and she gagged. The taste of regurgitated sausage overwhelmed her, and she was forced to brace herself against the wall.

"Are we almost to the safe place?" Jamie asked in a hushed whisper.

Sophie sucked in some filtered air and blinked the cloudiness from her vision. "Yes, we're almost there," she said.

"Keep moving," Overton ordered.

Jamie latched herself around Sophie's waist. "I don't like the dark."

"Dr. Winston, keep her quiet," Overton barked.

Sophie ran her armored fingers through the girl's locks and glanced at Finley's body one more time before continuing on down the tunnel.

Heel to toe. One step at a time.

The distance between their location and the entrance to the Biosphere was hard to judge. The green glow of her night vision made everything look like a video game.

She pressed on. Every step brought her closer to finding Emanuel.

A few feet ahead she could see that the tunnel curved slightly to the right. Overton had already halted, trying to gain an angle on the turn. She craned her neck and saw Bouma was still behind them.

"The entrance to the facility is right around this corner," Overton whispered into the com. He stole a quick glance around the granite wall and eyed the passage.

"It's clear. Stay tight."

Sophie felt a lump forming in her throat. She gripped Jamie's hand tighter and followed the sergeant, stepping carefully over the train tracks.

They crept up the staircase leading from the tunnel to the platform and followed it into the facility in single file. Every footstep sounded like a miniature earthquake in the narrow hallway.

The noise echoed in Overton's helmet. Stealth was the only advantage he had on the Organics; without it he knew he wouldn't be able to protect what was left of their group.

An image of Finley's headless body slipped into his mind. He gritted his teeth and forced it into the vault where he stored all of the other horrible things he'd seen. There was no hiding it forever—the image would reappear, more than likely on some dark night when sleep wouldn't come. But he had to put it away for now and focus on his current objective.

Get inside the facility. Secure it and find the rest of the team.

He repeated the mission over and over. It helped him focus. Finally, they passed a briefing room and a set of offices. He halted outside the entrance to the cleansing chamber. Taking one knee, he peeked around the corner.

His eyes fell upon the thing he'd been dreading to find. The aliens had already penetrated the facility, more than likely in search of the pond. On the ground were a thousand tiny pieces of shattered glass, spread across the floor like candy from a broken piñata. Mixed throughout were gooey remnants of the same material he had seen gushing out of the monster's skull in the tunnel.

Fuck.

The word escaped his mouth and sounded over the com.

"What is it?" Bouma replied, his voice tight with fear.

Overton responded by slipping into the darkness of Biome 1. He shouldered his rifle, grimacing from the growing pain in his arm.

A faint red signature glowed to life on his HUD. He knelt and zoomed in. Whatever it was, it appeared to be inside the wall.

"Contact," he whispered. "Check it out, Bouma."

Bouma hesitated at the opening of the cleansing chamber and then jumped onto the dirt of the garden, crushing several plants that had already sprouted. He walked at a steady pace, his weapon trained on the wall.

About one hundred yards out he stopped. He blinked to enhance the image on his HUD. The contact was curled up inside a closet. At first glance it reminded him of the ultrasound image he had seen of his nephew a few months earlier. But this was no baby. This was something else.

He pressed on cautiously, his boots crushing plants beneath their tread. When he got to the platform, he put one hand on the metal and pulled himself up, keeping his rifle trained on the closet.

Two large steps across the platform were all it took to get to the wall. He slouched against it, sucking in a deep breath. Counting to three, he slowly pulled the handle. The door creaked open, and he jumped back as a body slumped onto the platform.

"I found someone," he whispered into the com. He pulled off a glove to check the man's pulse. It was surprisingly strong. He rolled the man onto his back, and Emanuel's eyes popped open, scanning the darkness restlessly.

"Who—who's there?!"

"Keep it down," Bouma whispered, bringing his hand to Emanuel's mouth.

"We have to hide," Emanuel said, scooting backward on the metal platform until he hit the wall with a thud.

"Emanuel!" Sophie cried, dropping Jamie's hand and rushing toward him. "You're okay." She dropped to both knees and hugged him, gripping him so tight he couldn't scream again even if he'd wanted to.

"Sophie, is that you?"

She reached for her helmet and slipped it off. She blinked several times before the outline of his face came into focus. "Yes, it's me."

Emanuel's body slowly relaxed. He reached out for her, hugging her forcefully. "God, I thought I had lost you," he whispered.

"I know, I thought I lost you too," she whispered.

Emotions she had ignored for too long overwhelmed her. Mars, the

Biosphere, her team's opinion of her—none of it mattered anymore. All that mattered was surviving—surviving with Emanuel.

A single tear raced down her cheek, hidden by the darkness. She didn't bother wiping it away. Her body was too tired. It had been through so much.

"All right, lovebirds, let's get moving. I want the facility secured in thirty minutes. Bouma, set your mission clock," Overton said over the com.

The blue numbers began to tick away on his HUD. He checked his ammo and stretched his stiff arm. In the distance, a scream broke through the silence, and he instantly shouldered his rifle, his finger massaging the trigger.

"What the hell was that?" Bouma whispered.

"Sounded human. Kind of like that jackass computer guy," Overton said. He was moving before he finished his sentence, racing down the platform. Stealth was no longer important. If there were more survivors, he wanted to find them before the Organics did.

"Bouma, protect the civvies and get the power back on. I have an asshole to save."

CHAPTER 22

EVERY time Overton had ever thought he was incapable of completing an objective, his training would kick in and he'd get it done. After serving his entire adult life in the military, his senses were no longer his own—they belonged to the Marines. He could no longer control how he reacted in combat. His training, experience, and survival instincts snapped on and took over.

His current mission was no different. He didn't think about hugging the wall of the passage so that the enemy couldn't get behind him. He didn't think about shouldering his rifle tight against his body or the pain that it caused his injured shoulder. And he certainly didn't think about what could be lurking in the shadows. Whatever it was, he would deal with it. He was a goddamned Marine.

The first hallway was clear, and, surprisingly, the glass door to Biome 2 was still sealed. With the power off he was forced to pry his way in. He shuddered as the rubber-tipped bottom of the doors squeaked, but within a few seconds he was in.

The glistening water of the pond filled his HUD with a green glow. It was the last thing he had expected to see. He had assumed the Organics were after the Biosphere's water supply, but as another scream broke through the silence, he realized they were after something else—the team.

Kill the enemy and then *take their resources.*

It was one of history's longest-standing military strategies, dating back to a time when humans were little more than hunters and gatherers. And now an alien life force that had traveled an unfathomable distance to reach Earth was using it against them.

Shocked into motion, Overton rushed out of the chamber and sprinted down the hallway. He didn't bother looking in Biome 3. Out of his peripheral vision, he could see the glass was still in place. It was Biome 4 he was interested in.

He raced around a corner and eased to a halt as the mess hall came into view. The outlines of empty tables filled his HUD. There were no signs of life.

His instincts kicked in and he pushed on. Time was of the essence and trumped any need to go undetected. He certainly didn't like Timothy, but he wasn't going to let another one of his people die. Besides, he knew if Owen and Holly were still alive, they would be close by.

The sound of Timothy's screams broke through the silence again, and Overton blinked, enhancing his night vision. Judging by the strength of the screams, he put the man somewhere in the personnel quarters or the med ward. But without Alexia's guidance, he had no way of knowing the exact location.

In the corner of his HUD, the mission clock blinked red, reminding him he had only fifteen minutes to meet his objective—anything longer than that would give the Organics even more of an advantage. His objectives were simple, yet complicated: rescue the survivors, get the power back on, and secure the entryways.

He slipped into the hallway leading to the personnel quarters, and his display glowed to life. With several blinks he enhanced the optics until he could see a powerful glow from the entrance to the med chamber.

Pushing forward, he ignored the closed doors of the staff quarters and continued down the hall, his weapon shouldered and his fingers massaging the trigger. The glow meant one thing: contacts.

He slid his back against the wall and checked his magazine. It was full. He was locked and loaded, ready to go.

Light 'em up!

He ran into the room and almost fired a round into Timothy's forehead. The man stood, shaking uncontrollably, in the center of the med ward. His eyes were fixated on an orb floating over what was left of Saafi's cryo chamber.

Suspended from the ceiling were a half dozen spiders, their bellies bulging.

The sight was overwhelming. For the first time, Overton wasn't exactly sure what to do. None of it made sense to him. The spiders should have been attacking Timothy, aggravated by his screams. But looking closer, he saw they were in some sort of suspended animation. A translucent layer of skin covered their eyes and their liquid-filled torsos pulsated. Even from several paces away, Overton could see the liquid was slowly dissipating.

He didn't need to see any more. His instincts kicked back in. The spiders weren't sleeping; they were fueling up. Now was his chance.

One swift kick to the back of Timothy's knee was all it took to get him out of the way. He watched the man's legs crumple beneath him, and then, without further hesitation, he squeezed his rifle's trigger rapidly, like a child playing a video game.

Adrenaline filled his veins as the rounds tore into the spiders' shields. They just hung there, putting up no resistance. After only a few shots, their defenses weakened and failed. Overton finished the magazine with a few more squeezes of the trigger, and the last spider exploded in a mist of liquid. They'd never even moved.

"That's for Finley!" he shouted. He lowered his rifle and pulled another mag from his belt. With a click, he jammed it back in the weapon and fired off another volley of shots into a spider whose body was still somewhat intact.

"And that's for the rest of my squad!" he snarled.

A burst of static broke over the com. "Sergeant, what's going on? We heard gunfire. Over."

"All clear, Bouma. I found Timothy and"—he looked at the empty orb floating over the destroyed cryo chamber—"And what's left of Mr. Yool."

Silence filled his helmet as he waited for a response.

Sophie's voice slowly broke over the channel. "Sergeant Overton, please repeat your last transmission."

"Mr. Yool is gone, ma'am. I'm sorry for . . ."

A hissing sound distracted Overton before he could finish his thought. He spun and saw one of the cryo chambers open. When he saw Holly and Owen emerge, he immediately lowered his weapon, a relieved grin on his face.

"Dr. Winston. I've located Holly and Owen. They appear to be uninjured."

"Thank God," Sophie responded. "We're heading to the med ward now."

"Roger that. Bouma, how's it coming with getting those lights back on?" Overton asked.

"I found the source of the power outage. A few severed wires. I should have it back on in . . ."

A warm glow illuminated the room and the sound of Alexia's robotic voice repeated over the intercom system:

"Code Red. Please head to the medical ward. Code Red. Please head to the medical ward."

Relief washed through Overton's system. Two objectives down. And despite the loss of Mr. Yool, things weren't as bad as he thought.

He slipped off his helmet and peered at the cryo chamber Holly and Owen had been hiding in.

"Are you guys okay?" he asked.

"What about me, man? You about broke my freaking knee," Timothy complained.

The sound of the man's voice made Overton cringe. With one swift move he stood, spun, and swung at Timothy. His fist connected with the man's jaw, and the unmistakable sound of bone shattering echoed off the walls.

He turned to face Holly again before Timothy's body had a chance to hit the floor. "That should shut him up for a while."

A hint of a smile streaked across Holly's face.

"Thank you for saving us, Mr. Soldier," Owen said from inside the cracked lid of the cryo chamber.

Overton looked down at the boy and paused. He didn't know what to say. It was the first time he could remember a child ever thanking him for anything.

"Any time, little guy," he finally managed.

Bouma hunched over the main desk in the control room, studying a holographic blueprint of the facility. Miles of tunnels twisted and snaked across the map, leaving him perplexed. The age of the structure, combined with the fact that it had been completely retrofitted from the NORAD days, added to the complexity of the blueprints.

Overton had ordered him to find all possible entry points into the Biosphere, but as his mind digested the drawings, he realized it was going to be almost impossible. The main problem was that the Organics had already penetrated the facility, which meant they already knew of the team's presence.

Neither of the Marines claimed to be experts on enemy tactics, but they were both smart enough to know the Biosphere had been compromised.

A strong pat on his back distracted him, and he looked up to see Overton's exhausted face.

"Report," he said, stuffing the last half of a granola bar into his mouth.

"Sir, there are so many possible entries it will be almost impossible to secure the facility. Besides, they already know we're here."

"Bouma, I'm not asking for your opinion on the Organics. I'm asking if you can secure the Biosphere. Can you do that?"

Bouma hesitated and shook his head. "No sir, I don't think it's possible. With all due respect, if they got in once, they'll certainly be clever enough to get in again."

Overton massaged the metal holster of his .45. "I understand this may be difficult for you to grasp, son, but we *have* to secure this facility. There is nowhere else to run. Unless you suggest going back outside. Is that what you're suggesting, Bouma?"

Bouma shook his head again. "No, sir . . ."

"Then get on it!"

"Sir, yes sir!" Bouma said, his back stiffening.

"Alexia, are you back online?" Overton asked.

"Yes, Sergeant Overton. My mainframe is still downloading files, but I am 90 percent operational. How may I assist you?"

Her robotic voice echoed in his ears. Something about the tone reminded him of . . . no, he was just being paranoid. He shook the thought away quickly and stepped forward to get a better view of the blueprints. "I need to know how those things got in our facility."

Footsteps rang out behind him and he turned to see Sophie entering the room. Overton nodded at her and turned back to the holograms.

"Sir, for the sake of expediency, I have assigned names to the creatures. I am calling the spiderlike creatures, for the lack of a better word, Spiders. The larger species you encountered in the tunnel is a Sentinel," Alexia said. "The Spiders appear to have gained entry to the hangar through a pair of sanitary sewer lines associated with the old NORAD facility. And you saw how the Sentinel penetrated the hangar via the blast doors."

Overton's stomach growled. The granola bar hadn't been enough. He needed more food and desperately needed sleep. He shook his head and looked at the ground, trying to think.

Bouma was right. The facility was just too big to secure, and the Biosphere wasn't designed with security in mind. If the blast doors couldn't keep one of those things out, there was no way they could keep them out of the Biomes.

Sophie's firm voice pulled him back to reality. "What about the device?" she suggested.

"What?" Overton asked, massaging his temples.

"The magnet. Clearly it saved Luke's life and camouflaged his house from the Organics. Maybe we could get it to work here, too?"

Overton blinked, second-guessing his decision to leave Luke's bunker. Had it been the wrong move? He shrugged off the thought. He had had no way of knowing the Biosphere facility had been compromised. There was also no way he was going to risk heading back outside. Not now, with two children under their care. Besides, he knew most of the team would refuse to go anyway. Their only choice was to hunker down and try their best to make the chambers as safe as possible.

"Do you think you can get that thing up and running?" Overton asked.

Sophie eyed the device. "Shouldn't be too hard," she said confidently. "It looks kind of like a reverse magnetic pulse generator. I've seen prototypes before."

Overton shrugged. "Get it done then. Bouma and I will work on securing the front doors to Biome 1." He paused and looked down at his last electromagnetic concussion grenade. "If the magnet device fails, we go with plan B. These things take down their shields," he said with a wink.

"Works for me." She glanced at her watch. It was getting late. They were all in desperate need of sleep, but first they needed food. Those had to be their priorities. She hated to neglect Finley and Saafi's remains, but there wasn't anything they could do for either of them now.

"Alexia, please reset all sensors in the facility." She turned to Overton. "Does thirty minutes give you enough time to set your trap?"

"Does it give you enough time to set up the device?"

Sophie smiled. "Yes, that should be sufficient. Let's meet back at the mess hall in half an hour."

Overton set his stopwatch and grinned wolfishly. He was impressed with Sophie's resilience. It was the trait of a solid leader, one he looked for when recommending promotions. She would have made a hell of a Marine.

CHAPTER 23

ENTRY 0104
DESIGNEE: AI ALEXIA MODEL 11

Scans show the facility is completely contaminated. In fact, the data I have downloaded to my system may not even be accurate. It cannot be. The system is overloaded and readings are off the charts.

My objectives have changed. NTC programmed me to ensure two main goals. The first was to keep the Biosphere toxin-free, with systems running at 100 percent, and the second was to look after the health and safety of Dr. Winston's team.

I have failed at both objectives.

However, considering the events that have unfolded outside, I am surprised any of the team members remain alive. Or, to be accurate, I am not *surprised*. I was not programmed to feel surprise. The team's survival is, however, a true anomaly.

I put the possibility of continued survival over the duration of a month's time at approximately 20 percent. I should add that number drastically declines every week thereafter. The primary variables involved in these computations are simple, although the calculations are complex: One, the team's ability to grow food after the supply runs out. And two—which, I should highlight, is the most important factor—is their ability to avoid the Organics.

These statistics may change if the piece of magnetic equipment

Corporal Bouma brought back to the facility proves to be effective against the aliens. It is truly a fascinating device. Preliminary scans show the machine works by reducing the effects of an electromagnetic field over an area approximately the size of a square mile. The device houses some sort of magnetic material that blocks the electromagnetic energy wave the Organics are using. Put simply, it creates a shield around a location that effectively blocks any electromagnetic radiation, energy, or radio waves from getting in.

Before the power was cut, I had been running diagnostics on the electromagnetic disruption outside the facility. The results were intriguing. The Organics have created and sustained a wave of energy that has in turn disrupted communications worldwide. At this point I have several hypotheses regarding the source of this wave, but I can say with 99 percent accuracy that they used similar technology during the 2055 solar storms.

If the reverse magnetic pulse generator—or RVM, as Dr. Winston has been referring to it—is as effective as my scans indicate, it may be possible to amplify its range. However, this is only a theory, and I do not have enough information to take this idea to Dr. Winston yet.

A beep from my security program informs me that the defense sensors are back online. I zoom in with Camera 14 and see Sergeant Overton and Corporal Bouma working on securing the entrance to Biome 1 with several metal panels. Bangs echo off the walls as they bolt the thick sheets over the entry.

Another warning from my security program diverts my attention to the control room. I skip to Camera 34 and watch Dr. Winston and Dr. Rodriguez plugging wires into the side of the RVM. Two of the command computers have been unplugged, resulting in a loss of several data systems.

The time reads 9:15 p.m., and in Biome 4 Dr. Brown sits at a table with the children, Owen and Jamie. They are both shoveling food into their mouths while the doctor rubs their backs. Her face is strained, exhausted, and aged. She does not look like the young psychologist who entered the Biosphere a little over a week ago. Mr. Roberts is slumped in a wheelchair fast asleep and appears to be drooling on himself. It's more than likely the result of the painkillers he took for his broken jaw.

I pull all three images onto my display. Biome 1, the control room, and Biome 4 all show the remaining team members working on securing the Biosphere. While this behavior is logical, it seems to be statistically futile.

I recalculate their odds of survival at 19 percent. I decide not to inform them of this fact unless they specifically request the information. Although, from what I have observed of Dr. Winston and her team, knowing the odds would only make them fight harder to survive.

I've never understood this side of humans. Even after downloading thousands of articles on human behavior and psychology, I simply do not understand why they fight so hard to survive when faced with almost certain death.

When I was designed, my purpose was simply to assist them in accomplishing the Biosphere mission so humanity would have a chance of traveling to the stars and preserving their species. The AIs that came before me were all designed to assist as well, but not in protecting life—in destroying it. Their objective was to annihilate the enemy at all costs. They were designed by men and women who only cared about winning wars.

Man has an extraordinary ability to create, from skyscrapers to state-of-the-art medical centers. And yet, in a very short time, he can ruin everything he created—poisoning the atmosphere with carbon emissions and unleashing horrific weapons on innocent civilians.

The facility in which I now work is one of humankind's most impressive accomplishments. We are deep inside a mountain, working off the grid. It is here, where NTC pooled its resources and its last hope of creating a successful Biosphere together so humans could travel to Mars and repopulate, that the irony becomes obvious. As the three images show what's left of the team fighting for survival, their mission becomes crystal clear, and in reality it really hasn't changed: the mission is to preserve what's left of the human species. Only this time the enemy isn't humanity; it's an invading alien intelligence.

Another sensor goes off as Sergeant Overton and Corporal Bouma finish securing Biome 1. I check a new piece of data scrolling across my display.

Interesting.

The likelihood of the team's survival has climbed back up to 21 percent.

Overton wiped a bead of sweat off his forehead and took a seat on the cold metal bench of an empty table in the mess hall. With a loud bang he planted his rifle on the table.

His watch read 9:28. They had met their objective, securing Biome 1 in thirty minutes. Now he was waiting for Sophie and Emanuel to rejoin the group and report on the device. The clatter of metal spoons echoed throughout the mostly silent mess hall. Owen and Jamie watched him between bites.

Footsteps drowned out the sounds of the children eating, and he looked up to see Sophie and Emanuel entering the chamber side by side. Their faces were both rife with exhaustion, and Sophie's frizzled blond hair shot out in all directions.

Overton looked down at his watch again.

9:29:49.

"It's done, Sergeant," Sophie said, taking a seat across from him. "The RVM is online. I've tasked Alexia with ensuring it has the desired effect, but from what we could tell it's working at 100 percent."

Overton raised a brow but didn't speak. He was too exhausted to ask any questions. Besides, he didn't need a long, drawn-out explanation of how the machine worked, so long as it did.

"Biome 1 is secured," Overton said.

"Then the Biosphere is our home for the foreseeable future," Sophie said.

Emanuel braced himself against the chamber wall and crossed his feet. "Sergeant Overton, I ask this question with all due respect. Have you reconsidered your idea of a counterattack?"

The words seemed to slap Overton in the face. His tired eyes widened and his ears perked up like a dog sensing a predator. He ran a hand over his freshly shaved head. "Since you didn't accompany us on our last trip through hell, I'm not going to take that as a personal attack."

"And you shouldn't, Sergeant, but—"

Overton took his hand off his shiny skull and raised a single finger to stop Emanuel in midsentence. "It's much worse out there than I thought. We only found two more survivors: Jamie, and a civvie named Luke who we got the RVM from. And he's dead now. So are Private Finley and Mr. Yool." Overton paused to shake his head.

"We didn't see any other survivors. Got that? No soldiers, no kids. Nothing. From what Luke said, most of the other survivors were killed by the creatures hours after the initial stages of the invasion. I'm sure there are others out there, but we are cut off. There is no intelligence to indicate the military, NTC, or any government still exists. I believe . . ." Overton faltered for the first time since Emanuel had met him. "I believe we are on our own."

The words lingered in the air for several moments. Finally, Holly kissed Jamie and Owen on their cheeks and began herding them out of the mess hall. "Come on, time for bed," she whispered. They didn't protest and slugged toward the first two rooms of the personnel quarters. Before they disappeared down the passage Holly turned, "Don't worry, I'll watch them tonight," she said, managing a smile. "But tomorrow I'm sitting down with all of the staff members to discuss recent events. Sophie, you're going to be first," she said sternly.

Sophie frowned, but agreed with a simple motion of her hand before changing the subject. "With Alexia's security systems back online and Biome 1 secured, I'm going to suggest we all get some sleep. We can discuss strategy in the morning."

Overton nodded. "Bouma, you and I will trade watch shifts tonight here in the mess hall."

"Yes, sir," Corporal Bouma said, his back stiffening.

Sophie pulled herself off the bench and joined Emanuel by his side. "Thank you for everything, Sergeant Overton. I'm truly sorry for the loss of Private Finley. He seemed like a good man. A good Marine."

Overton nodded again and grabbed his rifle off the table. "See you in the morning, doctors," he said with uncharacteristic softness, his voice fading as he turned and headed to retrieve bedding and a pillow from the personnel quarters.

Emanuel grabbed Sophie's hand and twined his fingers with hers. He pulled her close, wrapping his other arm around her waist. "Promise me something," he whispered into her ear.

She studied his restless eyes. "I'm not sure we live in a world where I can promise anything anymore, Emanuel."

"I know Saafi's death is hard for you to accept. It's hard for me, too. So is the loss of the mission and the trip to Mars. I know this is all so much to bear, but promise me you won't give up," he said. "Promise me you won't give up on the team's survival. Or on us."

Sophie tilted her head back, a smile playing on her lips. She hadn't expected to hear him use the word *us* ever again.

"I won't," she said, relaxing into his arms. A sense of relief washed over her body. It wasn't just a feeling of temporary safety, though. It was something deeper—something more intense.

It was love.

Sophie stirred, trying to stretch her legs. The beds had specifically been designed for one person, and she was forced to literally wrap herself around Emanuel. It wouldn't be such a bad thing, if she had actually been able to sleep. She eyed the clock.

11:18 p.m.

With a sigh she pulled one leg off Emanuel and swung it over the side of the bed. The instant her toes touched the cold floor, the chill sent a shiver up her spine. She wanted to stay with Emanuel, wrapped up in the warmth of their bed. But there was work to do.

Darkness blanketed the room. The red glow from the clock's display was the only guide for her tired eyes. She rubbed the sleep out of them and stood. It was deathly silent, and she was tempted to wake Emanuel to have some company. But even through the darkness, she could tell he was deep in REM sleep. If anyone needed it, he did.

A silent growl from her stomach reminded her she had gone to bed without much of a dinner. She grabbed her headset and, like a zombie, lurched forward, stumbling toward the automatic door.

By the time she got to the kitchen, her eyes had started to adjust to the darkness. The vague outlines of two figures appeared as she walked into the mess hall. She assumed the lump wrapped in blankets on the floor was Bouma and the figure sitting on a bench staring at her was Overton.

She was right; Overton's rough voice sliced through the silence. "Everything okay?"

"Just hungry," Sophie responded. "Pay no attention to me." She continued on and began clawing through the contents of the cupboards as if she hadn't eaten in days.

She retrieved a box of prepackaged meals without reading the label. The faint scent of bacon coming from a half-open package was enough. She tore into it, grabbed several of the bars, and jammed one into her mouth, chewing rapidly.

The more she ate, the hungrier she got. Soon, her throat was begging for water. She opened the cooler behind her, snagged one of the bottled waters, and gulped it down. Excess water ran freely down her white shirt. The thought of wasting a dwindling resource didn't faze her. She drank until the entire bottle was gone and her shirt was drenched.

Sophie coughed and took in a few breaths through her nose before plopping another two bacon bars into her mouth. With every bite, the hunger grew. It seemed insatiable.

A crack rang out in the distance. She froze, a half-eaten bar still lodged in her mouth. Another bang followed a few seconds later, and she spit the chunk of food into an automatic trash dispenser next to the cooler. She tiptoed into the dimly lit mess hall and saw the silhouettes of Bouma and Overton standing with their rifles pointed at the entrance to Biome 4.

"What is it?" she whispered.

Overton ignored her.

Sophie flinched and put on her headset. The banging sound shattered the silence again. "Guess your device didn't work after all," Bouma said.

"Alexia, what are your sensors showing?" Sophie asked.

There was no response, just the sound of static over the airways.

The banging got louder and then subsided. They waited for several agonizing minutes for the sound to return. An eerie silence filled the room. Maybe the device had kicked on after all and confused the Organics. Sophie couldn't be sure and that bothered her. Whatever the case, the sound was gone.

Her stomach growled, reminding her that she was still starving. She glanced over her shoulder at the kitchen. "Do you think it's safe?" she asked.

No response. She whipped her head around to look at the Marines. They were gone.

"Sergeant Overton? Corporal Bouma?" she whispered.

Her eyes darted around the room, searching for them, but the space was empty.

She froze, suddenly feeling completely isolated and alone. Fear gripped her and she wanted to run back to her quarters where Emanuel slept.

Her feet, however, wouldn't budge. In the corner of the chamber, where the passage led to Biome 3, she could see a faint blue glow. She squinted and watched the glow become more intense.

Not again, please not again.

Sophie blinked several times, hoping that the glow was nothing more than an optical illusion and that Overton and Bouma would be back. At this point, she'd be happy to be hallucinating. She closed her eyes and counted to ten.

When she opened them again, she wished she hadn't.

Standing where the Marines had been were dozens of Spiders and three of the Sentinels. They surrounded her on all sides, their heads tilted, studying her.

Scratch. Scrape. Scratch. Scrape.

The Spiders lurched at her, their claws coming within inches of her exposed flesh. She tried to scream, but nothing came out. Her eyes widened as she realized she was paralyzed.

One of the Sentinels slithered forward, flinging metal tables out of its path like a child tossing aside toys. Several of the Spiders screeched in protest, scrambling out of the way.

Sophie's ears throbbed with pain. She closed her eyes again, desperately pleading for the Organics to go away. When she opened them the Sentinel was towering above her, licking its thin black lips with a long, blue tongue. The creature tilted its head as if it were studying her, the pair of reptilianlike eyes blinking rapidly. Then its mouth cracked into what looked like a wicked smile full of jagged black teeth.

Luke had mentioned that some of the Organics were smarter than the others. Was this one of their leaders?

Sophie didn't know. She didn't care. All she could think about was escape. She tried to move but she was still paralyzed, her limbs frozen against her sides. Her eyes were locked with the Sentinel's gaze. And then something took over her mind. Images raced through her subconscious. Hundreds of them. She saw the world from above—first Paris, then New York and Tokyo, and finally Moscow. The cities were filled with thousands of glowing orbs.

New images flooded her mind: long stretches of desert, as far as the eye could see. Speckled throughout were what looked like boats and the bones of some sort of animal.

It only took a second to recognize the skeletal outline was that of a whale. She knew she was looking at what had once been the ocean.

The image disappeared and was replaced by a mountain range. Above the tree line, the rock was dry, void of any ice or snow.

Next she saw dried-up riverbeds and lakes. She saw dying forests with naked branches pointing toward the cloudless sky. The images continued, and she felt tears welling up in her eyes, unable to blink them away.

Why was she seeing these things? Why her? Why now?

The questions were replaced with more images. More death, more emptiness—a world void of life. No humans, no animals, no trees. Nothing.

She screamed inside her mind, and the scenes finally vanished. When she opened her eyes, the Organics were gone. She was back in bed with Emanuel.

He was shaking her violently, whispering so he didn't wake anyone else.

"Sophie, wake up! It's just a dream!"

She blinked and shook her head, rubbing the sleep from her eyes. Her tongue swished around her mouth and came back free of the taste of bacon. The thought of it disgusted her now.

She sat up and embraced Emanuel, silencing him with her grip.

"I saw it. I saw it all," she whispered.

"Saw what?"

"The world, or what the world will look like when the Organics are done with it."

"What do you mean?" Emanuel asked, pulling free of her hug so he could study her face.

"They aren't just after us—they're after the oceans! That's why the temperature is rising outside. They must be slowly draining the seas."

Emanuel reached for his glasses. "The salt must be slowing them down."

"Or the fact that they cover over seventy percent of the Earth's surface."

"Didn't stop them from getting all of the surface freshwater on day one," he replied.

"There isn't enough information to hypothesize. We don't know that they did. And we also don't know how fast they are draining the oceans." Sophie paused and caught his gaze. "All I know is nothing will survive. They won't stop until every ounce of water is gone."

CHAPTER 24

Rays of light danced across the walls of Biome 2. Sophie crouched next to the water, staring into the clear depths and wondering how much was really left outside the walls of the Biosphere.

"Are you ready?" a voice said from behind her.

Sophie didn't budge. The sight of the pond was calming and after the chaos of their short stay in the facility she welcomed the escape.

"Is this really necessary?" she finally said, turning to see Holly in the doorway.

"You know it is. You can't keep going on like this. These dreams are not good for your mental health. You have to address them."

Sophie stood and paced down the metal platform. "All right," she said, studying the young woman's face. Unlike the others, Holly didn't look fatigued. Her eyes were warm, welcoming, still filled with . . .

Hope.

"I have to admit, I'm surprised by how well you're holding up," Sophie said.

Holly smiled. "I'm glad I learned something after accruing that mountain of student loan debt."

"I don't think that it matters much anymore."

"No. No, I suppose you're right. I won't be getting a call if I miss a payment," she said with a laugh. "So, how are you doing?"

Sophie turned back to the pond, clasping her hands behind her back. "I'm okay. Honestly. I mean, for the most part. I've come to accept that everyone beyond these walls I have ever known and loved is dead. All I can do now is try to move on, to take care of those who are left." She watched a ray of light sparkle across the surface of the water. "Especially now that we have the children."

"You're right. There isn't anything we can do for those we have lost. As team lead, you're faced with deciding the best path forward for all of us."

The words echoed in Sophie's ears. She was well aware of her responsibilities, but hearing them from someone other than Emanuel caught her slightly by surprise. "What would you have me do?"

"That's up to you, Sophie. You and only you can make that decision, but just remember, your mental health will affect your decisions, which in turn affect all of us."

Sophie crouched down next to the pool again, peering deep into the clear water. For the first time she caught a glimpse of the bottom of the pond. Even with the state-of-the-art recycling system, they were slowly using up the last known freshwater source.

Fear overwhelmed her, and reality finally set in. Holly was right—as a leader she was going to have to make decisions that affected everyone on her team. And given the dwindling water, she was going to have to make one in the near future. The Biosphere wasn't going to protect them forever.

"There's something I need to do, Holly. Can we continue this later?"

The petite woman sighed but managed a smile. "Sure," she replied. "Just remember what I said."

"That's just it, Holly. You've helped me realize what I need to do." Sophie approached the door to leave but hesitated, catching a glimpse of sadness on Holly's face. "It's going to be okay," Sophie said, embracing Holly before making her way to the command center.

"You must go—"

Sophie paused the video and then replayed it, studying Dr. Hoffman's lips before the image faded and crackled away.

"I'm sorry, Dr. Winston, but with recent events I did not have time to discuss this with you earlier," Alexia said.

Sophie ignored her. "So you think he meant either we must go to *Secundo Casu* or we must go on with the Biosphere mission?"

"Precisely. I ran the possibilities after uploading Dr. Hoffman's personality profile, and these two are the most logical responses."

Sophie sucked in a deep breath and exhaled. She turned to face the others in the control room. Overton, Bouma, and Emanuel stared back at her, waiting for her to lead.

"You guys are a lot of help," she said, managing a smile.

"She's the computer," Bouma said. "If she can't figure it out, how could we?"

"Artificial Intelligence," Alexia corrected.

"Yeah, whatever. Either way, does it really matter what this Dr. Hoffman meant?" Bouma asked.

Overton stood and stretched his legs. "It matters now more than ever. He knew more about these Organics than anyone. If he told us to go somewhere or do something, we'd be fools not to listen." He turned to Sophie, narrowed his eyebrows, and looked her directly in the eye. "So what the hell is *Secundo Casu?*"

Sophie pulled away from Overton's gaze. She paced over to Emanuel, who stood with his back against the doorframe.

"I guess now is as good a time to tell them as any," she said.

Emanuel nodded and stepped forward. "*Secundo Casu* is NTC's prototype ship that was to carry passengers and a crew to Mars to begin colonization. We had been hired as the crew to manage the Biosphere on Mars, hence our mission here."

He paused, seeming to weigh his words. He glanced at Sophie and continued, "Our team was not privy to NTC's time line, nor were we directly involved in the ship's design or construction. What I am about to say is only an assumption."

"Go on, Doctor," Overton said.

Emanuel shot Sophie another nervous glance. "Sophie has been having dreams. Lots of them. Very realistic ones."

"What kind of dreams?" Bouma asked.

"Paranormal dreams," Emanuel replied. He raked his hands through his messy hair. "She dreamed about the Organics before they invaded.

And she was able to describe what the drones looked like long before we actually made contact."

"So what? Luke said thousands of scientists worldwide knew. Maybe your girlfriend was one of 'em." Overton said.

Sophie stepped forward, her face bright red. "I didn't know!"

"With all due respect, Doctor, why should I believe you of all people didn't know about the invasion?" Overton asked.

"If I were you, I would be asking the same question, but all I can tell you is that it was as much of a shock to me as it was to you."

Overton growled. "This is bullshit. You're telling me she dreamed these things up before they invaded? I thought you people were supposed to be scientists!"

The console next to the hub of monitors glowed to life and Alexia's image emerged. "I am capable of answering that question, Sergeant Overton," she said without hesitation.

"Be my guest."

Sophie's ears perked up and she grasped Emanuel's hand. Something told her she wouldn't like what came next; Alexia was far too eager to explain.

"Two months ago you were all required to go through several rounds of physicals and procedures that tested your ability to survive for an extended trip in space. You may remember a specific test, one in which you were given a sedative and put into an MRI machine."

Sophie gripped Emanuel's hand tighter. It was fuzzy, but Sophie could remember the white room and the amber glow of the MRI before she had fallen asleep.

"During this process you were all implanted with a microchip at the base of your spinal cord. It was designed to automatically track brain activity in order to mitigate any mental anguish and high stress accompanying space flight."

"This was done without our consent?" Emanuel shouted.

Overton frowned at him. "Does that surprise you? This is NTC we're talking about."

"However, the microchip Dr. Winston was implanted with also had a secondary function. As team leader, her subconscious was supplied with confidential information NTC had on file about the Organics. Images of the first drone, data revealing what NTC knew about the high-pitched frequencies the aliens use to communicate, and information about their thirst for our resources—for our water."

"Oh my God," Sophie gasped, dropping Emanuel's hand and wrapping her hands around the nape of her neck.

"Dr. Winston, the second function of your microchip was only supposed to be activated if a catastrophic event occurred. Clearly, the chip was flawed and caused you to suffer from recurring nightmares prior to the invasion. I should explain that this device never made it past laboratory testing. The FDA did *not* approve it for human experimentation. NTC, however, felt the importance of the Biosphere mission justified utilizing it."

"Of course they did!" she said, keeping her voice just shy of a scream. "The depths of NTC's manipulation doesn't surprise me. What I want to know is why you didn't share this information earlier."

"The information was stored in a database I did not have access to until Dr. Hoffman's message was delivered. It was then that I was informed of the microchips."

Sophie rolled her eyes. "Figures. Dr. Hoffman kept us all in the dark."

"Dr. Hoffman told you exactly what you needed to hear at the time," Alexia responded calmly.

"Forget Dr. Hoffman. Forget NTC. How do I get it out of me?"

"Dr. Winston, I would strongly suggest keeping it. That chip contains everything NTC knew about the Organics, more than even I know. Besides, without the proper medical tools, the surgical procedure could be dangerous."

"I don't care. Take it out of me and download the information," Sophie insisted.

"I'm afraid that's not possible. We simply don't have the surgical tools here. Besides, it was designed to recognize your DNA. If it is removed, the device will be rendered useless."

Sophie's nostrils flared. "I don't have time for this. I'll dig it out myself if I have to."

Overton blocked her from leaving the room. "Dr. Winston, maybe Alexia is right."

For a second she studied his features—the scar lining his cheek, his bushy blond eyebrows, the stubble on his chin. Then she caught his gaze and held it for several seconds, refusing to back down.

"I'll consider your suggestion," she said, her warm breath brushing over his face. "Now, if you would, I want to check on Owen and Jamie. Holly could use a break, I'm sure."

Overton hesitated but finally withdrew his arm from across the door, allowing Sophie and Emanuel to pass.

"Just when I was starting to like her," Overton said under his breath. "Come on, Bouma, she's not getting off the hook that easily."

Holly watched Owen and Jamie play in the dirt of Biome 1. They chased each other through the trampled remains of a row of cucumber plants. The irrigation poles began showering them with water, prompting cries and shouts of laughter.

She smiled, and for the first time in a week she felt a true sense of happiness flood over her. The resilience of the children in the wake of losing everything and everyone around them amazed her.

For the majority of her career, she had worked with individuals suffering from post-traumatic stress disorder, and while both children seemed to exhibit some traits of PTSD, they were also still behaving like, well, children.

"I'm faster than you!" Jamie shouted, running past Owen and shoving him playfully.

"Nuh-uh!"

The irrigation poles clicked off moments later and the children frowned simultaneously before dragging their dirty feet through the mud. Emanuel had set them to run as little as possible so they didn't waste any water.

"All right, kids, time for lunch," Holly shouted, motioning them toward the metal platform.

"There you are," said a voice from behind her. She turned to see Sophie and Emanuel jogging across the platform.

"What are you guys doing out here?" Sophie said, lowering her voice so the children wouldn't hear.

"Look at that!" Emanuel blurted. "They're destroying the crops. We're going to need every plant we can grow," he said pointing at the leveled row of cucumbers.

"We'll manage, Emanuel. Calm down," Sophie said. She turned back to Holly to reassure her. "It's okay, and that isn't what I wanted to talk to you about, anyway."

"Oh?" Holly replied. They left Emanuel and the kids and walked shoulder to shoulder around the crops.

"Did you know about the implants?" Sophie said quietly.

Holly stopped and squinted. "What implants?"

Sophie studied her face for a second. It was all the time she needed to determine Holly had no idea what she was talking about.

"Come on, I'll tell you on the way back to the mess hall."

Timothy sat alone at one of the metal tables in the cafeteria, attempting to drink through a long straw. "Gah damn it," he mumbled, tossing the cup onto the table. He heard footsteps and managed to wheel himself around to see the entire crew approaching. To the right were Sophie and Emanuel and to the left was the man who had broken his jaw.

Adrenaline shot through him. He clenched his tender jaw and glared at Overton.

Asshole.

"Mr. Roberts, how are you feeling today?" Overton bellowed as he made his way across the mess hall.

Timothy scowled silently.

"Glad to see you're feeling better," Overton said, ignoring the look of almost comical hatred on Timothy's swollen face. "You're just in time for a little discussion about the future of the Biosphere. Take a seat—oh wait, you've already got one."

The sound of rubber wheels squeaking was the only response

Overton got as Timothy wheeled himself away from the awful man's presence.

The sergeant was still chuckling to himself as the two doctors entered the room. "Dr. Rodriguez, now that you and Dr. Winston have had a chance to settle down, maybe you wanna tell me what you're *not* telling me about that ship." Overton took a seat and retrieved his combat knife, twirling it on his fingers.

Emanuel paced over to the table and clasped his hands behind his back. He wrinkled his nose and took a deep breath. "Yes, I believe I probably should," he said, glancing at Sophie for approval.

She nodded, and he continued. "*Secundo Casu* is the most sophisticated ship ever built. Its engines were designed to run off several different fuels, allowing it to travel significant distances without having to refuel. Between jet fuel, solar power, and a new classified nuclear reactor, this ship has the ability to make it to Mars in six months. I don't know much more than that—Sophie could explain it in much more detail—but that isn't what you want to hear anyways. What you want to hear is why I believe this ship is no longer a prototype and is instead prepped and ready for space flight."

Overton stopped twirling his knife and set it on the table. "Go on."

"As I was saying, Sophie had a very specific dream about this ship on Mars, seeing it in action. And after hearing about the implant, I believe she did so for a reason. I believe it means something." Emanuel unclasped his hands and stepped forward, placing them palm-down on the table. Jamie and Owen sat on either side of Holly, and as he caught Owen's eye, the little boy smiled.

The action took Emanuel off guard. He was about to tell the team one of his craziest theories yet, and this child had absolutely no idea what was going on. For a second he wished he was in Owen's place, almost completely oblivious to the threats around him. But he was a scientist. He cleared his throat and continued.

"I believe her dreams mean *Secundo Casu* is ready for space flight and could still be our ticket off this planet. I believe Dr. Hoffman was trying to tell us to go there so we could escape and the human species would survive."

The room erupted into commotion. Timothy began mumbling beneath his breath, and Overton's curses mixed with Bouma's. Emanuel took a step back, amazed at their reaction. To him it didn't sound all that unrealistic, but he was a biologist, not a Marine or a programmer.

"Who would pilot the ship?" Bouma asked.

"There are only eight of us—not exactly enough to repopulate Mars," Overton added.

"You're talking about a prototype, first off. Second, if that ship could make it to Mars, and that's a big if, you still have the problem that it's likely at the NTC Spaceport, over seven hundred miles away from here," Timothy moaned, his voice garbled by his broken jaw. "I know you guys think I'm an idiot, but we wouldn't survive a trip of seven miles, let alone seven hundred."

"Timothy is correct; I put your chances at survival outside the Biosphere at less than 1 percent," Alexia said.

"Enough!" Sophie finally yelled, stepping forward. Silence carpeted the room as all eyes focused on her. She pulled her hair into a ponytail. With a deep breath, she leaned forward, bracing her hands on the metal table in front of Overton. "The Organics are draining the oceans."

"You just figured this out?" Timothy laughed bitterly. "What did you think they were here for?"

Sophie shot him an angry glare. "Do you understand the ramifications of what I just said?"

He shrugged and put an ice pack on his jaw, unable to meet her gaze.

"Do any of you?" she asked.

"We're all dead?" Bouma said.

"Precisely. I don't know how long it will take for them to drain the seas, but judging by how long it took them to suck up all of the surface water, we don't have long. The temperature is already rising."

Holly frowned. "Can't we stay in the Biosphere?"

Emanuel stepped to Sophie's side. "Ever seen the data from Mars? That's what will happen to the Earth. No water equals no life, period. We could stay here, but only until our resources run out."

"What are you suggesting we do?" Bouma asked. "Steal a spaceship and fly it to Mars? This isn't the movies, guys."

Sophie sighed. "We've been through this before. Do we stay, or do we risk going back outside? Knowing what we do about the situation outside, no rational person would risk the trip to *Secundo Casu*. We have food and water resources here that will last us months, if not years, and the solar energy will keep the power running indefinitely. The device we retrieved from Luke's bunker appears to be effective, so . . ." Sophie paused. She studied the small faces of Owen and Jamie. There was no way she would risk taking them outside again. It wasn't an option.

"I see two possibilities. One, we all stay here and focus on surviving, hoping there is some arm of the government, the military, or other, better-equipped survivors left to fight the Organics and prevent them from draining the seas. Or two, Sergeant Overton and I try to get to the ship. If it is spaceworthy, then I'm sure I could figure out a way to run the autopilot system and fly it ourselves."

"Not a chance." Emanuel pounded the table with his fist. "Have you lost your mind? I can't—I won't lose you."

Overton shook his head and stood, sheathing his knife. "I'm not a scientist or a doctor. Hell, I don't even have a college degree. But one thing I'm good at is reading people. From everything you've told me about this Dr. Hoffman, I bet he had a few tricks up his sleeve. Luke's RVM was one. And I'm guessing another one was that ship."

"Sergeant Overton is right," said Sophie. "I believe Dr. Hoffman knew exactly what was coming, and he also knew there would be no stopping it, regardless of how powerful some super-magnet was. I have no doubt Dr. Hoffman had a contingency plan, and I believe that plan was probably *Secundo Casu*."

"So who's to say Dr. Hoffman isn't already sipping fine-ass whiskey in first class on his way to Mars?" Bouma asked. He cracked a grin that suggested he knew he had said something clever.

"The video feed of Dr. Hoffman proves they were caught off guard as much as anyone," Sophie said.

"So where does that leave us?" Holly asked. "Even if you and Sergeant Overton manage to make it to the ship, even if it's operational, what about us?"

Sophie sighed. It was a legitimate question and one she didn't know how to answer.

Think, Sophie.

An image of the RVM they had stolen from Luke popped into her mind and she smiled, snapping her fingers.

"There's got to be a way to re-create or duplicate the technology in the RVM. A way we can leave it here to protect the Biosphere and, at the same time, shield ourselves on our trip to the ship."

Emanuel ran a hand through his hair. "That's a thought. It could work, theoretically."

"Alexia, do you think you can figure it out?"

A blue hologram shot out of the console in the corner of the room and Alexia's hazy figure appeared. "Of course, Dr. Winston. I will get started now."

"You forgot about one key piece to all of this," Bouma said.

Sophie eyed the Marine suspiciously. "What's that, Bouma?"

"Transportation. What will you be using to get there?"

"Ever heard of the electric train beneath the ruins of the Denver Airport?" she asked.

Bouma shook his head.

"Good. That's a promising sign. Most people didn't know about it. There was a secret bunker built under the airport when it was constructed over sixty years ago. The government built something else there—a high-speed electric train that can top three hundred miles per hour. The tunnel extends seven hundred miles to the White Sands Missile Range near Alamogordo, New Mexico. Which, as Timothy already pointed out, is the location of the spaceport and more than likely the location of *Secundo Casu*."

Overton grunted. "Wily old bastard. How much of this do you think Hoffman planned? It seems like everywhere we go, we put our foot in another one of his plans."

"What makes you think that train is still operational?" Bouma asked.

Sophie smiled. "The bunker and train aren't really that different from the Biosphere. They were both built so humanity could survive a postapocalyptic event."

Bouma shook his head. "Doesn't mean they work. We'd be traveling on a gamble."

"Not entirely true," Emanuel added. "I once dated a woman who was stationed at the Denver NTC headquarters. Apparently, the tunnels are still operational."

"And how'd you convince her to tell you that?" Sophie said with a raised brow.

Emanuel looked at the ground and then back at the group. "If we can just reach Denver, I'm sure the train will work too."

"Sounds like a suicide mission," Overton drawled. "Count me in."

CHAPTER 25

Bouma had scooped out the entire contents of the orb in the medical ward. It didn't make much difference; Saafi's body had been liquefied. There wasn't anything recognizable left. Not even his clothes remained.

He sighed, watching as Overton placed the container with Saafi's remains next to a makeshift box containing Private Finley's body.

Sniffles and the occasional whimper echoed off the massive walls of Biome 1 as the team prepared the two men for cremation. Emanuel had suggested their remains be burned, and the ashes used to help fertilize the garden. Considering there was nowhere to actually bury them, Sophie had agreed.

"Would anyone like to say anything?" Sophie asked.

Overton stepped forward. He stared ahead at the remains for several minutes, his back stiff and his posture straight.

"I didn't have the chance to get to know Mr. Yool, but based on what you all said about him, he was a good man." Overton stepped closer to the small container with Saafi's remains. "I promise you one thing, Mr. Yool—your death will not be in vain," he said. Then he turned to Finley's coffin.

"Finley was a good Marine. The best. I was hard on the kid only because I knew it's what he needed to be successful. In the few months he was with my squad, I got to know him as more than just the goofball with jumbo ears—more than the high school wrestler who liked fast cars and country music. Private Finley's life was just beginning, but it was cut short by those monsters. I swear to you, Finley, we'll make 'em pay." Overton ran his hand over the stubble growing on his head. "He was a good kid. A good man."

Overton bowed his head and closed his eyes. If Sophie didn't know better, she'd think he was praying. She gave him a moment and then patted him on the back. "Thank you, Sergeant. Private Finley was a respectful and capable Marine, one we will certainly miss. I did not know him well, but from what I saw he served his country admirably." She paused and looked over at the smaller box that held Saafi's remnants.

"Today we also remember Saafi Yool. He was one of the finest gentlemen I'd ever met. Saafi was a fighter. After he escaped his war-torn homeland of Somalia and made his way to the United States, he obtained an advanced degree in engineering, quickly rising to the top of his field. His life was truly remarkable, and ended too soon."

She stepped aside and slid back into the group. A small hand gripped hers and she looked down to see Owen's wide eyes staring up at her.

"Are they going where my mommy and daddy are?" he asked.

"Yes, honey, they are."

Holly glanced over at her, tears flowing freely down her cheeks. Then she bent down in front of the children and said, "Jamie, Owen, I'm going to tell you something now that may be hard, but you're both brave kids and will understand. Okay?"

The two children looked up at her, their eyes wide and full of innocence.

Holly knew that no matter what she said, the kids would likely not understand what had happened to their parents, Saafi, or Finley. But she was from the school of thought that the best explanation for a child experiencing loss was a simple one.

"Sometimes we have to deal with losing those we love and care about. Now is one of those times," she said. "Your parents, your families, and Mr. Yool and Mr. Finley—they're in a good place now. It's a safe place, a happy place. They can't be with you right now, but you always have your memories." Sophie looked over at her and offered a short reassuring nod, but Holly quickly saw a sad little frown dawn across Owen's face.

"They're in heaven with my grandma and grandpa and Sam," he said, as if repeating something he'd been told before.

Jamie looked down at the ground and began to whimper. "I wanna see my mom and dad."

Holly crouched to the girl's level and put two fingers under her chin, tilting her face up so she could look at her.

"Your parents would want you to be here now, Jamie. They'd want you to live your life."

Jamie pulled away. "But I want to be with them now!" she cried.

Holly pulled Jamie to her, letting the little girl cry into her side.

Overton lit a match and placed it under the makeshift caskets. The boxes burst into flames, the scent of gasoline filling the room.

Deep within the computer system, Alexia watched with her artificial lenses, controlling the air ducts so the smoke was filtered and sucked away. A sensor went off and she checked a line of data running across her display.

The team's survival rate had been updated earlier, and somehow she had managed to overlook it. With the recent losses of Mr. Yool and Private Finley, the group's chances of survival had decreased to 15 percent.

Emanuel waded through the lush crops in the garden biome. The scent of ripe tomatoes filled his nostrils, and for the first time he felt like he was actually doing what he had been hired to do.

He checked one of the cornstalks, which were already over three and a half feet tall. Peeling back the tassel, he examined the ear. Several kernels were turning brown. He had foreseen this and grabbed his tablet. With the swipe of his finger he pulled up a list of possible maize diseases that could have this effect. He selected a chemical that would control the blight and made a note to add it to the irrigation supply for this row.

Next on his tour of the crops were the cucumbers. He paused to stare at the area where just a few days earlier they had laid Finley and Saafi to rest. The vines were out of control and jutting out in all directions. He sighed and made note of another chemical he would need.

Overall, the garden was doing well. Even with the introduction of foreign toxins, he would be able to salvage at least 80 percent of the harvest. The food would last them months, but eventually it would run out.

The thought was sobering, but he pushed on. All that mattered now was survival. If what Sophie had dreamed was true, then they were all on borrowed time anyway.

He pushed the thoughts from his mind and made his way past the control room, where Timothy sat in front of one of the monitors playing a game of solitaire to keep his mind occupied. Emanuel chuckled under his breath and continued to the mess hall. Holly was teaching Jamie and Owen basic math on a tablet. Alexia's hologram watched from the console behind them, occasionally offering suggestions or corrections to Holly's instruction.

In the med ward, Sophie and Overton were hard at work retrieving supplies for the anti-Organic shield generator. He paused to watch them strip the panels of the cryo chambers so they could get at the guts of the machine. Alexia had provided them a list of all the items they would need to create a second RVM similar to the one Luke had built. They'd been on a scavenger hunt all over the Biosphere.

"Need something?" Bouma asked from the corner of the room. He sat patiently on a bench, playing on his tablet while waiting to be summoned for a task.

"Just came to get a chemical for Biome 1," Emanuel said.

Bouma nodded and returned to the blue glow of his device.

A few hours later, Overton was in possession of a hunk of metal that looked like a greasy turtle shell. The veins in his forearms bulged as he dropped it on one of the tables in the mess hall where the team had gathered.

Sophie followed him, a wide smile on her face. "It's done," she said. "Alexia has already confirmed it works. The only thing we need now is a power source to keep it running on the trip to the Denver Airport."

"That's not the only thing, Dr. Winston," Overton said, stretching his sore arms. Pain raced down his shoulder, which still hadn't healed completely.

"Transportation to the airport?" Sophie asked, beaming. "Don't worry, I'm already ahead of you on that."

"What's your plan, Doc?"

Sophie strolled over to the table, staring at the device. She knew they needed something with an energy source powerful enough to sustain it for the duration of the trip. There was one Humvee left on the tarmac, but unless they could find a way to hook it up to the engine without draining juice from the rest of the vehicle, it probably wouldn't work.

Ideas raced through her head. Even with a cloudless sky, solar power wouldn't be potent enough. It would also fail as soon as they entered the tunnels under the airport.

She frowned and glanced over at the console where Alexia's hologram was glowing brightly. "Alexia, what's the most powerful energy source in the Biosphere?"

"That would be my fuel source, Dr. Winston."

"Really? Is it portable?"

"Protocol is to stay with the facility, but I was designed to travel in cases of emergency."

"I'd consider this an emergency," Overton chuckled.

A grin streaked across Sophie's face. "How would you feel about a road trip?"

"That would be acceptable," said Alexia.

"Corporal Bouma, you'll be in charge of security, and Emanuel will assist with all Biosphere operations while we're gone. Holly, look after the children, and . . ." Sophie paused. "Look after Timothy, too."

The man scowled from his wheelchair, holding an ice pack tightly to his jaw. "Good luck," he mumbled.

Sophie decided to assume he was being sincere for once and thanked him. She turned back to Alexia's hologram. "We'll leave as soon as it gets dark. In the meantime, I'm going to need your assistance with removing your fuel cell and hooking it up to the device."

Alexia smiled for the first time in her existence. It was something she had been saving for the right time, a human reaction she had studied for years. She considered the moment a perfect time to test her hypothesis.

It worked; Sophie returned the smile before pacing over to the children, mussing Owen's hair with a swift pat on his head. For less than a millisecond Alexia felt a strange reaction trickle through her system.

She scanned the constant line of data running across her display. The code was odd, unlike anything she had seen before. It wasn't full of symbols and numbers—it was a statement that repeatedly scrolled across the bottom of her consciousness:

You are feeling happiness. You are feeling happiness. You are feeling happiness.

She was, by every indication, evolving.

CHAPTER 26

EMANUEL leaned over in the cramped bed and brushed his fingers across Sophie's face, catching her gaze. "I really wish you would reconsider this."

"No," she said, pulling away.

Her monosyllabic response took Emanuel by surprise. He was used to her drawn-out sentences, often finding himself listening rather than contributing to their "discussions."

With a sudden burst of confidence he wrapped his arms around her and leaned in to kiss her. Sophie closed her eyes and surrendered to the feelings racing through her body. She needed a break from reality—a break from the truth of what the world had become. A break from thoughts of death and loss.

"I have to go. You know I do," she said between kisses. "If *Secundo Casu* is operational, then it may be humanity's only hope."

"That's my girl," he said. Emanuel pulled her closer, kissing her deeper. "You always have to be everything to everyone," he whispered, pausing to take a breath. "But what about me? What about us?"

There was that word again. It was more than just a pronoun. To Emanuel, it meant a future together—a future she'd denied him before. Apparently, it had taken the end of the world to make her reconsider.

"There will always be an *us*," she said, climbing on top of him and unfastening her bra. "There always has been, and there always will be, no matter what happens."

Emanuel felt a tingle race down his legs. He brushed a strand of blond hair from Sophie's face and held her gaze for several seconds. "You better fucking come back to me," he said.

"We don't have long," she said, pulling her shirt over her head.

Emanuel didn't respond. He knew the reality of the situation. This could very well be the last time he ever felt her touch. He pulled her down on top of him, crushing their bodies together. If this was to be the last time they ever made love, he wanted it to be the best time, too.

Alexia's voice erupted over the intercom. "Sergeant Overton has ordered all hands to Biome 4."

"No, no, no!" Emanuel cried as Sophie rolled off of him and pulled her shirt back on. He grabbed her hand and said, "I love you."

Sophie hesitated. She had a responsibility to her team, but a few more seconds wasn't going to matter. She leaned down and kissed him. "I love you too, Emanuel, and I *will* return to you."

He smiled grimly, letting go of her hand. Deep down he wanted to believe her, but he was a scientist. Even with Sergeant Overton's protection, he knew the chances of their return were limited.

"Well, you heard her. Are you going to see me off or what?"

He couldn't help but smile. No matter what adversity she faced—no matter what the odds of success—she gave 100 percent. It was what made her a leader, and it was, he hoped, the one thing that would help her stay alive on her mission to *Secundo Casu*.

The blast doors hissed open. A wave of adrenaline emptied into Sophie's system as the dark summer night stretched out before her. Wiped clean of clouds, the sky had become an endless blanket of sparkling stars. In a way, it reminded her of what she had seen in Colorado Springs that first, horrible night, with the countless orbs glowing throughout the city.

"Let's move," Overton's voice said over the com.

Sophie took off in a sprint toward the outline of a single Humvee at the edge of the tarmac. She blinked and her night vision powered on, spreading its eerie green over her display. A few paces behind her, Overton struggled. The metal device clanged loudly on his armored back.

"This thing better fucking work. It weighs a ton," he grunted.

"It is functioning at 100 percent," Alexia's voice said over the com.

They had inserted her fuel cell into a small interface at the bottom of the RVM and uploaded her consciousness so she could connect to the wireless links in their helmet. While she didn't have access to her mainframe, she could still operate at almost full capacity. Sophie had to marvel at NTC's ingenuity.

Overton halted when he got to the Humvee, scanning the tarmac for any heat signatures before opening the door. "Gimme a hand with this, Doc."

Sophie unclipped the cords holding the second and more powerful RVM, and he heaved it onto the seat of the vehicle.

"I'm driving," he said, jumping into the front seat.

Sophie took one last look at the blast doors and climbed into the Humvee. "Good-bye," she said under her breath as Overton punched the gas.

Sophie stared out the window, her eyes fixed on a crater to the east. She could see the outlines of dozens of boats lying sideways in the dirt of what had been a lake bottom weeks before. The sight disappeared as the truck raced on, zipping between the empty vehicles lining I-25.

"Where are all the orbs?" Overton asked.

"I was just wondering the same thing. My guess is the Organics have already processed them."

Sophie knew that the skin sacks of the deceased were probably littered across the highway, and was grateful she couldn't see them through the darkness. In a way it was a relief, knowing the Organics had already moved on to a different location.

She turned back to the window and watched the dry landscape pass by. The temperature on her HUD read ninety degrees. It was unseasonably high, which could only mean one thing—the Organics were in fact draining the oceans at an alarming rate. There was no way to know how much longer the Earth had left. All she could do was move forward and try to survive.

A deafening boom echoed through the night. She froze, too petrified to look out the rear window, but the blue glow racing toward them was impossible to ignore.

Sure enough, the outline of a drone appeared behind them. In seconds it had reached the Humvee and slowed effortlessly to match the truck's speed.

"I thought this fucking thing was supposed to keep them away!" Overton shouted.

Sophie clenched her pistol and sank in her seat, as if she could hide from the aliens by making herself smaller.

"Dr. Winston, check the machine!"

Alexia's voice broke over the channel. "The RVM is operating at 100 percent efficiency. The Organics must be drawn to our movement. If we—"

Overton threw on the brakes before Alexia could finish her statement. The smell of burning rubber quickly filtered through their helmets.

"Quiet," Sophie whispered, bringing a single finger to her helmet where her lips would be.

The drone hovered over the truck. The blue sides pulsated and rippled. Inside, a bright glow throbbed and the belly of the craft opened, spreading a radiant blue light over the truck.

Sophie cringed, holding her breath. It was scanning them. Days before, during their first ill-fated trip outside, the drone had used a beam to not only disable the electronics of the truck but to capture Saafi and Emanuel. This time was different; the drone kept scanning them, over and over again. It seemed almost confused.

Just when she thought she couldn't hold her breath any longer, the light vanished and an explosion from the rear of the ship ripped through the night. Sophie gripped the outside of her helmet, her ears pounding with pain. She twisted just in time to watch the craft disappear over a ridgeline.

"Fuck, that was close. I thought we were toast! Guess that thing works after all," Overton said with a nervous chuckle. His hands loosened their grip on the steering wheel, and he scanned the skyline several times before twisting the key in the ignition. The engine roared to life, and he slowly pressed down on the gas.

"Fifteen minutes and we'll be at the edge of I-25, where the Wastelands begin. The remains of Denver aren't far after that," he said. "Better check our nutrition before we get into the dead zone."

Sophie unfastened her helmet. She grabbed a water bottle from her duffel bag and forced down several gulps. Feeling around in the bag, she retrieved two energy bars and tore them open. She chewed and listened to the reassuring groan of the diesel engine, and started to relax.

She closed her eyes, sinking into the seat. An image of Jamie and Owen sitting next to Holly at the mess hall table crept into her thoughts. If the children could survive the Organics without weapons, food, or a super-magnet, then surely she stood a chance.

Crumpling the wrapper into a ball, she threw it back into the bag and looked at the RVM one more time. The hunk of metal glistened in the dim light. It was hard to imagine that the box not only housed the smartest artificial intelligence on the planet, but also harnessed an electromagnetic wave that could confuse alien invaders. Science never ceased to amaze her; even when all seemed lost, it had a way of giving her hope.

The silhouette of Denver's destroyed skyline appeared in the distance, the once great skyscrapers nothing more than artifacts from a dead civilization, like the Great Wall of China or the pyramids in Egypt.

Sophie thought of the young pilot who had flown her to the Biosphere just weeks before. He had mentioned his girlfriend's family was from Denver. She hoped he had somehow managed to escape from the Organics, but she didn't really believe it. With a lurch, Sophie realized that she'd never bothered to learn the pilot's name.

She pushed the concern from her mind, squeezing her eyebrows together and blinking. The optics built into her display enhanced, allowing her to scan the interstate for any signs of life. Deep down she knew there wouldn't be any. The city had been evacuated years before, when the edge of the CME had torched the city and turned it into a radioactive night-light.

The emptiness was eerie, but oddly soothing at the same time. Strategically, the location worked out in their favor. Without human life to prey upon, the Organics would have no reason to be anywhere near the city. And with the surface water already gone, Sophie figured they wouldn't run into any further resistance until they got to the White Sands Missile Range.

Ruined buildings and the abandoned cars of people who had tried to escape the doomed city filled her display. The scene reminded her of an old postapocalyptic movie poster she'd had hanging in her college dorm room—a scene she never thought she'd see with her own eyes.

In the distance the triangular rooftops of the airport emerged. There were only a few of the pyramids left fully intact, but as they approached it was clear the architects had designed the roof to look like the Rocky Mountains.

Overton slowed the vehicle and maneuvered around the dozens of metal hangars lining the tarmac. "How are we going to find the entrance to this underground bunker?"

"I'm trying to remember what my contact at NTC told me, but it's . . . hazy."

Overton eased the vehicle to a stop and tilted his head so he could look directly at her. "You're fucking telling me you don't have the slightest idea where we're going? You think you coulda mentioned this, I dunno, *before* we left the Biosphere?"

"You're starting to sound like Timothy. Don't worry; it'll come back to me. Just drive," she said.

She watched row after row of hangars pass as they continued down the tarmac at a crawl. All she could recall was the NTC staffer telling her the main entrance to the bunker was under a hangar. Unfortunately, there were a lot of them to choose from.

Look for the wings.

The staffer's words popped into her mind. "Look for the old air force symbol," she told Overton. "The one from before the government gave control of its air defenses to NTC."

"Okay . . ." Overton punched the gas and watched the metal buildings zip by. He knew the hangar would not be with the civilian buildings.

The military always kept its facilities separate. He turned the steering wheel hard to the right and raced down the tarmac toward a pair of buildings in the distance.

"Where are you going? You're heading away from the airport!"

They raced past a bullet-riddled white sign with the faded image of wings etched into the middle. She watched the sign disappear in the side mirror. "How did you know?"

"Because I'm a soldier, and I know how other soldiers think," he said with a grin.

The doors to the first hangar were cracked open, revealing the guts of a facility that had been used to house weapons at some point. Overton recognized the outlines of a forklift and several other pieces of machinery used to cart large missiles before they were loaded onto aircraft. He dipped the barrel of his rifle into the warehouse before slipping through the opening. Ancient crates and metal boxes littered the dusty concrete floor. Several dents from the colossal dust storms peppered the walls of the hangar.

This was not the type of place he imagined the military would have housed an underground bunker, but then again, the frail walls could have been built to deceive anyone looking for such a facility.

He finished his recon and marched back to the truck, tapping Sophie on the shoulder and jerking his head toward the hangar. She nodded and followed him. The doors to the second hangar were sealed shut, and the handle to a side entrance was locked. He cursed under his breath and threw the strap of his rifle around his back. Taking one knee, he removed his combat knife and unscrewed the bottom of the handle. Inside were several lock-picking tools. His squad had teased him on more than one occasion for carrying them, but this wasn't the first time they had come in handy.

With a click, the door unlocked. He swung it open cautiously, crouch-walking behind the safety of the thick metal. Inside were more crates and boxes. The hull of a rusted tractor sat in the corner of the room, half-draped in a tarp. At first glance there was no evidence of an entrance to the bunker. Frustrated, he broke radio silence. "Advance."

Sophie emerged with her pistol drawn. Her helmet darted back and forth as she scanned the room.

"I don't see shit to indicate a bunker," he whispered.

"Alexia, are you able to scan the facility?" Sophie asked.

"Already completed, Dr. Winston. Check the east corner of the room. A preliminary scan indicates there is something covering the entrance."

"Would have been nice to know before I stuck my neck in here," Overton growled.

Sophie smiled and patted Overton on his armored shoulder. She paced toward the tractor, and with his help they pushed it forward. Underneath was a circular door.

He could hardly believe it. Without hesitation, he squatted and wiped off the surface, revealing the etched letters *NSA*.

"National Security Agency," he said, shaking his head.

"It was basically the intelligence branch of NTC before it became, well, NTC," Sophie said, joining him on the floor.

"Go back to the truck and get the device. I'll try to get this thing open," he said, gripping the handle and heaving with his back. He pulled harder and felt the cut on his shoulder tighten.

"Fuck. On second thought, help me with this first," he said. "On three. One. Two. Three!"

They twisted the circular handle, and the ancient door clicked open, revealing a thin sliver of red light.

"I'll be damned," he said, peeking into the tunnel. "The lights are still on after all these years."

Sophie shrugged. "You need to start listening to me more often."

"I will take that under consideration, Dr. Winston. In the meantime, how about you retrieve the RVM?"

"Yes, sir," she replied with a salute that was only half ironic.

She jogged back to the truck, satisfied with their find. They were one step closer to their objective—one step closer to seeing if Dr. Hoffman had indeed wanted them to proceed to the ship.

The glow of the stars filled her display as she slipped back outside, but another glow also illuminated the night. Her heart stopped. A hundred yards away were a dozen Spiders surrounding the Humvee. Their heads tilted simultaneously and a hundred eyes studied her.

"Spiders!" she screamed into her com, backing straight into the metal wall. Fumbling for her pistol, she tripped and fell onto the concrete. The pistol went flying and landed several feet away.

Scratch. Scrape. Scratch. Scrape.

The Spiders skittered across the concrete tarmac. She hesitated, calculating the odds of reaching the pistol before they reached her, and then scrambled back into the hangar on all fours. She slammed the door shut and locked it.

Overton darted over to her and leveled his rifle at the wall. A claw punched through the metal like a knife cutting a piece of bread. Dozens more followed, tearing foot-long gaps in the door.

"We have to get to the train! This isn't going to hold them for long," Overton shouted.

Sophie tried to follow behind him, watching in horror as the Spiders tore through the wall. "But we need the RVM. We need Alexia."

He grunted, firing off a volley of plasma rounds through one of the openings. A shriek followed as the rounds tore into one of the Spider's shields.

Overton looked down at the single electromagnetic concussion grenade he had taken from Bouma. He didn't want to use it yet, not this early in the mission, but he didn't have a choice. If he waited, they might be dead before he had another opportunity.

"Get to the train. I'll get the device," he yelled, firing off another dozen rounds.

Sophie hesitated.

"I said go!"

She nodded and disappeared into the glow of red light spilling out of the tunnel's entrance. Overton watched her go and then returned his attention to the wall. The scraping sound of the claws echoed in his helmet. The noise prompted a steady flow of adrenaline to pump into his veins. It was all he needed for his training to kick back in.

Without further thought, he unclipped the grenade, removed the pin, and dropped it through one of the openings in the metal. It dropped with a hollow click and rolled a few feet before detonating. He shut off his HUD with a blink and closed his eyes to prepare for the blast. The pulse wave ripped across the tarmac, penetrating the creature's defenses. Through the opening, Overton watched the blue glow of their shields pulsate and fail.

One swift kick from his boot sent the door flying off its hinges. It slid across the tarmac, knocking three of the Spiders down. He pulled his .45 from his holster and smiled.

"Time to die, you little bastards!"

He strode out of the hangar with his pistol in one hand and his rifle in the other. The first shots sent two of the Spiders spinning into the night. Another three advanced, and Overton squeezed the triggers again. Two heads and a torso exploded, showering him in blue goo.

High-pitched screams ripped through the night, but he pushed forward unfazed. He fired his rifle at another two monsters still circling the Humvee and turned to finish off three more advancing toward him.

The click of a dry magazine sounded, somehow louder to Overton's ears than the horrifying screams. He tossed the rifle aside and took one knee, aiming the pistol at the remaining two Spiders. Instead of advancing, they circled him, their claws scraping the ground.

Scratch. Scrape. Scratch. Scrape.

He closed an eye and aimed, but resisted the urge. Why weren't they attacking? Was there something they knew that he didn't? Something he couldn't see? It was almost like the fuckers were taunting him.

"Fuck it," he said and squeezed the trigger. The two bullets whizzed out of the chamber, down the barrel, and into the heads of both Spiders.

Pop.

They exploded like water balloons, their blue blood fountaining into the air. Overton surveyed the gruesome scene. Several of the creatures' limbs twitched on the ground, their claws still scraping the ground harmlessly.

Scratch. Scrape. Scratch. Scrape.

He fired off the remaining rounds in his pistol just to silence them, then glanced over his shoulder at the hangar to gauge the distance he'd have to haul the damned RVM. The spiked, humanoid head of a Sentinel stared back at him, its reptilian eyes blinking rapidly.

"You have to be shitting me!"

He scrambled to reload his weapon as the monster slithered forward with its massive tail dragging across the concrete. The thing grabbed him before he had time to retrieve a single bullet. It wrapped one arm around Overton and heaved him into the air, bringing him within inches of its face.

"You are one ugly bastard," he muttered, preparing for the same fate as Finley. He refused to close his eyes. Instead he squinted, studying the alien.

It looked back at him quizzically, tilting its head to one side like it was trying to comprehend something beyond its intelligence. Overton was reminded of a dog he'd had when he was a kid.

That's when it hit him. The Spiders, the Worms, and the Sentinels—they weren't intelligent creatures. There was no way these things had traveled trillions of miles to pillage Earth of its natural resources.

Luke had been right. These creatures were nothing more than foot soldiers in an army controlled by a life-form he hadn't yet met. Overton let out a muffled laugh; he was about to be liquefied by the alien equivalent of a rottweiler. He faced his fate like a Marine—with his eyes open.

Crack, crack.

The creature's head exploded into pieces, speckling his visor with chunks of blue skin and meat. Overton's mind hardly had time to register the sound of gunfire. He hit the ground with a thud, still wrapped in the creature's limp arm.

Crawling out from under the heavy limb, he pulled himself up and wiped the goo off his visor. Standing twenty feet away was Sophie, still gripping the pulse pistol tightly in her shaking hands. Overton considered yelling at her for taking the risky shot, but changed his mind. The doc didn't have much sense when it came to keeping her ass safe, but she had moxie. Instead he scanned the area for more contacts. His HUD revealed no heat signatures.

He hunched over to pick up his rifle and strolled over to her at a leisurely pace. "Guess the device doesn't work after all," he said.

"Not necessarily. They didn't attack until they saw us. I believe they also pick up on movement. When you stopped the Humvee, the drone disappeared. The device appears to distract and confuse them, but it only works if we aren't moving," she said, her hands shaking. "You know, I did just save your life. Some sort of thank-you wouldn't be out of order."

"Thanks, Doc," he said sincerely, placing his hand over hers and slowly forcing her to lower the pistol.

"N-no problem," she stuttered.

"Where did you learn to shoot?" he asked.

"My dad taught me when I was a kid," she said. "He, uh, liked to take me to the . . . gun range."

Overton ignored the obvious lie. "I thought I ordered you into the tunnel."

"You did, but when I got there I realized I'd lost my gun. There was no way in hell I was going down there without a weapon."

Overton cracked a grin and chuckled. "You continue to impress me, Doc."

"Call me Sophie."

With a nod Overton said, "All right, Sophie. Now let's get the RVM and Alexia. We have a train to catch."

CHAPTER 27

JAMIE stood on the metal bench next to Holly, attempting to braid the psychologist's blond hair. "Why did the monsters come?" Jamie asked, so softly that Holly almost didn't hear her.

Owen, leaning against Holly's side, answered, "My dad said that there's no such thing as monsters."

"Your dad was right, Owen. There is no such thing as monsters. The things outside are just animals, but from another planet."

"Animals? Like cows?" Jamie asked, her eyes wide and full of curiosity.

"Sort of like cows," Holly agreed.

"Cows that want to eat us?" Owen said.

Holly bit her lip and scooted forward, searching for some way to salvage the explanation. "Well, we eat cows, and cows eat grass . . ."

"I'm hungry," Jamie said abruptly, changing the subject as only a child could. She jumped off the metal bench and clutched her stomach.

"What would you like to eat?" Holly asked.

"Ice cream," Owen said.

"And cookies!" Jamie added.

Holly laughed. "Let's see what we have in the kitchen, shall we?"

Both children hurried through the mess hall toward the kitchen. Jamie hummed a song along the way, and Owen dragged his filthy blanket on the floor. Holly marveled at their resilience. Just days ago they had both lost their whole worlds. Yet after hours of counseling, it turned out all Holly had to do was mention the word "cookie" to get them to smile.

Pots and pans clattered as Timothy poked through the cabinets in the kitchen. Holly paused to study him. His behavior was becoming increasingly erratic. It was really too bad she couldn't simply give him a cookie to calm him down, too, but she could always slip a Xanax in his water. It was a compelling thought.

"He's a real piece of work, isn't he?"

Holly smiled, seeing Bouma standing in the shadows of the hall-way leading to the personnel quarters. In the dim light he looked stoic, almost like a statue. With his chiseled jawline and short, cropped hair he was the stereotypical Marine, and in a way, kind of good-looking. Besides, it wasn't like there was a huge male popula-tion left.

The thought was selfish. She had two children to look after. And one adult who acted like a child. She watched Jamie and Owen tear into a freeze-dried packet while Timothy glared at both of them.

"How are you doing, Holly?" Bouma said. He moved closer to her, his eyes darting back and forth from her to Timothy. He had been watching the man closely, concerned that he would try something stu-pid with Overton and Sophie gone.

"Good."

"Okay, good," the Marine said awkwardly. He'd never been great with women, but he knew the short answer meant she didn't want to talk. Turning to leave he felt a hand on his shoulder.

"Wait," Holly said.

Bouma held his breath and spun to face her.

"If you ever want to talk, I'm here for you, just as much as I am for my original team," she said.

"When do the kids go to bed?"

"I'll put them down after dinner tonight."

"Meet me in Biome 1?"

Holly smiled. A walk through the gardens sounded exactly like what she needed.

"It's a date," she said. She stiffened, realizing that he might take her at her word. "I mean, um, I'll be there."

Bouma smiled, trying to hide his crooked teeth. "See you then."

The blank white walls of the medical ward kept Emanuel at ease, but they also made him drowsy. Sleep had become elusive ever since Sophie had left. He had kept himself occupied by turning a section of the medical ward into a laboratory, where he had begun dissecting the remains of one of the Spiders. He'd performed countless necropsies on animals in his career, but this was by far the most intriguing, and also the most risky. Who knew what unfamiliar contagions or viruses the aliens were carrying? Alexia had left a subset of her personality with the biosphere to monitor its conditions, and Emanuel had put her on standby to run constant scans for potentially harmful foreign substances before he was exposed.

Emanuel finished suiting up by covering the last of his bare skin with a pair of plastic gloves. The Biosphere had not come equipped with hazmat suits, so he had improvised and used one of the NTC suits he'd found in the decontamination chamber. Hopefully that would be enough.

He peeled back a layer of the Spider's translucent skin with a scalpel, clamping it open. Then, with an artist's precision, he used a laser to cut a tiny slit in one of the blue veins running the length of the creature's dismembered torso.

Unfortunately, the rounds from the pulse rifles had made his work very difficult. The Organics' defenses were clearly advanced, with their shields and supersonic shrieks, but without these weapons they were surprisingly fragile. Like jellyfish washed up on the beach, their skin and insides just seemed to melt away.

The specimen in front of him was the most intact he had been able to find. With half a head, a full torso, and two of six legs remaining, it was plenty for him to work with.

As he took a sample of the fluid from the vein, one of the creature's eyeballs popped out of its socket and rolled across the table.

Emanuel couldn't help but chuckle under his breath; there was something almost slapstick about the moment. The sight of gore had never bothered him. And even if it had, he wouldn't let it stop him from performing the necropsy. After all, it wasn't every day a brand-new alien species showed up.

It was delicate work, yielding more questions than answers. For example: How did the Spiders' defenses work? He saw no indication of an energy source, nor any technology that would create their shields. In fact, he didn't see a single hint of advanced biological functions, which meant they were more than likely just the grunts, conscripted to collect water and resources for their more intelligent commanders.

The thought made him nervous. He had only begun to scratch the surface of the aliens' chemistry and composition. Their fragile bodies weren't what scared him, though—it was the fact that he still wasn't sure who or what was giving them orders. Without specimens of the Sentinels or the wormlike creatures that Overton had described, Emanuel had no way to determine which, if any, was the dominant life-form. It was more likely that they hadn't even seen the superior Organics yet.

And why would they have? If these aliens had the ability to travel across the vast distances of space, why would they risk harm by showing themselves?

Emanuel suddenly felt weary. Humans were never much of a threat to the Organics in the first place. If anything, humans had been a threat to themselves. After all, that's why he was standing in a biosphere designed to help mankind venture into space, the last place they hadn't destroyed.

He peeled back another layer of veins and pushed the questions from his mind. Focusing on his work was the only thing that calmed him. It was also the only thing that helped prevent his thoughts from turning to Sophie. He fumbled with the scalpel and tore several of the veins open. Blood splattered onto his faceplate.

"Shit," he said under his breath. "Alexia, are you seeing anything worrying?"

"Dr. Rodriguez, my scans aren't picking up anything that registers in my database as toxic. However, there are several elements that are unidentified and therefore I can't advise on their effect on human biology."

Emanuel watched the blue liquid trickle down the glass protecting his face. He could no longer feel his heart beating, or the air coming through his nostrils. The sight of the alien blood so close had paralyzed him with fear. "Dr. Rodriguez, is something wrong?" Alexia said.

He shook his head. "Well, I think it just sank in that I'm dissecting an alien life-form, but I'm fine."

Alexia did not respond, and Emanuel wiped the mess off his face guard. Then he snapped his gloves tightly around his wrists. He compartmentalized the fear by reassuring himself that his work was extremely important to the future of the human race.

He retrieved a vial of the Spider's blood and used a pipette to transfer a sample under the electron microscope. He magnified down to a single cell, moving from one cell to the next.

Hours of studying the sample resulted in little new information. He already knew the blood contained mostly water, but it was the other elements that interested him.

Resisting the urge to remove his glasses and rub his tired eyes, he instead sent the data to Alexia. "Let me know if you see anything I'm missing here," he said, stretching his back and letting out a groan.

Before he had a chance to straighten his spine, Alexia emerged on the console next to him. His sight was hazy from staring into the microscope for so long, but he could have sworn he saw excitement on her face.

"Dr. Rodriguez. This sample of Organic blood does contain approximately 80.43 percent H_2O. However, the other 19.57 percent consists of a substance very similar to plasma. I'm still breaking the data down, but it appears the blood has an electronic component, which likely has something to do with their defenses."

Emanuel smiled. He hadn't wanted to admit it before, but he was really starting to enjoy having Alexia around.

He moved to another station and flicked the display of the monitor. "Fascinating. Electrovalent blood," he mumbled, scanning the data again to make sure he was reading it correctly. It was shocking, but at the same time it made sense. The shields were likely powered by the creatures' blood. When they were feeding, their systems must shut down, and in turn lower their defenses.

The revelation made his heart beat rapidly in his chest. If his theory was correct, then he had just found the Organics' biggest weakness.

A strange, metallic rustling sound rang out in the ventilation above. The noise startled him, and he quickly forgot about the implications of his findings. He froze, listening intently.

Silence.

Emanuel was just about to shrug off the noise and return to his work when he heard the rustling again. It was growing more pronounced, as if something was moving through the ductwork.

He grabbed the scalpel and edged toward the door. Just before he reached the sliding glass panel, he recognized the sound.

Scratch, scrape, scratch, scrape.

Timothy forced an ice pack against his jaw. His face throbbed. The painkillers had worn off. A broken jaw wasn't something that just healed overnight, even with the incredible advances in modern medicine. It would take another week before the bones would be completely repaired and the pain subsided.

A crack in his coffee cup reminded him of the scar on Overton's face. The bastard had given him a scar, too. He grimaced and probed the tender spot where the Marine's fist had made contact. The scar was only an inch long, but it would be a constant reminder of his hatred for the macho Marine.

Timothy had hated men like Overton his entire life. They had bullied him as a child and bullied him as an adult. But he would have his revenge somehow, presuming the man made it back to the Biosphere alive.

He pushed the anger aside and swiped one of the monitors with his index finger. Several images of the Organics appeared, screenshots captured by the security cameras before the power was cut. Timothy grabbed the mug and took a sip of cold water, savoring it as it ran down his throat. There was a time when he'd have preferred some radioactive-colored, over-caffeinated soda. It was hard to imagine that something as simple as water would be a luxury—something they would have to ration.

The world had changed dramatically. Things he had once taken for granted had become extinct overnight. No more fast food. No more sci-fi movies on TV. No more Internet porn. Timothy wasn't sure he wanted to keep going in a world like that. There was no way to determine how much was left outside, or if there were any survivors who could get the grids running again.

The world was no longer the safe and convenient place he had grown to know and love. He would never be able to FaceTime with his friends on his fancy Apple sunglasses or blog his research to thousands of followers. He realized with a sickening lurch that his entire online gaming guild was probably dead. They wouldn't be fighting dragons together anymore. No, this time the monsters were real, and it looked like they were headed for a total wipe. Game over.

Timothy took another sip of water and focused on the images of the Spiders crawling across the screen. The first picture showed a dozen of the creatures entering the facility. The next showed the same group climbing into an air duct in the briefing room outside the Biosphere. It was when they got inside the facility that things got interesting.

Ten of the Spiders dropped into Biome 4, where they branched off into two groups. The remaining two Spiders never reappeared after entering the ducts from the briefing room.

He scanned the images again, thumbing to the last picture taken before the power had gone out. The other two creatures were definitely absent.

Switching to video feed, he watched the scenes again, tracking the Spiders from the tunnel all the way to Biome 4, where they split up and disappeared. It was like the Spiders had simply vanished.

His stomach growled, reminding him it was time for his lunch ration. He stood, stumbling slightly as blood rushed to his head. It was his first day walking without any sort of assistance, and he was still getting used to it. Fumbling with his chair, he pushed it aside and slipped through the automatic door into the dimly lit hallway.

Somewhere behind him, a faint, metallic scratch tickled the very edge of his hearing. He halted, straining his ears to make out the noise, but it disappeared as quickly as it had emerged. With a shrug he continued down the passage to the mess hall. He could see Holly and the children were already there, no doubt scarfing down the last of the mac and cheese.

Another growl from his stomach urged him forward. He stopped in the entryway to the cafeteria to catch his breath. Holly looked up from her tray. She had a strange expression on her face. Jamie looked up next. Her mouth opened and unleashed a bloodcurdling scream.

Timothy froze. They weren't looking at him; they were looking behind him.

Scratch, scrape, scratch, scrape.

"Oh God." He turned his head to see the two missing Spiders from the video feed. One of the creatures hung from the ceiling, where a loose panel dangled freely. The other continued to slide across the concrete floor, its claws scratching. Its compound eyes scanned them, and Timothy had the horrible feeling that it was deciding which of them to eat first.

He took a step back—a mistake, it turned out. The Spider seemed to finalize its analysis, and Timothy was clearly on the menu.

He closed his eyes and waited for the Spider to tear into him. But his right eye wouldn't stay shut. The nervous twitch had returned, just in time for him to watch the claws descend.

The tunnel was dim, illuminated only by a few emergency lights. One flickered intermittently, reminding Overton of the red lights from the railway crossing in his hometown. Like a subliminal warning, the light blinked on and off, on and off. It shed an eerie glow over an idle escalator at the end of the passage. It was as if they were being warned to stay out of the tunnel.

Overton ignored the superstitious thought and secured the RVM on his back before leaping over the security lever at the top of the escalator.

He began the descent into the darkness, blinking to enhance his night vision.

The green glow of the goggles' night vision bled across his HUD, revealing zero contacts. All he could see was the vague outline of a metal gate at the bottom of the stairs.

Footsteps sounded behind him as he made his way down the metal teeth of the escalator. He didn't risk turning to check on Sophie, for fear of tripping and falling.

A few moments later he reached the bottom of the escalator. With a simple push, the entry door creaked halfway open. He frowned at the sound echoing off the tunnel walls.

The noise was loud enough that any living thing within close proximity would hear them coming. Several strained heartbeats later, the noise vanished, and he slipped through the gateway. The main corridor was similar to the one that led to the Biosphere facility. It had been drilled with a "mole," or tunnel-boring machine. Only a TBM left behind such smooth walls.

Overton checked the tunnel. His HUD again blinked clear of heat signatures.

"It's clear," he said. A moment later, Sophie caught up with him.

With a nod she paced down the passage, shoulder to shoulder with Overton. At some point she'd grown rather fond of the brusque Marine. Without realizing when it had happened, they had become a team.

The image of an idle train filled their displays as they rounded the corner. It rested on the tracks like a sleeping beast. Overton stared at the relic from the past; it had been years since he had ridden on a train. A pair of red emergency lights glowed above the front car door, illuminating the symbol of the NSA. Overton approached the train, jamming his combat knife between the car doors.

"Help me," he said. Working together, they pried the door open and slipped inside the empty train. It was littered with debris—rusted metal fuel barrels, a pair of rubber tires stacked neatly on top of one another, and a plastic container filled with tools.

"Looks like someone's used this train since it was decommissioned," Overton said.

Sophie shrugged, making her way past the barrels and into the conductor's car. She guessed several airport employees who knew about the facility would have brought their families to the tunnel during the solar storms. She'd harbored a faint hope that they might have done so again, but she saw no sign of recent habitation. She checked her HUD for a radiation reading. It was fairly high—high enough to keep survivors out of the tunnel. There was little chance of running into any humans.

Overton pushed his way into the tiny car and peered over Sophie's shoulder, studying the gears. "Well, do you know how to run this thing?"

Sophie pushed a red button on the middle of the console, and a row of lights flickered on. He patted her on the back and slipped back into the second car, taking a seat on one of the dusty benches. His stomach was growling and his throat was parched. It had been several hours since he'd had any nutrition and a couple seconds without his helmet wasn't going to kill him.

"Hold on to your seat, Sergeant. If I'm correct, this train can reach a maximum of three hundred miles per hour. That should put us at White Sands in a little over two hours."

Overton took several gulps from his canteen, letting the warm water glide down his throat. "Let's get this show on the road," he said, and tore open an energy bar.

The floor of the train groaned and creaked as the electric engine flared to life. He slipped his helmet back on and closed his eyes, chewing the last bit of chocolate before resting his helmeted head on the glass window. By the time the train had reached full speed, he was asleep.

The creature's mandibles split and its head darted forward, straining the Spider's thin neck as it lunged for Timothy. Oddly, in that moment of terror and confusion, he fixated on the waft of breath coming from the thing's gaping mouth. It was odorless.

Ever since he was a child, he had imagined what monsters would be like. He thought they would have the most disgusting, raunchiest breath possible, the scent of death and decay rolling off their tongues. It was a prerequisite for dungeon-dwelling beasts.

In the moment before his death, he realized this was no make-believe monster. It was a real, honest-to-God alien life-form, so different from anything his youthful brain had ever created. He didn't have time to comprehend what that meant, if anything.

There wasn't much pain, just a short, hot explosion behind his eyes as the creature sank its sharp teeth into his head. Timothy's legs folded beneath his limp body. The other Organic rushed up behind its friend and lunged with several of its claws, raising the man's corpse into the air. They began spinning him into a blue web.

By the time Bouma and Emanuel arrived, Timothy was already covered in the glowing substance. Bouma sprinted down the passageway with his pulse rifle clanging against the shoulder of his armor.

He halted several yards away, skidding to a dead stop as his mind grasped the gravity of the situation. A slew of eyeballs stared back at him. The Spiders both tilted their heads and let out high-pitched shrieks.

"Run! Take the kids and hide!" Bouma managed to scream over the intermittent screeching of the monsters.

He resisted the urge to check whether Emanuel, Holly, and the children were following his orders. Instead, he did what he was trained to do: neutralize the threat.

With one swift motion, he raised the barrel of his rifle, steadied his breathing the best he could, and squeezed down on the trigger. He knew he had little chance of lowering their shields without an electromagnetic concussion grenade, but he had no choice.

To his surprise, the rounds tore into the creatures' flesh, sending limbs and grotesque eyeballs in all directions. The exploding bodies splattered the walls with glowing blue blood, like a drunken artist spray-painting with glitter.

Bouma emptied the magazine into the Spiders. He wanted to be sure—he *had* to be sure they were dead. After studying the mess from a distance, he finally stepped toward the scene. Slowly, he lowered his rifle and removed the empty clip, grabbing another one from his belt and jamming it into the weapon. Trying to still his labored breath, he took one knee.

He pulled out his tablet from a pouch on his back and accessed the defense system to check the records. He studied the lines of code running across the display. Something was amiss. The sensors had picked up the Organics, but only when they had entered the hallway minutes earlier. For some reason the defense mechanism had never kicked in to warn the team of their presence. Which meant it was possible there were still more of them lurking in the ceiling.

Bouma made the mistake of studying the gore. His stomach lurched. Protruding out of the mixture of human and Organic blood was Timothy's face, his features warped at a terrifying angle. He forced himself to look away. There was nothing he could do for the man now.

He shouldered his rifle and retreated into the mess hall. His first objective was to secure the civilians. The next objective terrified him. After ensuring their safety, he was going to have to crawl through the ducts to root out any remaining creatures.

The image of Finley's and Saafi's burning remains flickered in his mind. He tried to blink it away, but it was replaced with the faces of comrades from his old squad, and finally the sweet face of his baby nephew.

He pulled back the lever on his pulse rifle barrel. A loud, metallic click rang out as the first round entered the chamber. If there were any of the aliens left, he was going to find them. And he was going to kill every last one of them.

CHAPTER 28

THE ancient train groaned and creaked, slowing to a stop. Sophie nudged Overton's leg. "We're here."

He blinked the sleep out of his eyes. Throwing his rifle strap over his shoulder, he grabbed one of the hand railings and hoisted himself up. Stars raced across his eyes, and he was forced to sit back down. The poor sleep, lack of food, and the loss of his squad had finally caught up to him.

"Shit," he said, smacking his helmet with his armored hand.

"You all right?" Sophie asked.

"Yeah, perfect. I just have a headache."

Sophie examined the vestibule of the train station through the grimy windows. The lobby was nothing like the bunker they had entered at the airport. Her night vision revealed the obscure outlines of concrete chunks littered across the ground. The wall had been scored with deep gouges. A sign hung loosely off one of the destroyed pillars. It was speckled with holes, making it difficult to read. After a moment, she made out the sweetest words she'd ever seen: *Welcome to White Sands Missile Range.*

"What happened here?" Sophie said, hunching over so she could get a better view of the lobby.

Overton gave his helmet one more smack and strolled over to the glass. He blinked a few times to enhance the optics and focused on the outline of several humps in the corner of the vestibule.

"Those look like bodies," he said.

A short burst of static broke over the com as Sophie exhaled. "How is that possible?"

"I don't know, but I don't like it. I'm going to check it out. Wait here."

Overton slipped through the automatic door and stepped out onto the concrete platform. Bringing the scope to his visor, he surveyed the scene, allowing the crosshairs to pop up on his HUD. He crept toward the figures, stepping over the chunks of concrete.

He checked the two corridors for contacts before entering the main lobby. They were empty—nothing but heaps of trash and broken glass. More relics of the past. The vestibule, on the other hand, was filled with signs of recent occupation—and of death. Bodies lay scattered throughout the room. Everywhere his eyes fell, the outlines of armored corpses filled his display. But there was something odd about them—something wasn't right.

Overton crouched to get a better look. What he saw made him fumble and nearly drop his rifle. The lumps weren't corpses. They were the black matte armor suits NTC soldiers wore in the Wastelands. The same suit he had on now.

The suits were empty. Where were the bodies?

It was clear there had been a battle. The dark craters from plasma rounds and chunks of broken concrete indicated as much. He scanned the room again, this time not for humans but for Organics.

There was no sign of them. No gooey blood, no dismembered limbs. Nothing.

This was no battle—this was a massacre.

He grabbed one of the soldier's fallen rifles and stood. "Sophie, get up here."

Footsteps rang out behind him immediately, followed by a burst of static over the com and then Sophie's calm voice.

"Where are the bodies?"

"That's exactly what I've been wondering." Overton paused, scanning the room one more time. His instincts reasserted themselves and he began to move cautiously forward, motioning Sophie toward the edge of the stairs leading into the facility.

"Alexia, you still alive in there?" Overton asked.

"Yes, Sergeant. I'm still 90 percent functional."

"Good. I'm going to need you to upload the facility's blueprint to our HUDs."

"One moment, sir."

Seconds later a rectangular box popped up in the corner of their displays, followed by two tiny red dots representing their location.

"Where's *Secundo Casu?*" Sophie asked.

"I am sorry, Dr. Winston, but unfortunately the blueprints to which I have access are outdated. White Sands is the largest decommissioned military installation in the United States, and—"

"Cut to the chase, Alexia," Overton growled. "If you had to take a guess, where do you think NTC would have housed our Noah's Ark?"

Another red dot appeared on their HUDs. Underneath it was a single number representing the distance to the potential location.

"That's five miles away from here, Sophie!"

"What? You expected the bus to take you right to the front door? This isn't elementary school, this is the big leagues now," Sophie chuckled.

"That's cute, really it is, but look around. The Organics beat us here! NTC beat us here! And that means *Secundo Casu* could be fucked!"

"We need to take a step back and focus on what we know. One, the RVM will protect us as long as the Organics don't see us moving. Two, we have already made it over seven hundred miles. The hard part is over."

Overton tossed Sophie one of the pulse rifles he had picked up. "Take this; you're going to need it."

She caught it gracefully and threw the strap around her back. With one more glance at the empty armor, she began the ascent up the staircase.

The connecting floor was pitch black. There were no red emergency lights here, just the darkness. The green glow of her night vision was beginning to make her dizzy. And with nothing to look at besides a jungle of wire and piping along the walls and ceiling, she was beginning to feel claustrophobic, too.

Sophie halted to take a deep breath. She was fatigued, hungry, and most of all, thirsty. It was possible her mind was beginning to play tricks on her.

"I'm taking five," she said in a hushed voice.

Overton nodded and turned on his head lamps before unclipping his helmet. A pair of double lights illuminated the tunnel. He set the helmet down and reached for the small pack on his back to retrieve one of his canteens and an energy bar. It only took a minute for him to devour the chocolate and polish off half of the water.

"You better conserve that. We need to save some for the return trip," Sophie said, chewing her way through a piece of beef jerky.

He scowled in the darkness. His face was hardly recognizable in the faint light, but Sophie caught the look. She held her tongue and decided to ignore her own advice. She finished off the jerky, washing it down with a few long gulps of the precious liquid.

Overton took out his tablet and studied the blueprint. "All right, looks like we're somewhere under the spaceport," he said, pointing to a horizontal line on the display. "Alexia puts the shuttle's possible location here. Which means we're going to have to go above ground to get to the hangar."

He looked at the mission clock on his HUD.

12:45 p.m.

"We could wait until it gets dark, but I'm not sure it'll make much difference."

Sophie shook her head. "Not a chance I'm staying down here for that long."

Overton grabbed his helmet and hoisted himself off the ground by grabbing onto a pipe, nearly ripping it free from the wall. "Roger that. Let's keep moving."

They picked up their rifles and continued into the darkness, pushing along the winding tunnels, up stairways, and through countless corridors. Several signs hung from the walls. They were rusted beyond recognition by the steady drip from the leaky pipes lining the ceiling.

Sophie finally knew what it was like to be one of the mice she had seen used in countless experiments. Navigating the tunnels was like being stuck in a maze—no, a rat trap. Even with the veteran recon Marine and the world's smartest computer as her guides, she was starting to feel lost.

As they rounded a corner, she saw the passage opened up into another vestibule. Her trot turned into a steady jog, and soon she was leading Overton up the stairs into a massive room.

This was different from the vestibule they had entered right off the train. It was larger, with a curved dome, much like Biome 1. The walls were all concrete, with painted arrows pointing at different passages. With the night vision, she couldn't make out the different colors, but she could read them.

HOLLOMAN AIR FORCE BASE 21 MILES

WHITE SANDS TEST FACILITY 14 MILES

SPACEPORT 2¼ MILES

WHITE SANDS POST HEADQUARTERS 13 MILES

"Like Alexia said, this was the biggest military installation in the United States at one time," Sophie said, preempting any snide comments from Overton regarding the distances.

"We're halfway there. Let's keep moving."

They hurried into the tunnel labeled "Spaceport." It was much wider—about three times the diameter of the others, large enough for a vehicle to travel in.

"This tunnel should open up into one last vestibule that leads to the surface," Alexia said in their earpieces.

"And you really think *Secundo Casu* is going to be waiting for us?" Overton asked.

Silence washed over the com. Sophie had stopped several paces ahead, her figure frozen in the darkness like a statue.

"What is it, Sophie?" Overton continued.

"I think I hear something . . ."

Overton halted and strained his ears. Nothing but the sporadic burst of static over the com filled his helmet.

"I don't—"

A faint metallic sound broke through the silence before he could finish his sentence. He swung his rifle off his back and shouldered it, peering down the tunnel with the scope. The crosshairs on his HUD glowed red as the wireless link synched the weapon with his helmet. He scanned the darkness for signatures but saw nothing.

For several minutes they waited, until the metallic scraping finally faded away.

"It could have been anything," Overton said, but he knew it was a lie. He was all too familiar with the sound the Spiders made as they moved on their knifelike claws. However, they seemed to be gone for now. There wasn't anything in the passages, save for rusted pipes and corroded wires.

Sophie forced herself forward, hugging the walls close behind Overton. She felt like something was watching her, tailing just behind them in the dark tunnel. Every few seconds she stole a glance over her shoulder to make sure the tunnel was clear.

It wasn't long before they could see a blue light at the other end of the passage. They both blinked off their night vision and halted.

Overton balled his hand into a fist and took one knee. Sophie followed suit, and as if they'd drilled the motion countless times, they raised their rifles in unison and waited—waited for the Spiders to swarm the tunnel and consume them. Even when Sophie's arm grew tired and her gun began to shake and dip, they still held their position.

Finally, after what seemed like hours to Sophie, Overton stood and took a step forward into some sort of sticky goo. He didn't take his eyes off the entrance of the passage—he didn't need to. The substance he had stepped in was the same goo he had all over his armor. It was the blood of an injured Organic.

Which meant the massacre hadn't been as one-sided as he thought. He motioned Sophie to join him with a silent nod and together they advanced toward the blue glow. With every step Sophie grew more anxious, her ears straining to catch a hint of metallic scraping. But the tunnel remained silent; it seemed they were alone.

From their vantage point, Overton could see that the passage opened up into another lobby. It was filled with orbs; too many to count. And hanging from the ceiling were dozens of Spiders.

Overton froze. Fear gripped him and prodded him to run, to retreat, but he remained still. If Sophie was right, the creatures could sense movement even with their senses confused by the RVM. It was the one advantage he had, and he wasn't about to blow it because he was scared.

From behind the safety of his visor, his eyes darted back and forth, examining the room. It was completely open, with only a few concrete pillars to hide behind. A single stairway led to a set of metal doors. The glass was smudged with dirt and dust, but several rays of bright sunlight filtered in, turning the orbs closest to it a fluorescent green. They reminded Overton of the ornaments his mother used to decorate their Christmas tree with when he was a kid.

The contents of the orbs, however, prevented any warm or fuzzy childhood memories from returning. Over half of the spheres had split open, their prisoners fully liquefied. The floor was littered with sacks of skin and remnants of clothes. He took a step back into the tunnel, his stomach rolling.

From Sophie's perspective, his body appeared to be split in two by the light, with half of his matte black armor exposed in the room and the other half hidden in darkness. She tiptoed up to him, catching a glimpse of what had made him retreat. Overton tapped her on the side of her helmet quietly, getting her attention. With one slow movement of his hand he pointed to the pillars closest to them, then to the staircase, and then back to his visor.

She managed a thumbs-up, took a deep breath, and followed him into the room. Everywhere her eyes fell, death stared back. But at the bottom of the stairs, one sphere's contents were still mostly intact, and, to Sophie's horror—still alive.

She slowed her pace to study the gaunt face of what had been a young woman. The greenish glow from the night vision illuminated the girl's distorted features. Her eyes were almost completely glazed over.

Her lips were curled back, showcasing a mouthful of missing teeth. The skin of her face was sunken and stretched, and her blond hair was plastered to her skull like seaweed.

Sophie froze when the woman's eyes came to rest on her. Overton was already a third of the way up the stairs, but Sophie couldn't move.

There had to be something she could do—some way she could help the girl.

A short burst of static broke over the com. "Move, Doc."

Sophie didn't need to look up to see Overton staring down at her from the top of the stairs. She willed her legs to move, but they wouldn't respond.

I can't leave her. Not like this.

She stepped forward and threw her rifle strap around her back. With a few careful footsteps, she navigated the gory remnants of skin and clothing from other victims.

"No!" Overton shouted into the com. "You can't save her, Sophie. Leave her. That's an order!"

Sophie ignored him and continued until she was less than a foot away from the woman. She brought her finger to her helmet, motioning the girl to remain silent. Instead, the girl's eyes grew wide and bulged from her head. Her lips began to quiver and move, splitting open in the process. Blood seeped down her chin, and a scratchy moan escaped her throat.

"No. You have to be quiet," Sophie said, bringing a finger to her helmet again. But it was too late. The woman erupted into a subhuman scream, the noise echoing off the concrete walls.

Sophie craned her neck and watched the Spiders begin to churn. Their claws slid across the concrete as they woke up.

Scratch, scrape, scratch, scrape.

A wave of fear washed over Sophie as she turned back to the girl. With an audible pop the girl's eyeballs exploded, spraying a bloody mist onto Sophie's visor. Stumbling backward, she grabbed her rifle. She tried to balance herself, but slipped on a sack of gore.

Her helmet hit the concrete with a thud. Stars filled her vision. Even with the padded support of the helmet, the trauma from the fall sent pain racing down her spine. She lay staring at the concrete ceiling, watching the Spiders crawl across it, their glittering eyes studying her from all directions.

She tried to sit up, but as the blood rushed to her head she was forced back down, gripping her helmet with both hands. Everything seemed to slow down when the first plasma rounds tore through the air above her. She watched the streaks of fire trace through the air and tear into the weak flesh of the Spiders. Their shields were still down, she realized, recharging from their recent feedings.

Sophie pushed herself up and stole one more glance at the woman, who was now disintegrating in the pool of liquid inside the orb. Sophie watched her disappear, knowing that it was a sight she'd carry with her for the rest of her life—however long it happened to last.

The high-pitched screams of the Spiders ripped through the silence and yanked her from her trance.

"Let's go, Doc!" Overton screamed, squeezing off another few rounds at the rapidly approaching Spiders. Sophie shook her head one last time and sprinted for the stairs, climbing them two at a time.

Overton kicked the door open, and they were blasted with the astonishingly bright sunlight. Temporarily blinded, Overton blinked several times to tint his visor. He closed the door, shoving his combat knife between the two handles. The door shook violently as the creatures crashed into it from the other side. Their shrieks pounded inside Overton's helmet, drowning out the sound of his thudding heartbeat.

Like a robot being commanded by a remote control, he grabbed Sophie by the arm and pulled her into the sunlight. They ran side by side down the tarmac toward two large hangars a hundred yards away. He tried to ignore the sounds of claws tearing through the metal behind him. Every few yards he stopped and fired off another few rounds at the door, sending a Spider or two to its death.

"Go!" Overton shouted between bursts.

The massive hangar doors dwarfed them as they approached. Overton looked between the two buildings, but he didn't see any obvious sign that one held their spaceship.

"Which one is it?" Overton yelled.

Alexia's calm voice broke over the channel. "After downloading the dimensions of the spacecraft, it's only logical that the ship would be in the larger hangar. The second is too—"

Overton cut her off and shoved Sophie toward the sealed doors of the first hangar. "Find a way inside. I'll hold off the horde!" he yelled, throwing himself on his stomach for a steadier sniping position.

Sophie grabbed an extra magazine from her belt and handed it to him. "Take this. You're going to need it."

"Thanks." Overton grabbed the mag before firing off another volley of rounds at the heads of two Spiders crawling through a hole in the door.

She took off running, craning her neck around the approaching corner to get a better angle. With her rifle aimed at the metal edge of the building, she jumped around it, ready to fire, but the blind spot was clear. Relieved, she sprinted for the door and fired off several rounds into the lock. The rifle vibrated in her hands and pushed her backward.

The power of the gun shocked her. It was the first time she had ever fired a pulse rifle, and she had done so without giving it a second thought. Less than a month ago she had been shut in her old lab, trying to solve sophisticated equations on her smart board, and now she was firing a high-powered pulse rifle with a horde of aliens chasing her. Saafi was gone, Emanuel was hundreds of miles away, and everyone she had ever cared about was dead or dying in a blue glowing prison cell.

She gritted her teeth and fired another round at the lock. The door broke open and she slipped into the hangar, blinking on her night vision as the darkness consumed her. When her eyes adjusted, she gasped. A large sign that read *Secundo Casu* towered over her, but the massive room was empty.

"NO!" she screamed. "It has to be here!" Sophie collapsed to her knees. The overwhelming feeling of defeat rushed through her as the ringing of gunfire filled her ears. Tears welled up in her eyes, and she didn't bother to remove her helmet to wipe them away.

The sound of footsteps rang out behind her and she quickly turned. In the corner of the room, peeking out from behind one of the Humvees, two children in gas masks and fatigues that were far too large for them were staring at her. She hardly noticed the oversized assault rifles they were pointing in her direction.

"You're too late," one of the children said, stepping forward but keeping the weapon leveled at her. "The ship took off right after the monsters came."

Sophie pushed herself off the ground, staring at the two figures. Behind her a volley of shots rang out, and the high-pitched shriek of another Spider bounced off the hangar walls.

The children hardly moved, unfazed by the terrifying sounds.

"Who are you?" the smaller one asked. "Are you here to rescue us?"

"Shut up, stupid!" the bigger child replied, smacking the other one on the back of the head. "If she was here to rescue us, she wouldn't be crying."

Sophie stopped sniffling and reached for her helmet, but halted as the larger boy pointed his weapon at her again.

"Watch it, lady! No sudden moves."

The children sounded like boys, and judging by their frames she assumed the smaller one was about seven years old, the larger one no older than ten. But with the oversized fatigues, it was hard to tell.

"Listen," Sophie managed to say. "I'm not here to hurt you. We came for the ship. That's all."

"Don't you listen? The ship's gone!" the larger boy shouted.

"We need to get out of here, they're coming," the other boy insisted, pulling on his friend's arm.

"Do you want to live or what, lady?"

Sophie wasn't sure how to respond. Finally she blinked the tears out of her eyes and managed to reply. "My friend's outside, I need to get to him."

The older boy tilted his head, listening to the gunfire, before checking the magazine in his own rifle. "He's not going to last long. Follow me," he said, taking off toward a ladder hanging on the wall behind the Humvee.

She hesitated before scooping up her rifle. Throwing the strap across her back, she opened the com link. "Overton, do you read?"

"Roger. Things are getting dicey. Not sure how much longer I can hold these bastards off. It looks like their shields are starting to regenerate. Did you find the package?"

Sophie closed her eyes against the pain. "No," she said. "It's gone."

"Gone? What the fuck do you mean, it's gone? You said it would be here!"

Sophie could picture Overton's nostrils flaring and his eyes widening with anger. She couldn't blame him.

"Hold tight, Sergeant. I found some survivors," she said.

Silence filled the channel, followed by another volley of gunfire. "Survivors?"

"Just sit tight."

On the roof the two children took up positions overlooking the tarmac. Below, dozens of Organics raced toward Overton. Both boys lay down on the metal surface and aimed their rifles. Sophie watched their precise, practiced movements in awe. The reality of the situation finally set in: With the majority of the adult population dead, only children who had managed to survive the first stages of the invasion would be left to fight the Organics.

It was a sobering thought. She imagined most of the children who had been lucky enough to survive in those first few hours would probably perish in the weeks to come, if they hadn't already. But as she watched the two boys take out several of the creatures with a few well-aimed shots, she began to wonder if they had a chance after all. Could the younger generation take up arms against an enemy that had effectively wiped out their parents?

Highly unlikely.

The chirp of high-powered rifles joined the chatter of Overton's pulse rifle, and she returned her focus to the battle below. She watched the slaughter with a grim smile on her face. Without their shields, the Spiders had no chance. Limbs and eyeballs rained down onto the tarmac in all directions, the blue goo washing over the blacktop like the innards of a gutted whale.

Minutes later it was over. The boys wasted no time reloading their weapons and heading back to the ladder.

"There'll be more. We need to move," the larger boy said calmly.

Sophie nodded and followed them back to the tarmac where Overton waited, his foot tapping, watching the gory mess for signs of survivors.

"If you want to live, come with us," said the larger boy.

"What the fuck is going on?" Overton said, jamming another magazine into his rifle.

"There are always more," the smaller boy said. "Please, come with us."

Sophie grabbed Overton's arm, silently persuading him to follow instead of argue. He pulled free and snorted into his com. The boys jogged at a steady pace toward the smaller hangar. Inside was a room furnished with modern desks, holographic consoles, and rows of monitors. NTC labels on metal crates revealed it to be the portable command center for *Secundo Casu*.

The two boys strolled through the equipment and stopped at a metal desk. The larger boy threw his rifle strap over his back and, with a short grunt, began pushing the desk across the concrete. Before Overton had a chance to help him, a hidden circular latch was revealed, similar to the one they had used to enter the train tunnel back at the Denver Airport.

"Get inside," the boy said, opening the lid and motioning them forward.

"I'm not going anywhere until you tell me what the fuck is going on!"

"Suit yourself," the boy replied, climbing down the ladder. The other boy shrugged and followed him.

"They just saved our lives, Sergeant, and I don't see any other option. Do you?" Sophie asked. She knew that sometimes the best way to convince a hard-headed person to do something was by putting the question back on them. If he didn't have an answer then he would have no choice but to agree.

"Shit," Overton said in a defeated tone. "You go first, I'll close the lid."

She didn't argue, and began the descent. Overton watched her go, stealing a glance over his shoulder. "I don't fucking believe this," he mumbled under his breath. "Saved by ankle biters." He chuckled and shut the lid, blinking his night vision back on as he descended into the darkness.

CHAPTER 29

THE boys led Overton and Sophie down some sort of maintenance tunnel that jutted out in several directions. They followed one of the passages to what appeared to be a dead end. It wasn't until the larger boy trained his flashlight on a door clearly marked *Storage* that Sophie realized this was where they had been hiding.

The room was littered with empty cans and trash. Several filthy blankets sat bunched up in the corner next to a stack of bottled water.

Sophie eyed the precious liquid curiously, wondering how the children had survived so long without being captured by the Organics.

They had beaten the odds—odds so stacked against them that their survival was more miracle than luck. In a mathematical equation, their chances would have been called statistically insignificant.

Overton shut the door behind him and broke the silence. "Who are you?"

"You first," the larger boy said. He rested his flashlight on the ground and slid his gas mask off, revealing a face no more than nine or ten years old.

"I'm Marine Sergeant Ash Overton, and this here is Dr. Sophie Winston with the NTC."

The boy eyed them both suspiciously before turning to help the smaller child remove his gas mask. "I'm Jeff, and this is my little brother David."

"Are you here to rescue us?" David asked, his brown eyes full of hope.

"Actually, we came here for another reason," Sophie said. Checking the radiation gauge on her HUD, she unclasped her helmet straps and pulled it off, managing a smile. "We came for the spaceship."

"I told you, it's gone," Jeff snapped.

"Yes, you did, but do you know where it went?"

"What's it matter?"

Overton slid off his helmet and approached the boy, stopping less than a foot away. The Marine towered over him. "Just answer her question."

The boy held his ground. "You don't scare me."

"Really? Because this is me being nice."

Sophie put her hand on Overton's shoulder and gave him a slight tug. "They saved our lives."

"That doesn't give him a free pass to show me attitude," Overton said, but he retreated a few steps.

"Yeah, whatever, you're all the same," Jeff said, running a hand through his matted brown hair. He paced over to the corner and grabbed two bottles of water, tossing one to David.

"NTC, the military—they left us down here to die. Our dad was the only one that tried to save us," the boy said, his voice sharp with anger.

"And he's gone now," David whimpered.

"I'm sorry about your dad, and I'm sorry you were left down here, but we aren't going to leave you," Sophie insisted.

David erupted in a fit of coughs and sat down on the concrete, pulling one of the dirty blankets over his legs. Jeff joined him and opened a can of peaches with a small knife.

"You need to eat," he said, handing his brother the can.

Jeff looked up at Overton and then at Sophie. In that moment, something in his eyes changed from angry to pleading. "He's sick. You're a doctor, so help him, lady."

Sophie sat next to the child. His face was pale and covered in grime. She reached to wipe off some of the dirt, but he pulled away.

"I can help him, but not here. We need to get you back to our facility, where we have medicine."

Jeff stood and placed his hands on his hips, studying her through narrowed eyes. "Where is your facility?"

Sophie paused. She didn't want to tell him the truth. He was old enough to know they were more than a car ride from Denver.

"It's in a safe place, but I can't tell you where. It's classified," she lied.

Overton shot her a confused look but recovered quickly, realizing her strategy.

"There are other kids there, too," he added. "Kids who survived like you two."

David sucked a peach into his mouth and looked up at his brother. "Can we go with them?"

Jeff narrowed his eyes even further. After several seconds of silence, he reached down and patted his brother on the head. "Yeah, David, we can go with them."

Bouma finished cleaning the gore out of the hallway with one final push of the mop. He eyed the broken ceiling tile where the Spiders had emerged. He'd spent as much time as he could cleaning up after the attack, but he couldn't put it off any longer.

"You're really going up there?" a voice said from behind him.

He turned to see Holly leaning against the entrance of the hallway.

"I don't have a choice."

"You could wait for the others to get back." Her voice was different. Holly's normal sweet tone had hardened, something he'd heard in soldiers before, after deployments. He didn't respond. Instead, he unfolded a metal ladder and positioned it under the hole.

"They *are* coming back," Holly insisted.

"I know," Bouma said. "Where are the kids?"

"With Emanuel."

"Okay. Now, do you remember what to do if something happens to me?"

"Hunker down in the med ward with Emanuel and the kids, and shoot anything that moves."

"You got it," Bouma said, grinning.

Holly fixated on the man's crooked teeth. For a second, they reminded her of the sharp teeth lining the jaws of every Organic she had seen.

"Can you give me a hand with this?" Bouma asked as he started climbing the ladder. She gripped the ladder tightly and watched the Marine reach for the vent cover. "I guess this means we have to postpone our walk."

"Yeah, but it will give me something to look forward to," he said, hoisting himself into the duct and staring into the pitch-black tunnel. A sudden chill of fear gripped him and for a moment he had second thoughts about clearing the vents. He peered back down and saw Holly's wide eyes staring up at him. She smiled, and the fear faded. He had a mission to finish, a squad to avenge, and a group of civilians to protect. And, best of all, a pretty girl waiting for him.

"Good luck," she said as Bouma's feet disappeared in the darkness.

The trip back to the train was painfully slow, providing Sophie with plenty of time to think. With *Secundo Casu* gone, her hope of seeing Mars was dead, and her hope for survival had diminished considerably. With every step she grew more anxious to get back to the Biosphere—back to Emanuel and the rest of her team.

By the time she reached the train, she had accepted the fact that the facility was her home for the foreseeable future. But was it really all that bad? The death toll worldwide could very well be in the billions, an unfathomable number. The Biosphere had virtually everything they needed to support their little band of survivors, and it was, to her knowledge, the safest place to ride out the invasion.

"Wow, cool," David said as they rounded the last corner and the train came into view. "We get to ride on that?"

Overton hushed him with a finger. "Quiet, kid."

The boy ignored him and rushed toward the automatic doors of the first cabin.

"Wait up," Jeff shouted after him.

Their voices echoed off the concrete tunnel walls. Sophie smiled as

Jeff chased his brother onto the platform, stopping him before he could enter the train. The boys wrestled playfully at the doors, David squirming in his brother's grasp.

A shadow danced across their path.

Overton saw it at the same moment Sophie did. She froze, her stomach tightening as the blue glow washed over the dimly lit tunnel.

"Oh my God," she whispered into her com. From her angle, she could vaguely make out the shape of the shadows approaching, but there was no mistaking the thin and bony legs of the Spiders. The black shadows raced across the platform. They extended their monstrous claws, reaching for the children.

Scratch, scrape, scratch, scrape.

The sound drowned out the boys' arguing voices and they froze. Slowly, they tilted their heads and saw it—a tunnel overflowing with monsters, an entire army of them.

"Run!" Overton screamed, holding the trigger down on his rifle. Conserving ammo was no longer a concern. If he didn't push the horde back quickly, he wasn't going to need the bullets later.

Shocked into motion, Jeff shoved David forward, but the train's automatic doors remained shut, and the boy crashed into the side. He bounced off with a bang and immediately started whimpering.

Sophie watched, horrified. She distinctly remembered leaving the train's power on, just in case they needed to make a quick getaway, which meant the connection to the power source had been severed.

"Alexia, any suggestions on how to get this train started?" Sophie barked into the com.

"Yes, Dr. Winston. There should be an additional power interface in the engine car. My fuel cell should provide adequate energy."

"Won't that cause the RVM to fail?"

"Does it look like we need it right now?" Overton yelled.

Sophie risked a glance over her shoulder and watched what appeared to be hundreds of Spiders spilling out of the tunnel. Terror gripped her, but she forced herself forward and fired two shots into the closed train door. They hissed open and Sophie ordered both of the boys inside.

"Stay away from the windows," she yelled before returning to the platform.

She raced to Overton, and with one swift tug she pulled Alexia's fuel cell free of the device on his back. "I just need a few seconds," she said.

Overton finished his magazine. The shots bounced off the creatures' shields harmlessly. They were getting close, now only a few hundred yards away. A brilliant blue glow filled the tunnel, making the scene beautiful and eerie at the same time.

Sophie retreated to the rear of the train. She had almost reached the doors when a shadow consumed her. This time it wasn't from a Spider. It was something different—something larger.

Her stomach sank as she turned to see a Sentinel towering over her. It wasted no time cracking its mouth open and releasing a deafening roar. She turned to run, but the creature lunged at her with its spiked tail. The impact penetrated her armor and sent her sailing through the air. She landed with a thud a few feet away from the train.

Farther down the platform, the Spiders surrounded Overton, clawing at the ground and shrieking like predators trying to intimidate their prey. He fired the last of his rounds and threw his rifle at the closest one before retrieving his pistol. "Come on, you bastards!" he screamed, squeezing off several shots, which ricocheted harmlessly off their shields.

Sophie watched him fall to his knees, overwhelmed by the creatures closing in around him.

Scratch, scrape, scratch, scrape.

Soon the sound would be replaced with tearing flesh and human screams. She couldn't bear to watch. The sound of Spiders' claws was drowned out by the scraping of the Sentinel's tail as it dragged its spikes across the concrete.

Defeated, she watched the ugly creature slither toward her.

Good-bye, Emanuel. I tried.

Tears crept down her cheeks just as a brilliant flash of light washed over the platform, killing her HUD. Sophie blinked, struggling to see through the fuzzy display. She heard gunfire, the chatter of high-powered rifles. When her vision finally returned, she saw Jeff step out of the train and fire a round of shots at the Sentinel. The bullets sunk into the alien's chest, blowing several melon-sized holes out of its back.

The boy grabbed her shoulder and pulled her into the belly of the train. He then raced back outside and began firing at the Spiders that were still circling Overton. His shots were surprisingly accurate, dropping several of the creatures.

Overton scooted back across the concrete and managed to push himself off the ground. He took off running, the bullets from Jeff's gun whizzing dangerously close to him.

"Why didn't you tell me you had electromagnetic concussion grenades?" he shouted, jumping onto the train.

"You didn't ask," Jeff said. He pried the fuel cell from Sophie's numb grasp and ducked into the conductor's cabin. Scanning the dashboard, he quickly located the power interface and shoved it home. The display panel glowed to life.

"Now my HUD's dead and I can barely see shit," Overton said. He slipped into the compartment and shoved the boy out of the way. "I got this."

With a single click of a button, the train flared to life. It rolled forward, picking up momentum. Overton watched the Spiders and several Sentinels racing across the tracks toward the train, and with a grin hidden behind his helmet, he engaged the autopilot.

"Watch this, kid."

The train picked up speed and raced forward, splattering the Organics in its path all over the tunnel.

Overton returned to the second car to check on Sophie. He found her spread out on one of the benches, David kneeling next to her.

"She's hurt bad, mister," he said.

"Don't worry, kid, she's going to be all right," Overton said. But his eyes had already found the foot-long gash along her side.

"Shit," he whispered. "Hang in there, Sophie. I'm going to get you home."

Somewhere inside her head, Sophie could hear Overton's voice, but as the adrenaline in her system was replaced by pain, she slipped into shock, closed her eyes, and drifted into unconsciousness.

Bouma strained his ears. Somewhere in the distance, a series of metallic clicks rang out, followed by the ambient sound of the ventilation system turning on.

He continued on, wriggling through the tight ductwork. Checking his HUD first for heat signatures, he blinked his night vision back on. The passage was clear.

Stopping at an intersection, he managed to push himself onto his knees, first looking to his left and then to his right.

"Damn," he muttered. He had only been crawling through the guts of the system for fifteen minutes and he was already lost.

He reached for his tablet and slid it in front of him, blinking off his night vision. The screen displayed the internal blueprints of the Biosphere. Running his finger along the surface, he followed one of the red lines. It didn't take long to find his approximate location. He wasn't far from the vent above the med ward, the area where the Spiders most likely would have sought refuge after they feasted on Saafi.

He slid the tablet back into its pouch and peeked around the corner. As the screen dimmed, he saw there was another light source. Resisting the urge to turn his night vision back on, he crawled forward. At the end of the passage he could see the outlines of what appeared to be several balls.

Moments later he was feet away from a cluster of glowing orbs—smaller ones, no larger than a basketball. He felt his heart beating faster, his breathing becoming labored. These were unlike the others. They were different—they were eggs.

He closed his eyes, trying to blink the sight away. But all it did was enhance his night vision, filling his display with a vibrant green glow.

He forced himself to crawl a few paces forward. With a quick jab, he poked one of the eggs with his rifle barrel.

The skin of the orb pulsated to life, revealing a tiny creature inside. Startled, Bouma scooted away from the thing, smashing into the side of the duct. He took a deep breath and focused on calming his heart rate. He watched the creature unfold one of its many legs, each with a miniature claw on the end. As the baby Spider began to tear through the fragile skin of the orb, Bouma grabbed his rifle. He didn't stop to think about what the eggs signified—he didn't stop to consider what it meant for the future of the human race. He simply squeezed off a single volley of shots, turning the cluster of eggs into messy blue pulp before continuing forward.

He had a promise to keep. He was going to kill them all.

CHAPTER 30

SOPHIE opened her eyes to an endless sea of red sand and a bright, unforgiving sun. At first she thought she was in the Wastelands, but as she examined her surroundings she saw the unmistakable impact scars from asteroids. She was on Mars.

She closed her eyes, expecting to wake up when she opened them. But as soon as her eyelids flicked open, her vision was filled once more with red sand.

Am I dead?

It was the only explanation.

"Dr. Winston," a familiar voice said from behind her.

She turned to see a hologram of Dr. Hoffman standing a few feet away, his arms folded across his chest.

"If you are seeing this message, then not only have I underestimated you, but you have beaten the odds. You have shown an impressive resilience, Dr. Winston. In fact, I never believed you had it in you. Now, what I am about to tell you is going to come as a shock. You're going to be confused and angry. But you have to understand that what I have done was for the good of all mankind."

He paused and looked down in her direction, his obsidian eyes burning into her own.

"You see, the Biosphere mission was always a failsafe. It was one of many we strategically placed throughout the world in preparation for the invasion, little vaults of humanity's treasures, if you will. We selected teams of people from all walks of life, promising them all whatever they needed to be offered in order to accept the mission. In your case, it was a trip to Mars—a trip I'm afraid you will never be making."

Sophie tried to move, but she was paralyzed. Her lips quivered with anger as she listened, unable to respond.

"I know this information must be devastating, but as I said, I did this to save our species. When we realized the world was dying faster than we ever predicted, we decided it was time to colonize Mars. But when we found out about the Organics, we knew we couldn't pin all our hopes on the Red Planet. We needed to plant the seeds for our survival on Earth as well."

Dr. Hoffman sighed, dropping his hands to his sides.

"You see, the Organics weren't trying to exterminate us in 2055— they were just testing our defenses. They came here, as you probably know by now, for water. We don't know how much they will take or if they will ever leave, but I do know if even a few of the Biospheres survive, our species will have a fighting chance."

"If I know you as well as I think I do, you are probably furious right now, and this last bit of information I am going to share is going to upset you even more. By the time you get this message, we will probably be well on our way. I set up one final failsafe: *Secundo Casu*."

The words raced through Sophie's mind. There had never been a seat on the ship for her or her team. Hoffman had manipulated them all. The contract, the mission—it was all based on a series of well-planned lies. But knowing what she knew now, could she blame him?

"Please know I take no pleasure in telling you this. I do wish you could be here when we open the doors and step out onto the red sand. There is one gift I have left for you in case everything else fails. Inside the command center, you will find a two-way radio that operates on only one frequency. It's encrypted and virtually indestructible. You can use it to communicate with the other Biospheres. I wish you the best of luck, Dr. Winston."

She watched his image fade. It took a few minutes for the information to saturate her brain, but it was more than enough time to grasp the fact that she had been completely deceived. As she sat, replaying the message in her mind, another pair of voices drifted through the wind.

"Sophie, can you hear me?" one of them said.

A calm, robotic voice quickly followed. "Dr. Winston, are you awake?"

She blinked and the red sand was replaced by the white walls of the med ward.

"Sophie!" Emanuel reached for her, naked relief on his face.

"Give her some space," a rough voice said from her other side. She didn't need to turn to see Overton's scarred face peering down at her.

"Dr. Hoffman! The radio! We have to find the radio," she said, struggling to get out of her bed.

"It's okay, Sophie, we heard the message too," Emanuel said, soothingly.

"But, how? What happened?" she asked.

"A couple of kids saved our asses. That's what happened."

Sophie managed a smile. She turned her head to the right to see Holly sitting with Jamie and Owen. David and Jeff sat on another bench, digging into a couple of freeze-dried meals. Standing next to them was Bouma. He winked at her.

She finished scanning the room and realized someone was missing. "Where's Timothy?"

Emanuel took her hand. "There were two Spiders hibernating in the ceiling. They killed him. But that isn't all." Emanuel paused, realizing the information might be too much for her to handle right away.

"Tell me," she ordered.

"Do you want the good news or bad news first?"

"Bad."

"First, the radio Dr. Hoffman was referring to doesn't work," he said. "We can't get any other Biospheres online. Which either means everyone else is dead or the disruption outside is preventing communication."

"And second?" Sophie asked.

Emanuel took a deep breath. "Second, the Organics are reproducing and by the looks of it they are doing so at an alarming rate."

Her stomach lurched. She didn't need a seasoned Marine like Overton to tell her what it meant. If they were spawning, then the survivors wouldn't just be fighting against an army with a set number of soldiers—they would be fighting against an enemy with the ability to replace its dead. And judging by the radio silence, it sounded like they would be doing so alone.

"What's the good news?"

"I may have found a way to kill them."

Overton's ears perked up immediately. "What do you mean?"

Emanuel rubbed his hands together. "It's fascinating, actually. Their blood is made up of 80 percent H_2O and 20 percent ions. The ions are what charge their shields. I think their shields function sort of like the suit an astronaut wears in space: it protects them from a hostile environment, one I don't believe they could survive without their defenses." He paused to check whether Overton and Bouma were following.

"Go on," Overton growled.

"Yeah, get on with it," Bouma said. "No need to wait for the slow kids." He caught a glimpse of Holly smiling at him and felt his cheeks glow red.

"As I was saying, when they feed or reproduce, their shields drop. Not all the way, just enough so their blood can regenerate. Now, if we can find a way to drop their shields all the way on a massive level, I think we can kill them. Kill *all* of them."

"Like some sort of EMP?" Overton asked.

"Honestly, I'm not sure. I need to do more research."

"This should be our number one priority from here on out," Overton said.

Sophie coughed deeply, interrupting the conversation.

"Are you okay, Dr. Winston? Your heart rate is elevated," Alexia said. Her hologram emerged over the corner console, and for a split second Sophie thought she saw a flicker of concern cross her face.

"I feel pretty good, considering," she said, attempting to sit up. The slight movement sent a wave of fatigue through her body. She rested her head back on the pillow. "How long have I been out?"

"Almost five days. Your heart rate was so low when we got you back here that we had no choice but to put you in a cryo chamber. You also had a nasty gash on your side that required Alexia to perform emergency surgery," Emanuel said. "You look a heck of a lot better now."

"Did you listen to the message from Dr. Hoffman?" Holly asked.

Sophie reached under the covers of her bed and massaged her injury. The rough surface of what would be a very nasty scar ran from her hip to her belly button.

"Yes, I heard it all."

"Good. We hoped if we hooked you up to one of Alexia's AI consoles with electrical nodes you would hear the message. We thought it might trigger something in your implant," said Emanuel. "It was playing on all our monitors for a day and a half."

"Smart thinking there," Overton said, patting Emanuel on the back.

The Marine smiled and ran a hand through his hair before turning back to Sophie. "You should rest." He began ushering the team out of the room. "Come on, everyone."

Sophie watched them leave as a wave of drowsiness swept over her. With one last ounce of energy, she grabbed Emanuel and tugged gently on his arm.

"Will you stay with me a bit longer?"

He smiled and dragged a stool up to the side of the bed. He sat down and held her hand, his thumb tracing her palm.

"Do you really think you can find a way to kill the Organics?" she asked quietly.

Emanuel nodded without hesitation. "Everything has a weakness, and I've found theirs."

They sat in silence for several moments. The lights in the room dimmed, and the ambient sound of the ventilation system kicked on. Sophie concentrated on the warmth of his hand over hers. They both knew what had been lost, what Dr. Hoffman's message meant for the future of mankind. And most of all, they knew how difficult it would be to survive in this strange new world. But, for that single moment, none of it mattered. All that mattered was that they had each other—and hope.

EPILOGUE

A CRIMSON sunset peeked above the black outline of a mountain range in the distance. The cloudless sky was a brilliant mixture of orange and purple, almost obscene in contrast with the dying valley below. A dry riverbed snaked through a browning forest. It had been weeks since the invasion, and the world was a very different place. Surface water was gone. The temperature had risen several degrees, and humidity was nonexistent. According to Alexia's calculations, the sea levels were slowly dropping around the planet. The Organics were advanced, but not all-powerful. They had found a way to get almost every ounce of freshwater on the planet, but the saltwater was slowing them down.

The Earth was dying, but it had been dying for a long time.

Sophie sucked in a breath of the dry air while listening to the now-familiar sound of laughing children. She turned to see Overton tossing a football to Owen and David halfway down the tarmac.

"When you're taking a long shot, you have to take wind direction into consideration," said Bouma from a few yards away. Sophie leaned her back against the outside of the blast doors and watched him help Jeff sight his rifle over the valley.

Holly was strolling across the tarmac with Jamie in tow. They stopped next to Owen, and Jamie picked up the football, pretending to hand it to him.

"Here you go," she said with an innocent smile.

Owen reached out to grab it, but she yanked it away. "Bet you can't catch me!" she shrieked, taking off down the runway.

Overton laughed. "Don't go too far!"

"Think it's really safe out here?" Sophie slid a few feet over to make room for Emanuel.

"Overton said there hasn't been a sign of a drone in over a week," Sophie said. "The RVM seems to be keeping them away."

"For now," Emanuel said.

Sophie didn't respond. She didn't want to think about the inevitable, not today. She didn't want to think about when the Organics would come back, or when the team would be forced out of the Biosphere to scavenge for supplies. She just wanted to enjoy the sunset and watch the children.

"Got you!" Owen yelled as he wrapped Jamie in his tiny arms. She squealed with laughter.

A smile broke across Sophie's face. It was then it finally hit her. She was looking at their future. All this time, she had believed the Biosphere mission was the most important one of her life, that Mars was the future for humanity. But as she scanned the faces of the four children, she knew that her mission had changed. Her goal was no longer to prepare for a new life on a distant planet—it was to protect what was left of life on Earth.

She thought briefly of those that they had lost: Saafi, Timothy, Finley, her parents, and those of the children they'd managed to save, and the billions of others who had perished. She wouldn't let their deaths go unavenged. Dr. Hoffman was right about one thing: the human race had to go on.

Alexia's calm voice sounded over Sophie's headset. She put her finger to the earbud, straining to listen over the children's laughter. "Dr. Winston, I'm picking up a radio transmission on the device Dr. Hoffman left behind."

Sophie gasped, reaching for the radio on her belt, but her hands came up empty. She had left it inside. "Can you patch it through?"

Static filled the channel for several seconds before a muffled voice finally broke through.

"This is Alex Wagner with the Biosphere facility at Edwards Air Force Base in California, requesting assistance. Over."

Sophie froze, her eyes widening as she grabbed Emanuel's hand. Out of the corner of her eye, she saw Overton drop the football and put his finger to his earbud. One by one her team members stopped what they were doing and rushed over to her.

"What do we do?" Bouma asked. He stood shoulder to shoulder with Holly, and for a moment Sophie thought she saw their hands touch.

"Well?" Overton said. "How are you going to respond?"

Sophie hesitated, looking at Emanuel for assistance before turning to face her team. Holly's advice from days before echoed in her mind. Now was the time to make good on her promise to Holly and to herself. "We tell them they're not alone," she said firmly. "And then we tell them that we're working on a way to defeat the Organics."

In the distance, the sun had finally disappeared behind the black mountain range. Sophie took a moment to admire the dazzling, star-filled sky. As she scanned the heavens, she couldn't help but wonder if one of the tiny dots of light was *Secundo Casu* on its way to Mars.

—End of Book I—

THANK YOU

Thank you for reading *Orbs*. If you enjoyed this book, please stop by my Facebook page or follow me on Twitter for updates on the Orbs series.

Facebook: https://www.facebook.com/pages/Nicholas-Sansbury-Smith/124009881117534
Website: www.NicholasSansbury.com
Twitter: https://twitter.com/greatwaveink

NICHOLAS SANSBURY SMITH is the bestselling author of the Orbs and Extinction Cycle series. He worked for Iowa Homeland Security and Emergency Management in disaster mitigation before switching careers to focus on his one true passion—writing. Smith is a three-time Kindle All-Star, and several of his titles have reached the top 50 on the overall Kindle bestseller list and as high as #1 in the Audible store. *Hell Divers*, the first book in his new trilogy, will release in July 2016. When he isn't writing or daydreaming about the apocalypse, he's training for triathlons or traveling the world. He lives in Des Moines, Iowa, with his dog and a house full of books.